Written by **PAUL TOBIN**
Art by **RON CHAN**
Colors by **MATTHEW J. RAINWATER**
Letters by **STEVE DUTRO**
Cover by **RON CHAN**

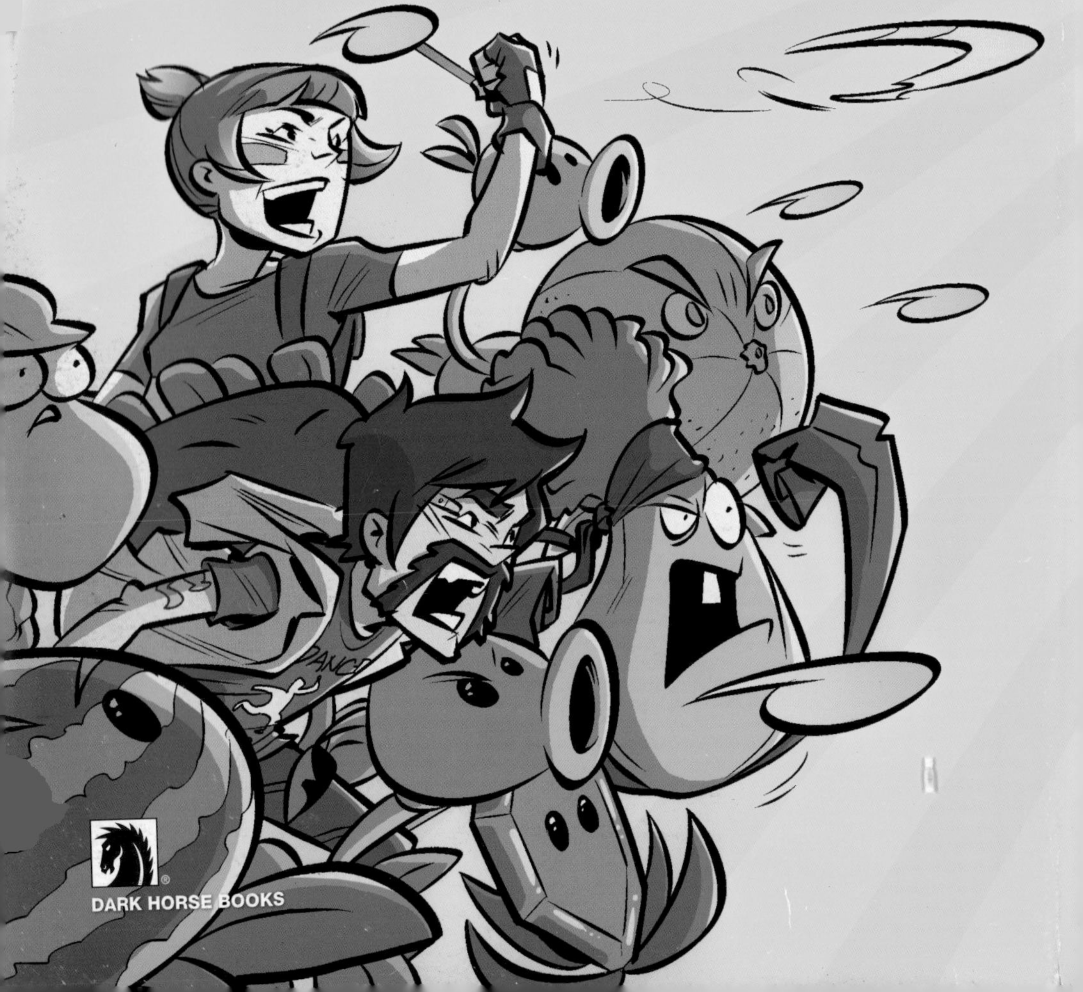

DARK HORSE BOOKS

**PLANTS
VS.
ZOMBIES**

TIMEPOCALYPSE

PLANTS VS. ZOMBIES™

TIMEPOCALYPSE

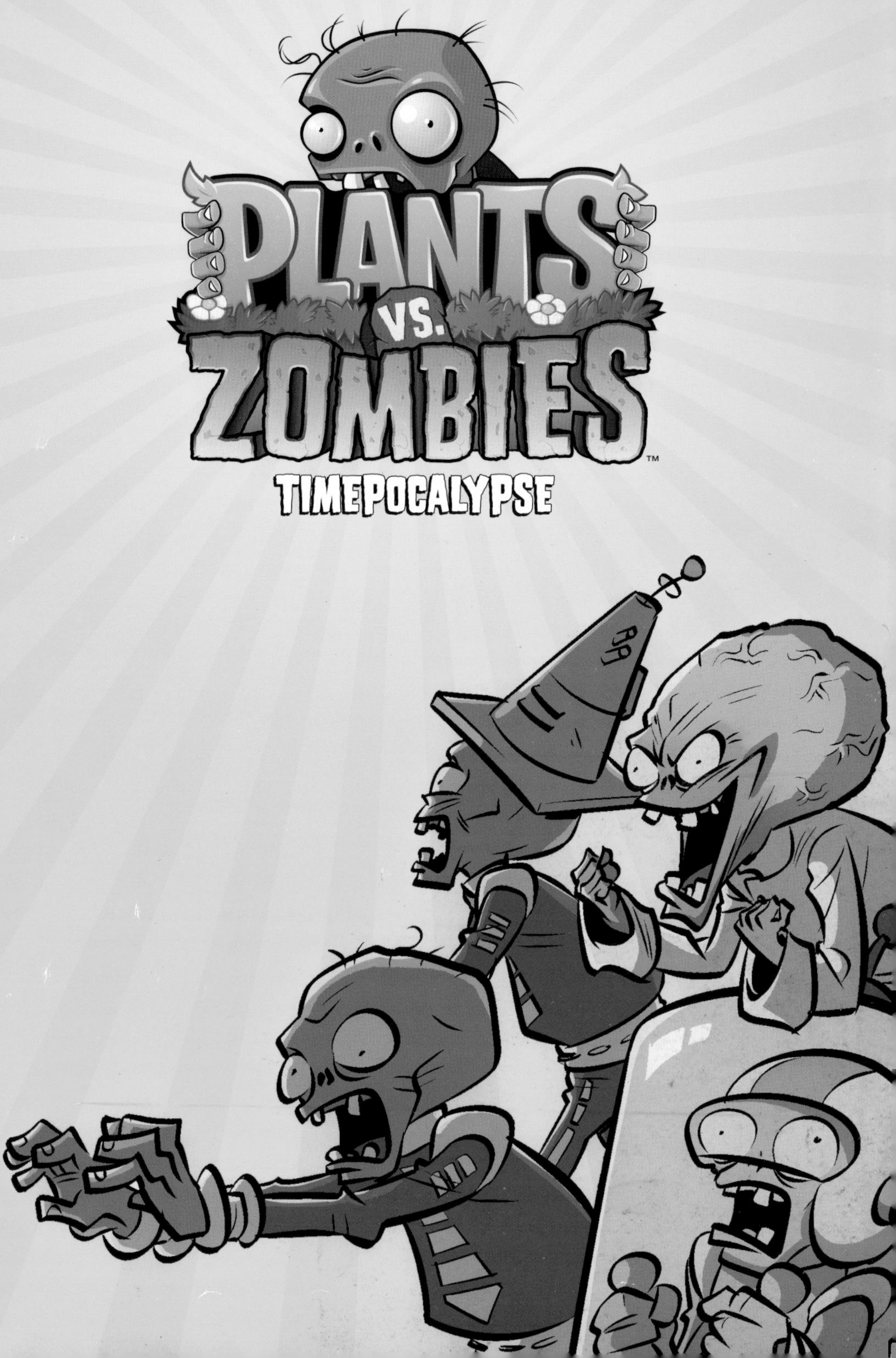

Publisher **MIKE RICHARDSON**
Editor **PHILIP R. SIMON**
Assistant Editor **ROXY POLK**
Designer **KAT LARSON**
Digital Production **CHRISTINA McKENZIE**

Special thanks to LEIGH BEACH, SHANA DOERR, A.J. RATHBUN, BRENNAN TOWNLEY, JEREMY VANHOOZER, and everyone at PopCap Games.

First edition: January 2015
ISBN 978-1-61655-621-1

10 9 8 7
Printed in Italy

DarkHorse.com | PopCap.com

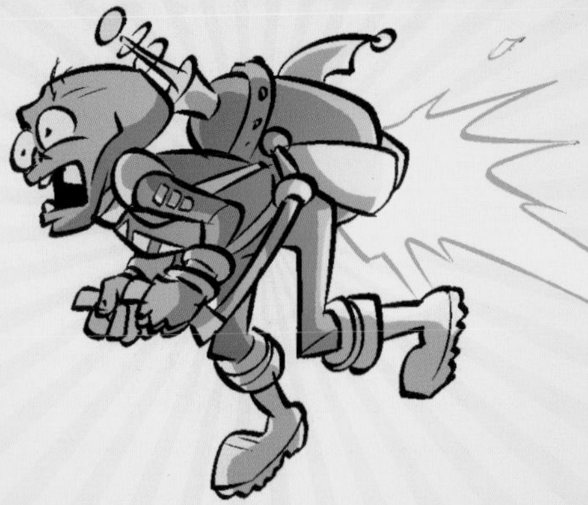

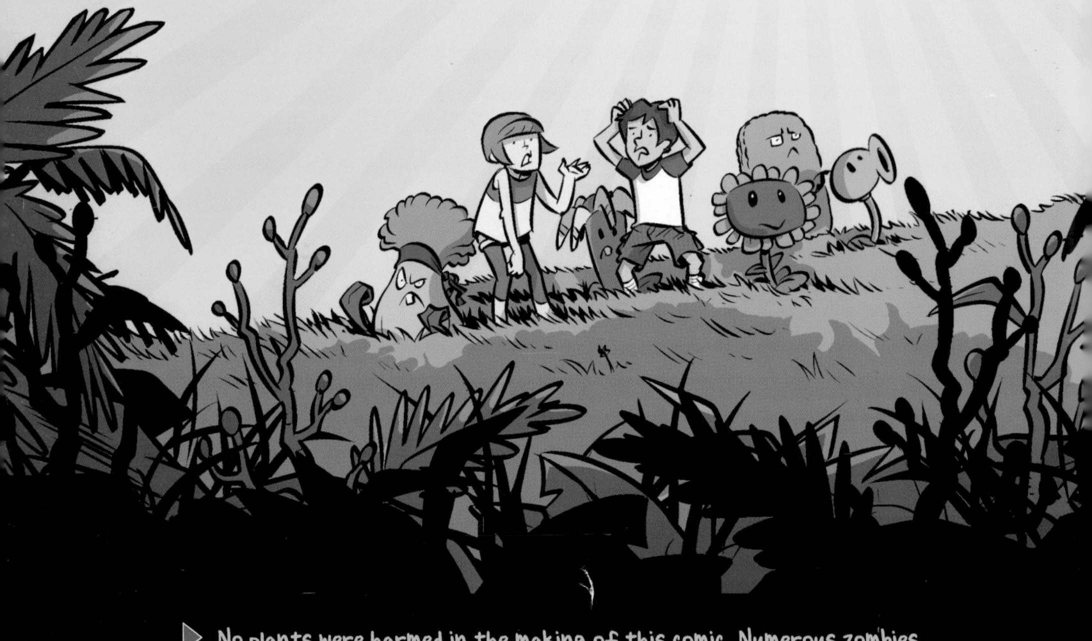

No plants were harmed in the making of this comic. Numerous zombies from various time periods, however, definitely were.

This volume collects *Plants vs. Zombies: Timepocalypse* #1–#6, originally serialized by Dark Horse Digital. | Published by Dark Horse Books, a division of Dark Horse Comics LLC, 10956 SE Main Street, Milwaukie, OR 97222 | International Licensing: (503) 905-2377 | To find a comics shop in your area, visit comicshoplocator.com | **PLANTS vs. ZOMBIES: TIMEPOCALYPSE.**

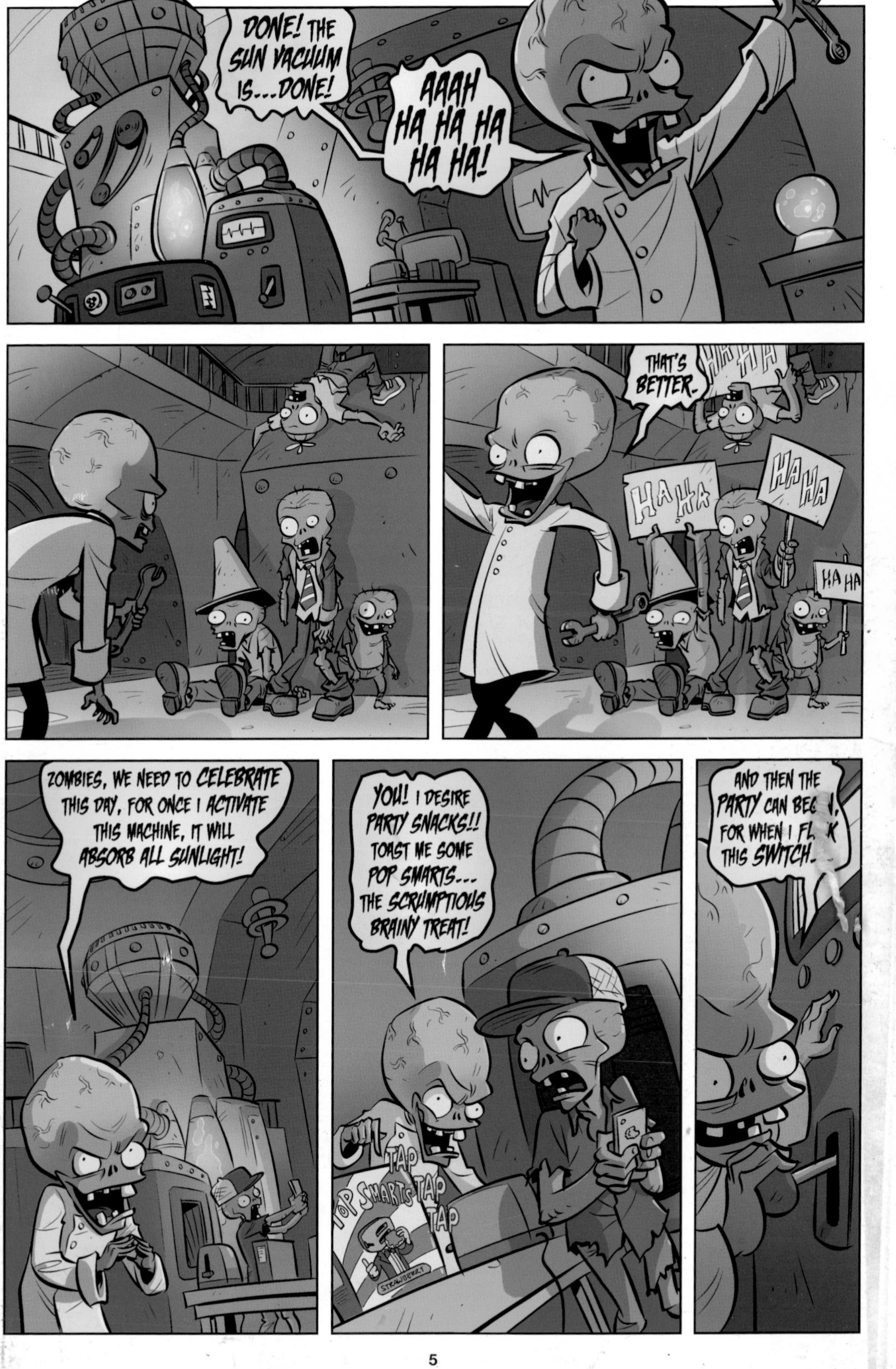
DONE! THE SUN VACUUM IS...DONE!
AAAH HA HA HA HA HA!
THAT'S BETTER.
HA HA
HA HA
HA HA
HA HA
ZOMBIES, WE NEED TO CELEBRATE THIS DAY, FOR ONCE I ACTIVATE THIS MACHINE, IT WILL ABSORB ALL SUNLIGHT!
YOU! I DESIRE PARTY SNACKS!! TOAST ME SOME POP SMARTS... THE SCRUMPTIOUS BRAINY TREAT!
TAP TAP TAP
POP SMARTS
STRAWBERRY
AND THEN THE PARTY CAN BEG
FOR WHEN I FL K THIS SWITCH

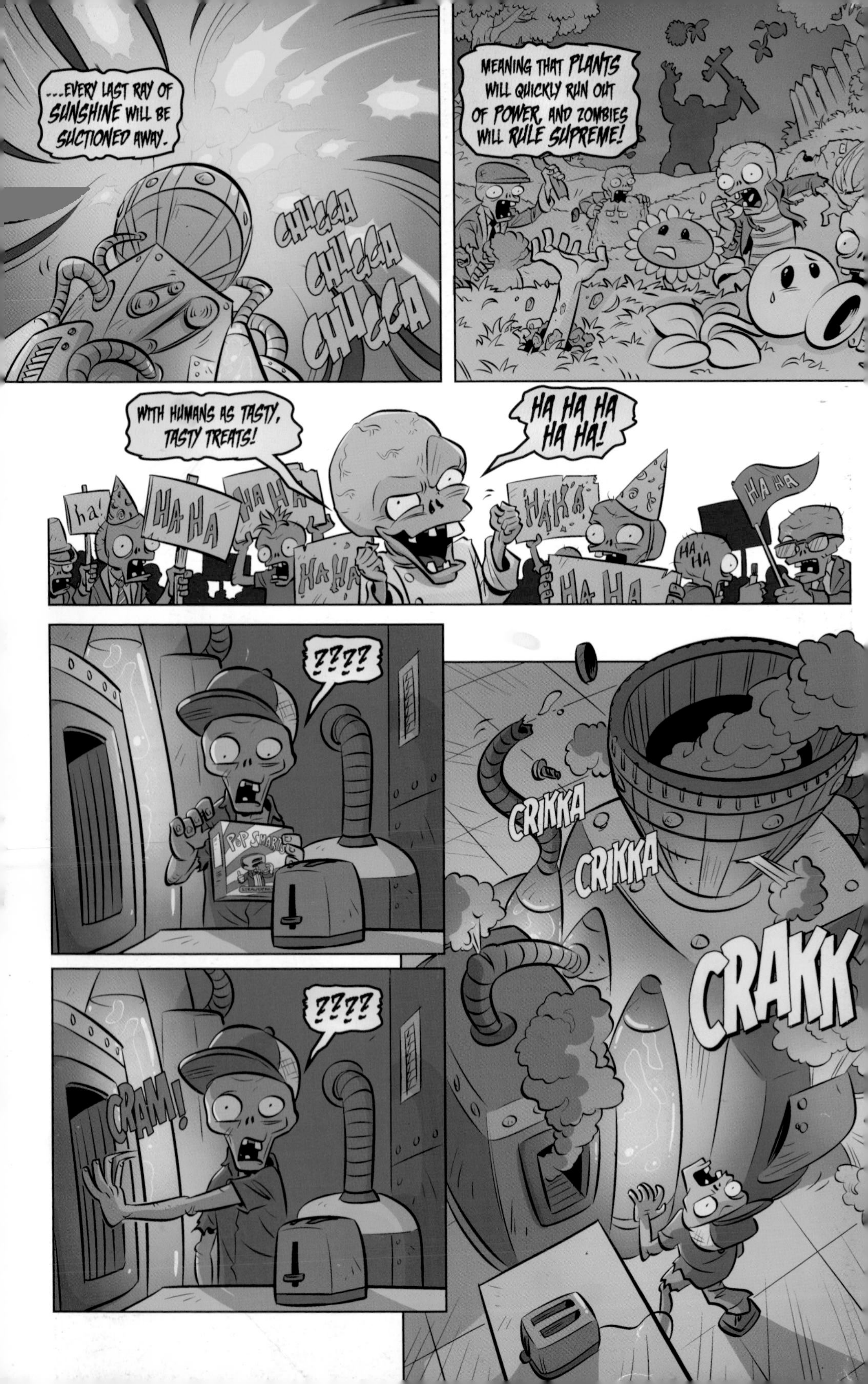
...EVERY LAST RAY OF SUNSHINE WILL BE SUCTIONED AWAY.
CHUGGA CHUGGA CHUGGA
MEANING THAT PLANTS WILL QUICKLY RUN OUT OF POWER, AND ZOMBIES WILL RULE SUPREME!
WITH HUMANS AS TASTY, TASTY TREATS!
HA HA HA HA HA!
ha!
HA HA
HA HA
HA HA
HA HA
HA HA
HA HA
HA HA
HA HA
????
POP SMARTS
????
CRAM!
CRIKKA
CRIKKA
CRAKK

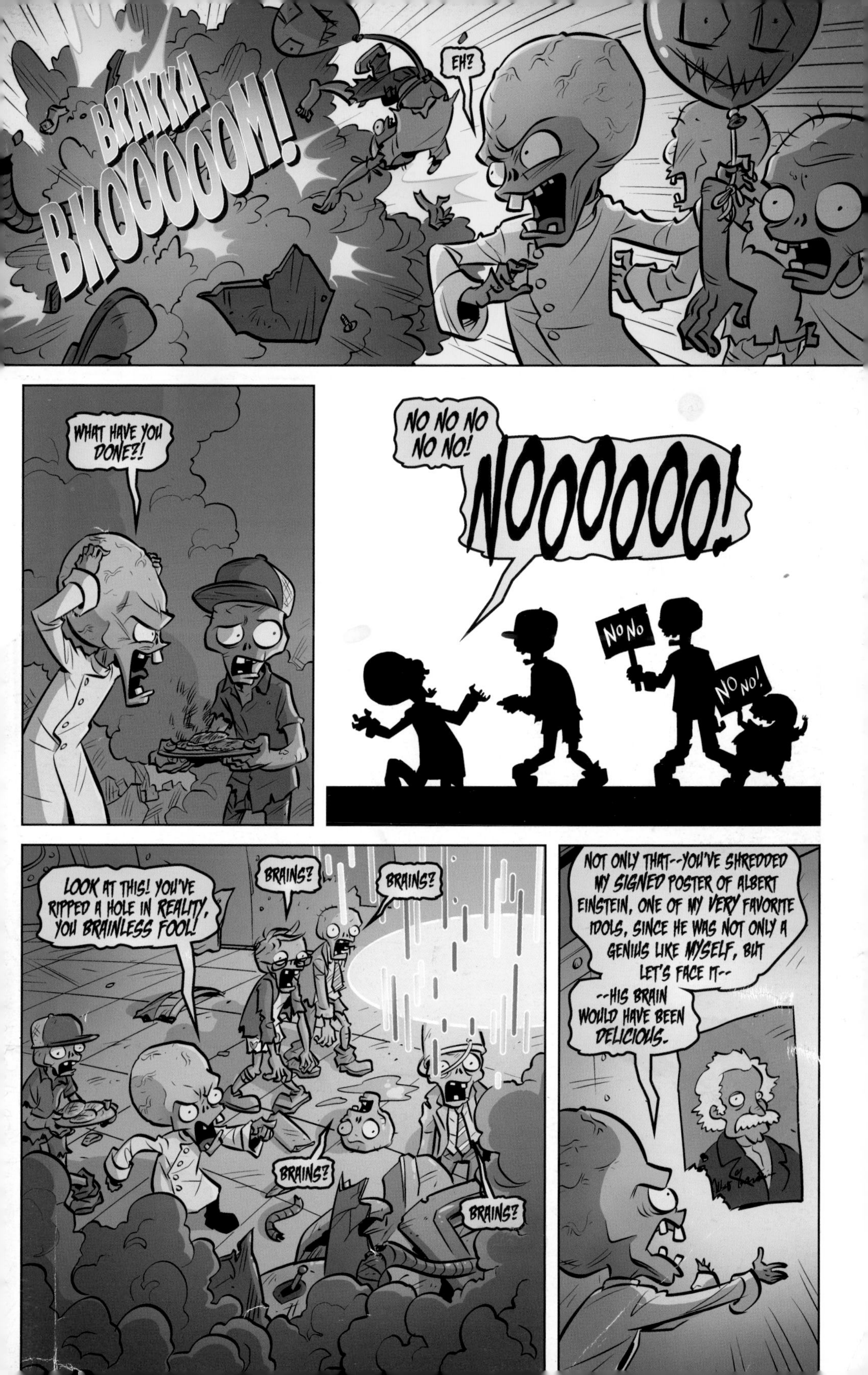

BRAKKA BKOOOOOOM!
EH?
WHAT HAVE YOU DONE?!
NO NO NO NO NO!
NOOOOOO!
NO NO
NO NO!
LOOK AT THIS! YOU'VE RIPPED A HOLE IN REALITY, YOU BRAINLESS FOOL!
BRAINS?
BRAINS?
BRAINS?
BRAINS?
NOT ONLY THAT--YOU'VE SHREDDED MY SIGNED POSTER OF ALBERT EINSTEIN, ONE OF MY VERY FAVORITE IDOLS, SINCE HE WAS NOT ONLY A GENIUS LIKE MYSELF, BUT LET'S FACE IT--
--HIS BRAIN WOULD HAVE BEEN DELICIOUS.

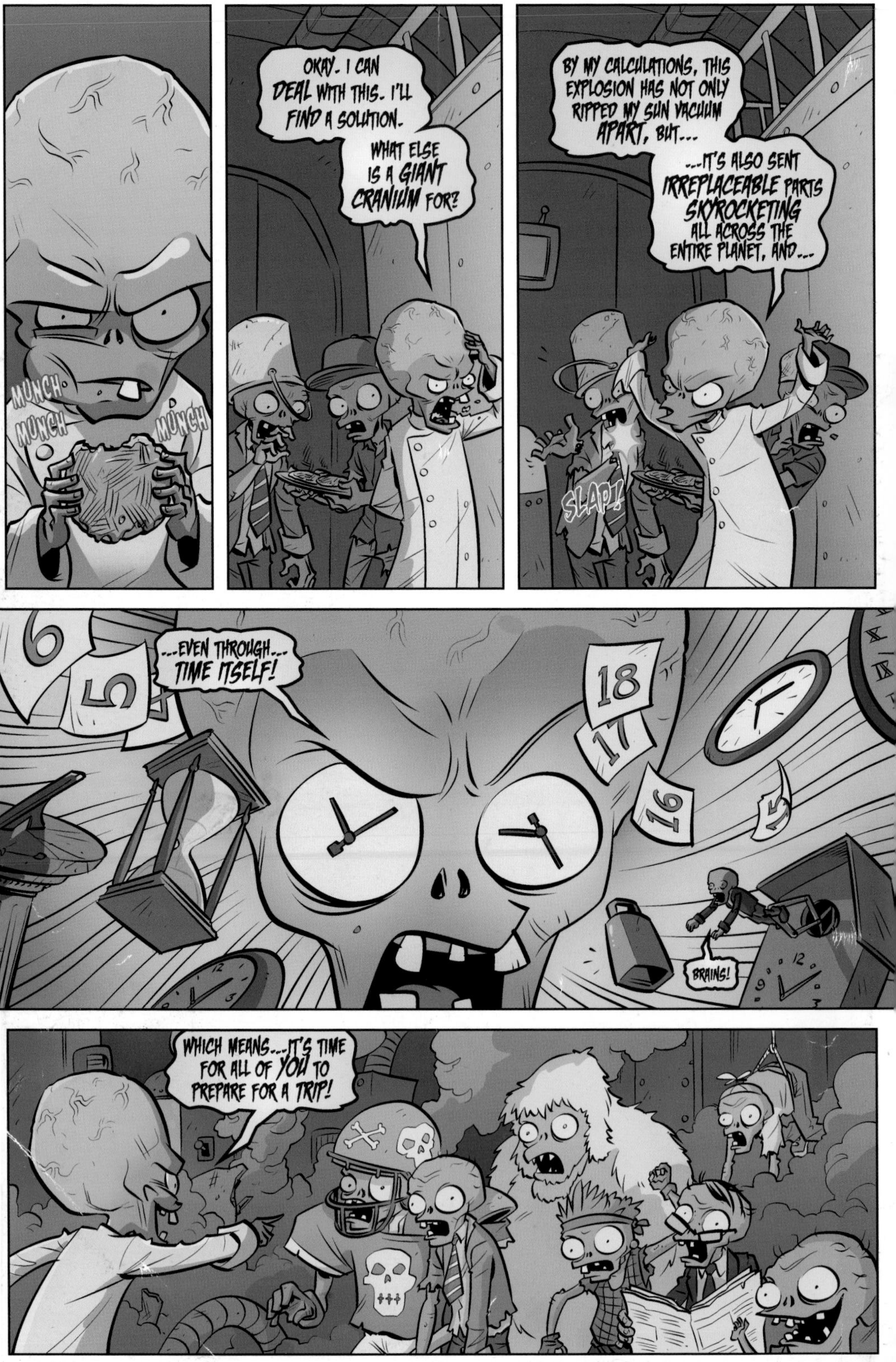
MUNCH
MUNCH
MUNCH
OKAY. I CAN DEAL WITH THIS. I'LL FIND A SOLUTION.
WHAT ELSE IS A GIANT CRANIUM FOR?
BY MY CALCULATIONS, THIS EXPLOSION HAS NOT ONLY RIPPED MY SUN VACUUM APART, BUT...
...IT'S ALSO SENT IRREPLACEABLE PARTS SKYROCKETING ALL ACROSS THE ENTIRE PLANET, AND...
SLAP!
...EVEN THROUGH... TIME ITSELF!
BRAINS!
WHICH MEANS...IT'S TIME FOR ALL OF YOU TO PREPARE FOR A TRIP!

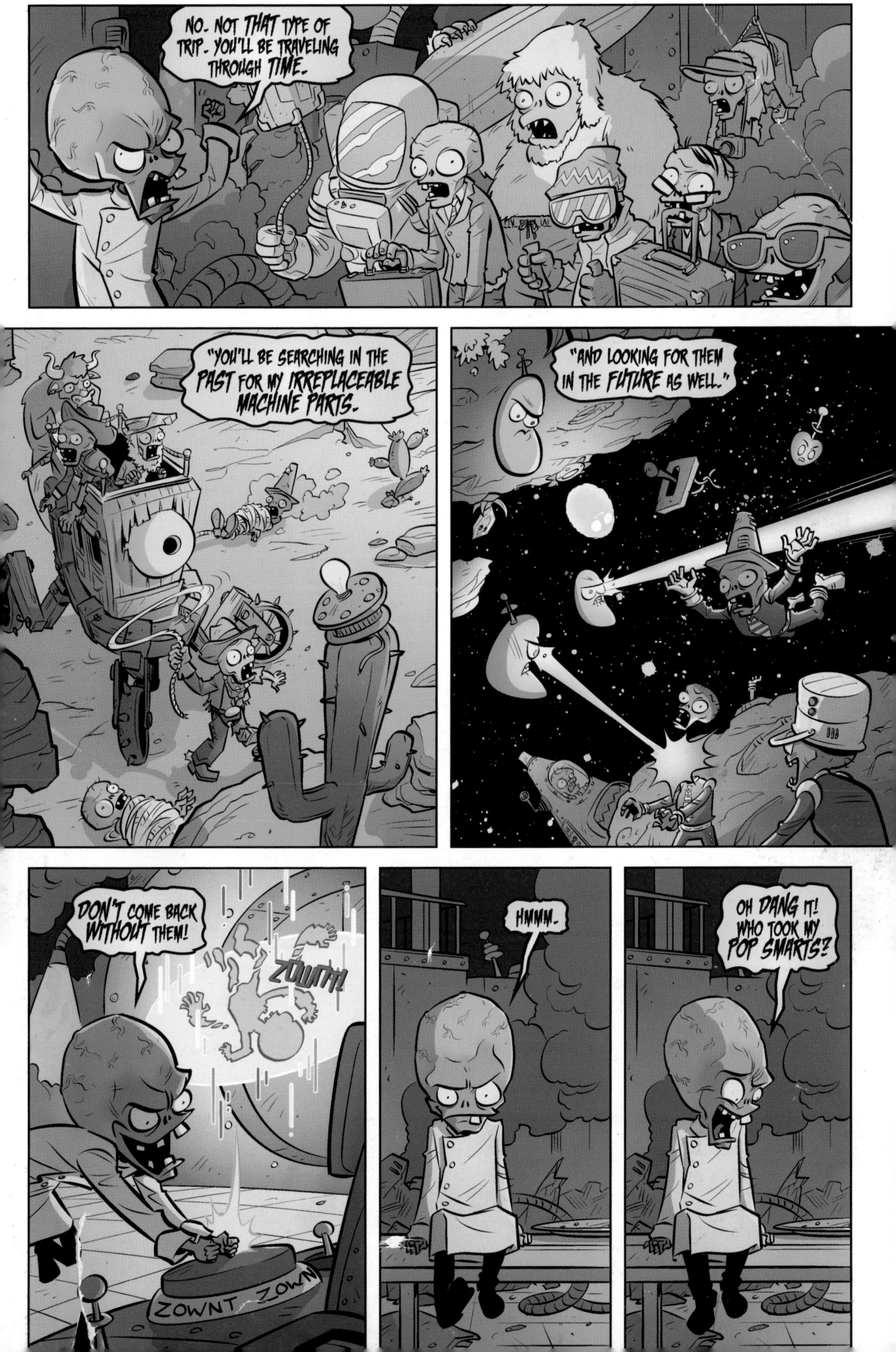
NO. NOT THAT TYPE OF TRIP. YOU'LL BE TRAVELING THROUGH TIME.
"YOU'LL BE SEARCHING IN THE PAST FOR MY IRREPLACEABLE MACHINE PARTS.
"AND LOOKING FOR THEM IN THE FUTURE AS WELL."
DON'T COME BACK WITHOUT THEM!
ZOWRRT!
ZOWNT ZOWN
HMMM.
OH DANG IT! WHO TOOK MY POP SMARTS?

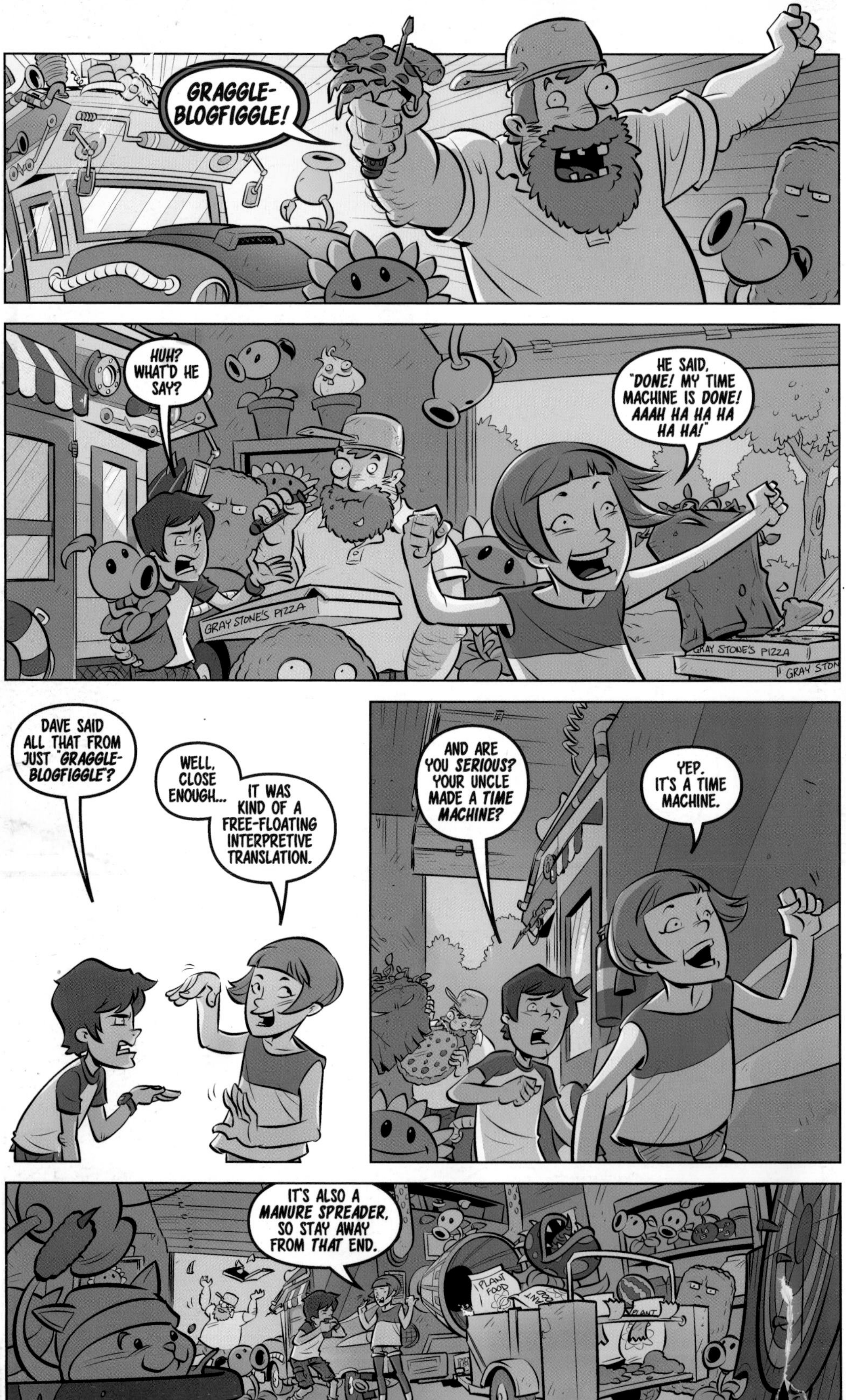
GRAGGLE-BLOGFIGGLE!
HUH? WHAT'D HE SAY?
HE SAID, "DONE! MY TIME MACHINE IS DONE! AAAH HA HA HA HA HA!"
GRAY STONE'S PIZZA
GRAY STONE'S PIZZA
DAVE SAID ALL THAT FROM JUST "GRAGGLE-BLOGFIGGLE"?
WELL, CLOSE ENOUGH...
IT WAS KIND OF A FREE-FLOATING INTERPRETIVE TRANSLATION.
AND ARE YOU SERIOUS? YOUR UNCLE MADE A TIME MACHINE?
YEP. IT'S A TIME MACHINE.
IT'S ALSO A MANURE SPREADER, SO STAY AWAY FROM THAT END.
PLANT FOOD

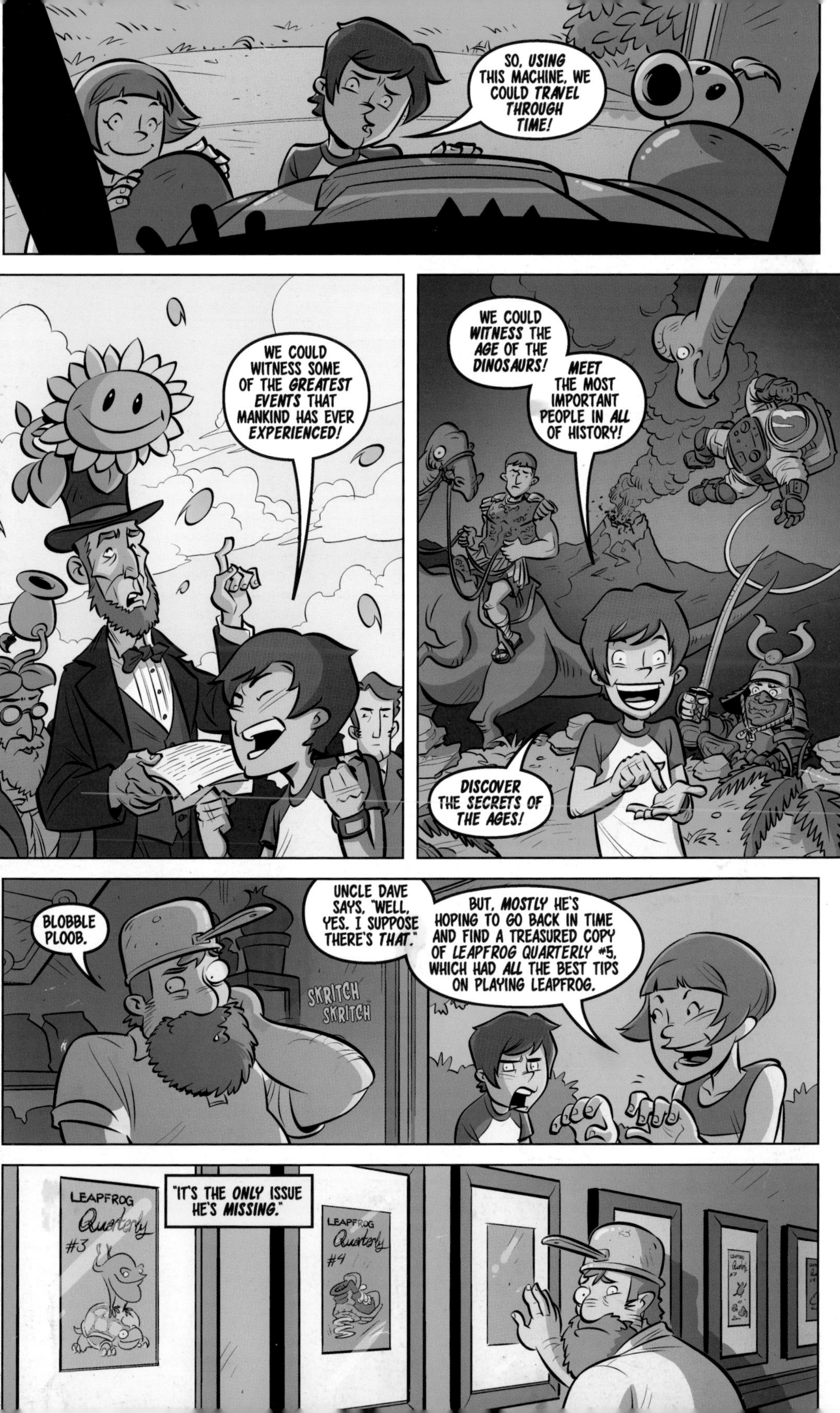
SO, USING THIS MACHINE, WE COULD TRAVEL THROUGH TIME!
WE COULD WITNESS SOME OF THE GREATEST EVENTS THAT MANKIND HAS EVER EXPERIENCED!
WE COULD WITNESS THE AGE OF THE DINOSAURS!
MEET THE MOST IMPORTANT PEOPLE IN ALL OF HISTORY!
DISCOVER THE SECRETS OF THE AGES!
BLOBBLE PLOOB.
SKRITCH SKRITCH
UNCLE DAVE SAYS, "WELL, YES. I SUPPOSE THERE'S THAT."
BUT, MOSTLY HE'S HOPING TO GO BACK IN TIME AND FIND A TREASURED COPY OF LEAPFROG QUARTERLY #5, WHICH HAD ALL THE BEST TIPS ON PLAYING LEAPFROG.
LEAPFROG Quarterly #3
"IT'S THE ONLY ISSUE HE'S MISSING."
LEAPFROG Quarterly #4

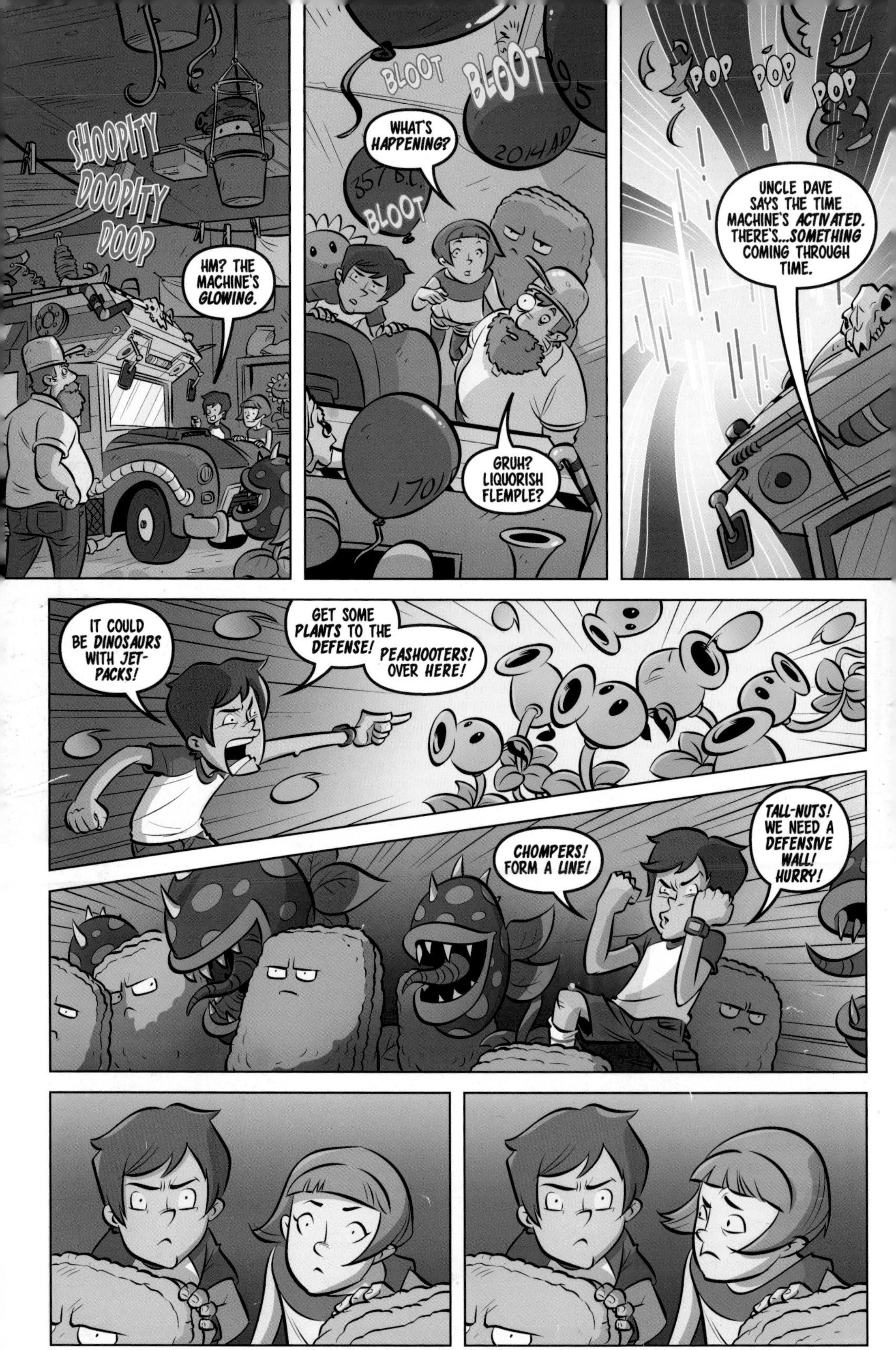
SHOOPITY DOOPITY DOOP
HM? THE MACHINE'S GLOWING.
BLOOT BLOOT
WHAT'S HAPPENING?
BLOOT
GRUH? LIQUORISH FLEMPLE?
POP POP POP
UNCLE DAVE SAYS THE TIME MACHINE'S ACTIVATED. THERE'S...SOMETHING COMING THROUGH TIME.
IT COULD BE DINOSAURS WITH JET-PACKS!
GET SOME PLANTS TO THE DEFENSE!
PEASHOOTERS! OVER HERE!
CHOMPERS! FORM A LINE!
TALL-NUTS! WE NEED A DEFENSIVE WALL! HURRY!

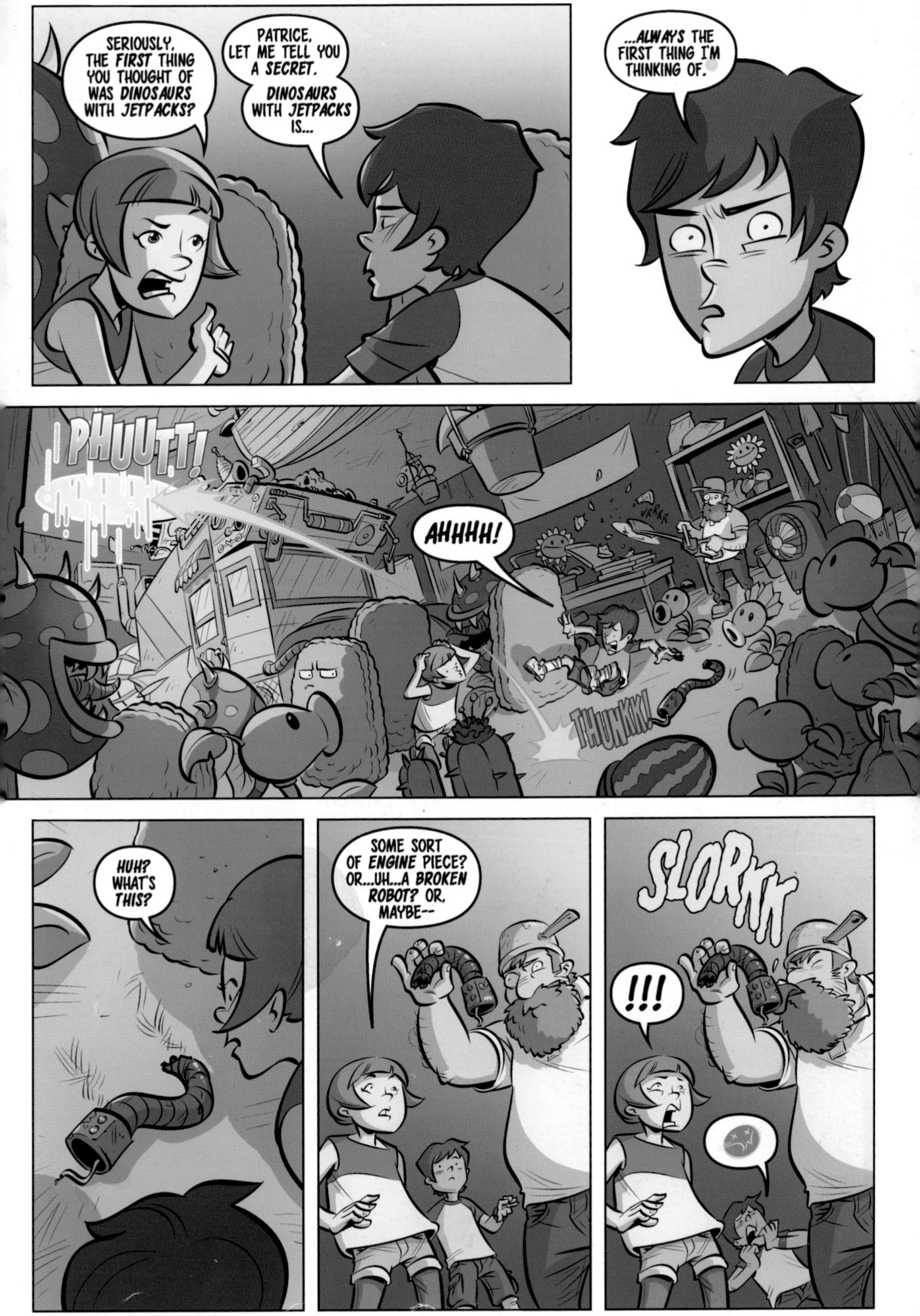
SERIOUSLY, THE FIRST THING YOU THOUGHT OF WAS DINOSAURS WITH JETPACKS?
PATRICE, LET ME TELL YOU A SECRET.
DINOSAURS WITH JETPACKS IS...
...ALWAYS THE FIRST THING I'M THINKING OF.
PHUUTT!
AHHHH!
THUNKK!
HUH? WHAT'S THIS?
SOME SORT OF ENGINE PIECE? OR...UH...A BROKEN ROBOT? OR, MAYBE--
SLORKK
!!!

GRA-GORGLE! FLING GRAK GRAK NARRRRRRR.

HUH, WHAT'S CRAZY DAVE *SAYING?*

WHAT MY *UNCLE* DAVE SAID IS THAT THIS IS A *MACHINE PART* FROM A *SUN VACUUM*—A MACHINE THAT CAN ABSORB THE SUN'S RAYS.

THE TYPE OF MACHINE THAT ONLY DR. *EDGAR ZOMBOSS* WOULD BUILD.

BUT HE SAYS THERE'S AN *AFTERTASTE* THAT MEANS THE MACHINE HAS BEEN *BLOWN UP,* SOMEHOW, WITH ALL THE PARTS *CATAPULTED* THROUGHOUT TIME.

AND THESE *SCRATCHES* MEAN THAT ZOMBOSS HAS SENT HIS ZOMBIE MINIONS *ALL THROUGHOUT TIME,* SO THAT THEY CAN *REBUILD* THE MACHINE AND *RULE THE WORLD.*

CRAZY DAVE CAN...I MEAN, YOUR *UNCLE* DAVE CAN GET ALL OF THAT JUST FROM *ONE CLUE?*

YEP. ALSO...

$$24.1x = \frac{\Omega\ IV}{.0146}$$

4.13

...DR. ZOMBOSS PUTS TOO MUCH *MACHINE OIL* ON HIS SUN VACUUM, AND HIS FAVORITE FLAVOR OF POP SMARTS IS *STRAWBERRY.*

PTUI!

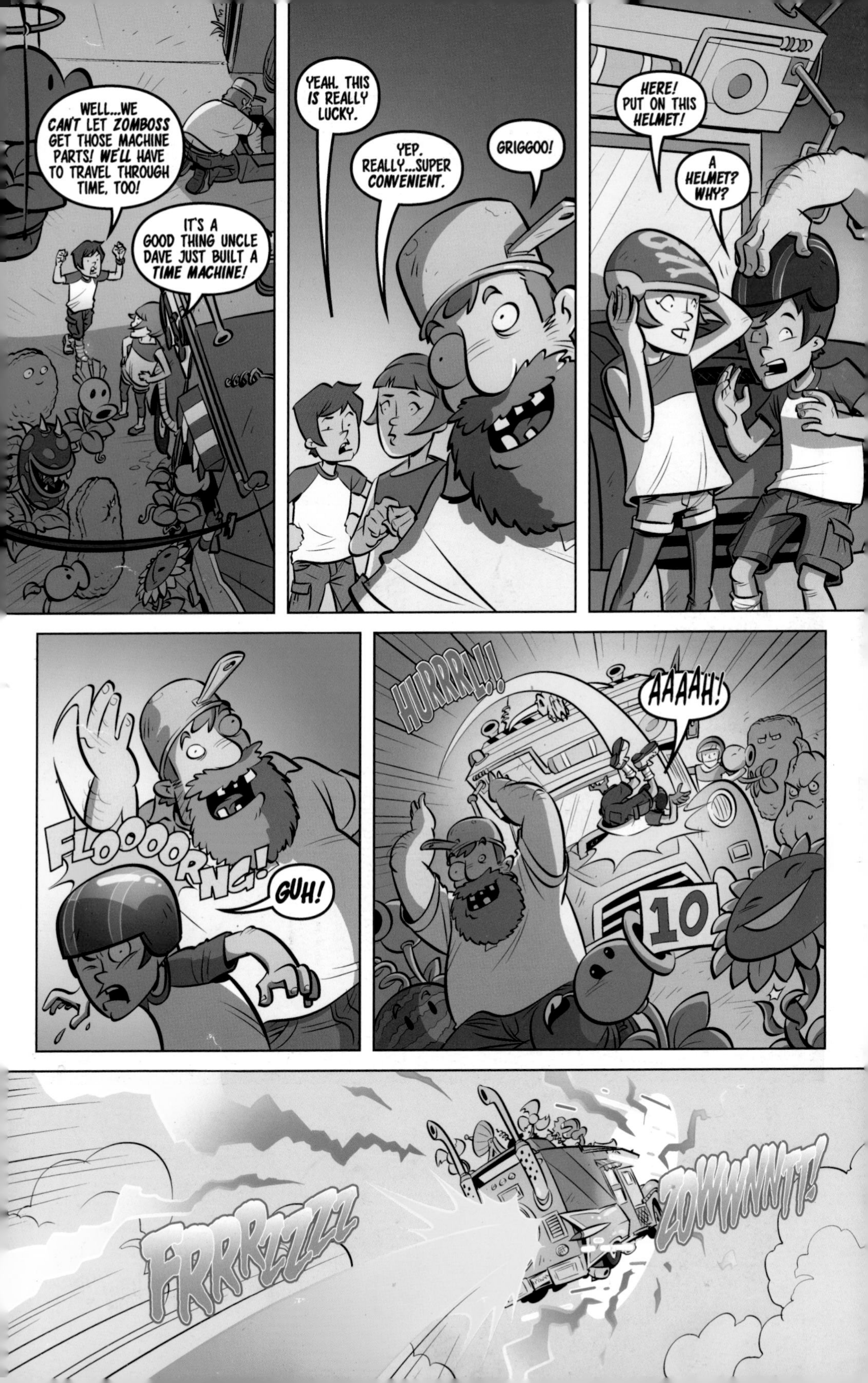
WELL...WE CAN'T LET ZOMBOSS GET THOSE MACHINE PARTS! WE'LL HAVE TO TRAVEL THROUGH TIME, TOO!
IT'S A GOOD THING UNCLE DAVE JUST BUILT A TIME MACHINE!
YEAH. THIS IS REALLY LUCKY.
YEP. REALLY...SUPER CONVENIENT.
GRIGGOO!
HERE! PUT ON THIS HELMET!
A HELMET? WHY?
FLOOOORNG!
GUH!
HURRRL!!
AAAAH!
10
FRRRZZZZ
ZOWWNNTT!

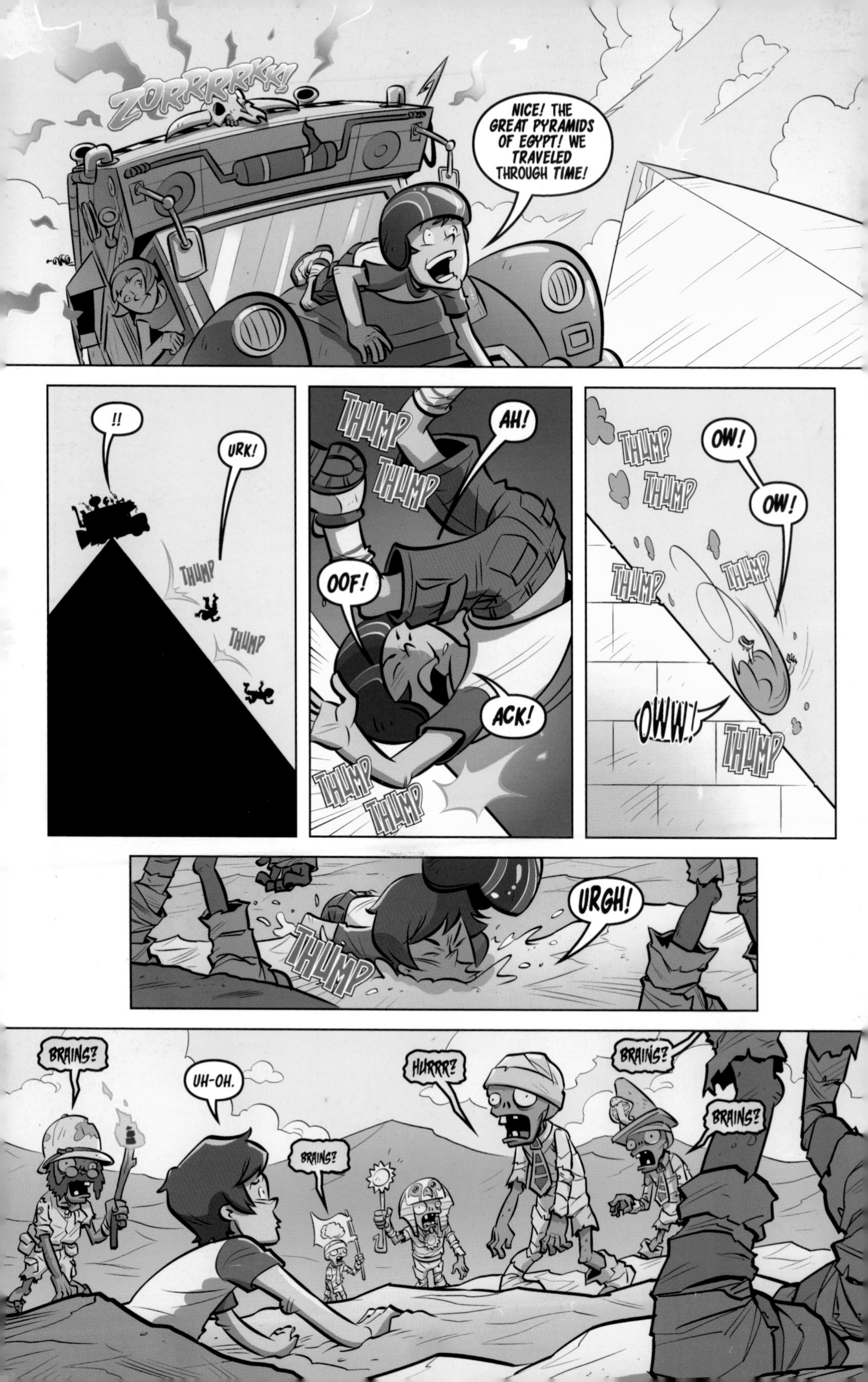
ZORRRRKK!
NICE! THE GREAT PYRAMIDS OF EGYPT! WE TRAVELED THROUGH TIME!
!!
URK!
THUMP
THUMP
THUMP
AH!
THUMP
OOF!
ACK!
THUMP
THUMP
THUMP
OW!
THUMP
OW!
THUMP
THUMP
OWW!
THUMP
URGH!
THUMP
BRAINS?
UH-OH.
BRAINS?
HURRR?
BRAINS?
BRAINS?

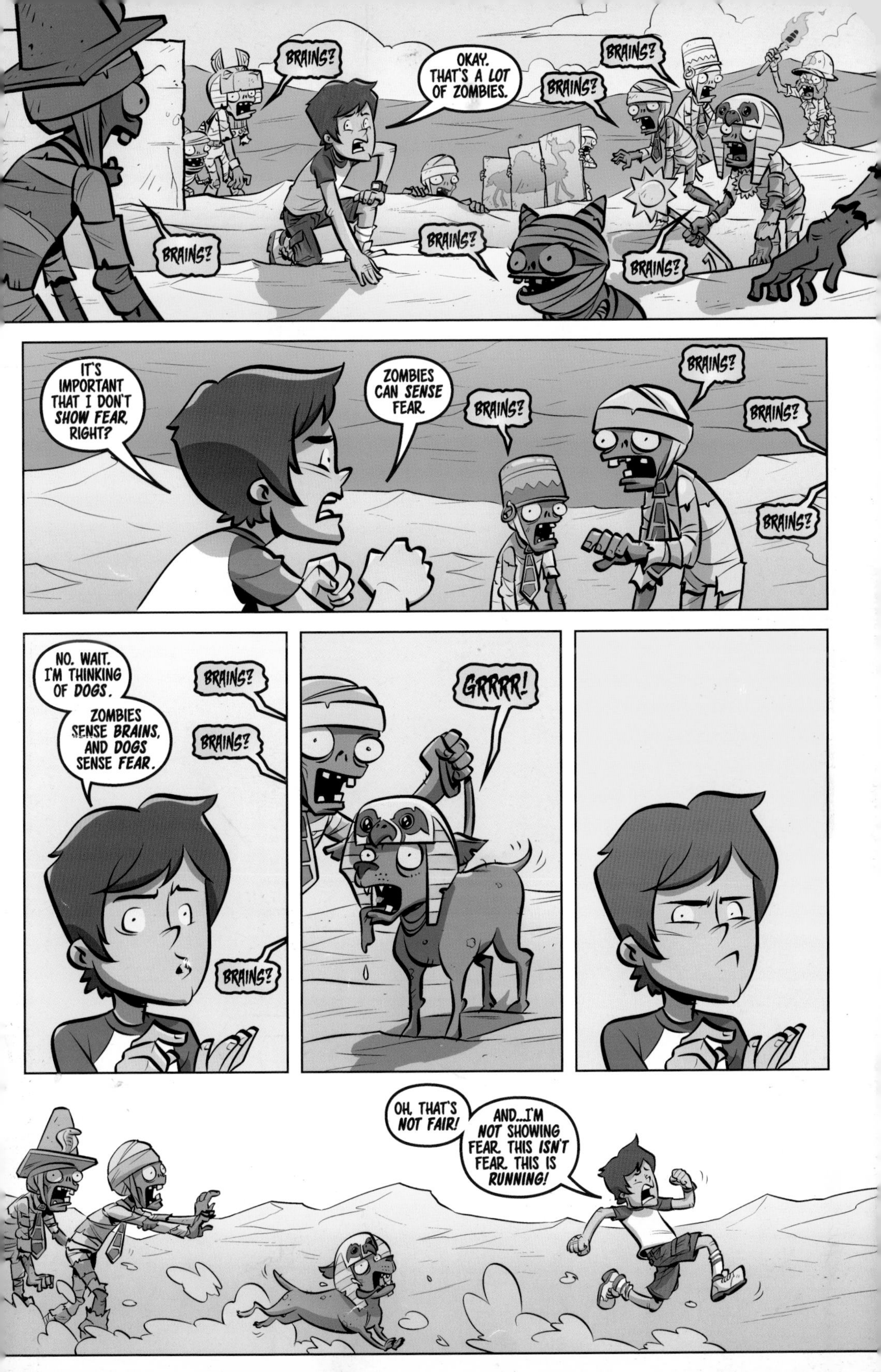
BRAINS?
OKAY. THAT'S A LOT OF ZOMBIES.
BRAINS?
BRAINS?
BRAINS?
BRAINS?
BRAINS?
IT'S IMPORTANT THAT I DON'T SHOW FEAR, RIGHT?
ZOMBIES CAN SENSE FEAR.
BRAINS?
BRAINS?
BRAINS?
BRAINS?
NO. WAIT. I'M THINKING OF DOGS.
ZOMBIES SENSE BRAINS, AND DOGS SENSE FEAR.
BRAINS?
BRAINS?
BRAINS?
GRRRR!
OH, THAT'S NOT FAIR!
AND...I'M NOT SHOWING FEAR. THIS ISN'T FEAR. THIS IS RUNNING!

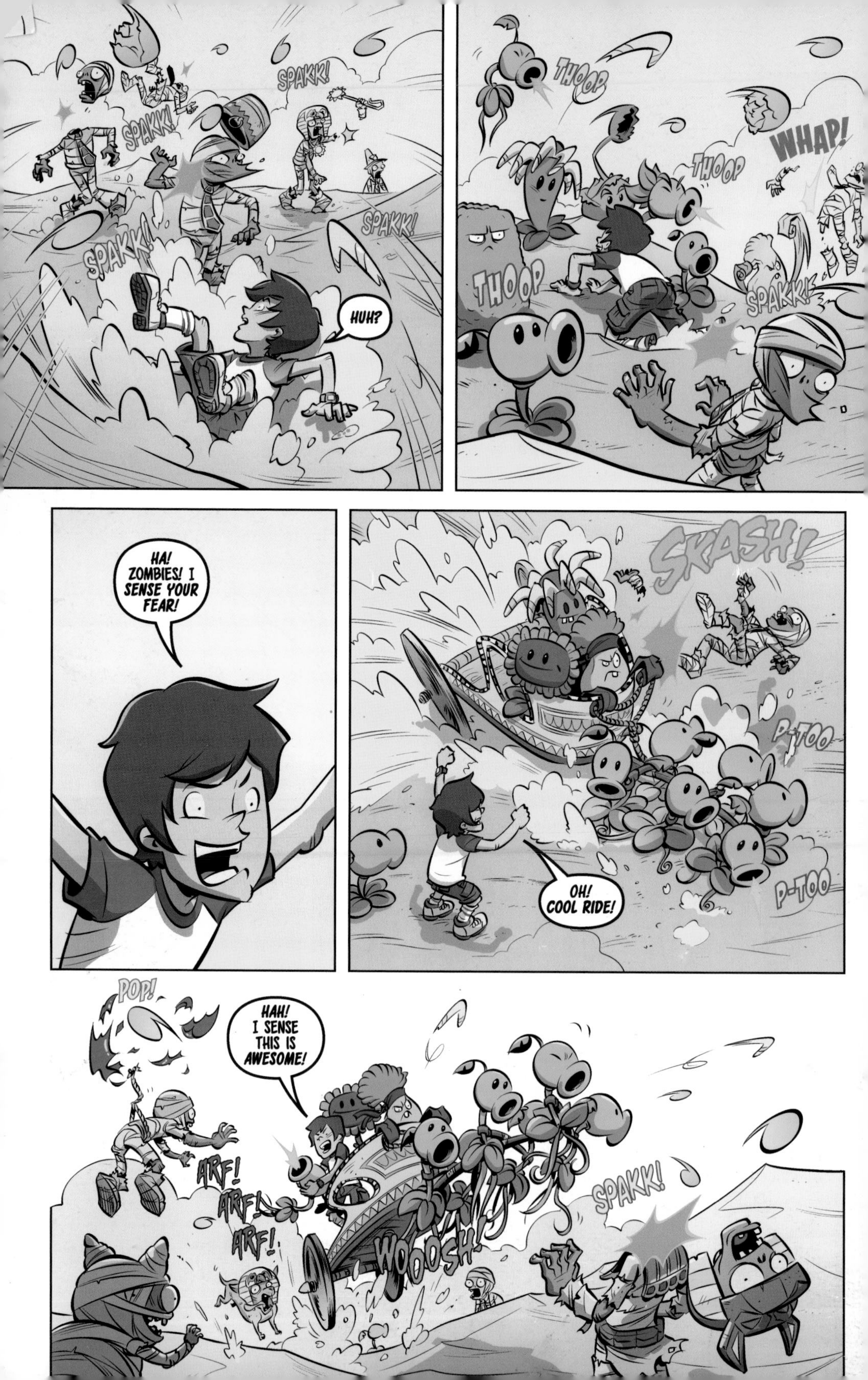
SPAKK!
SPAKK!
SPAKK!
SPAKK!
HUH?
THOOP
WHAP!
THOOP
THOOP
SPAKK!
HA! ZOMBIES! I SENSE YOUR FEAR!
SKASH!
P-TOO
OH! COOL RIDE!
P-TOO
POP!
HAH! I SENSE THIS IS AWESOME!
ARF!
ARF!
ARF!
WOOOSH!
SPAKK!

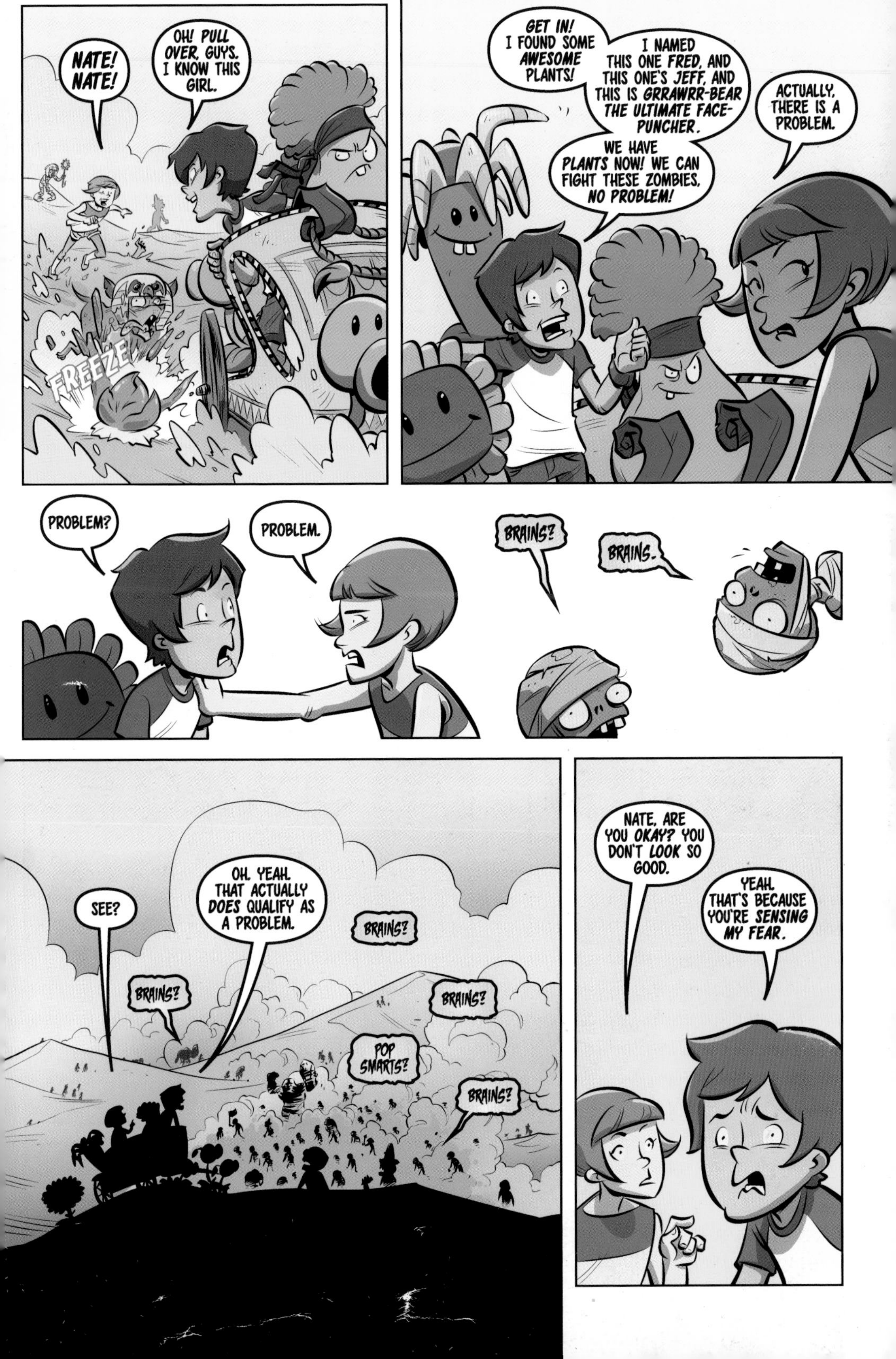
NATE! NATE!
OH! PULL OVER, GUYS. I KNOW THIS GIRL.
FREEZE
GET IN! I FOUND SOME AWESOME PLANTS!
I NAMED THIS ONE FRED, AND THIS ONE'S JEFF, AND THIS IS GRRAWRR-BEAR THE ULTIMATE FACE-PUNCHER.
WE HAVE PLANTS NOW! WE CAN FIGHT THESE ZOMBIES, NO PROBLEM!
ACTUALLY, THERE IS A PROBLEM.
PROBLEM?
PROBLEM.
BRAINS?
BRAINS.
SEE?
OH. YEAH. THAT ACTUALLY DOES QUALIFY AS A PROBLEM.
BRAINS?
BRAINS?
BRAINS?
POP SMARTS?
BRAINS?
NATE, ARE YOU OKAY? YOU DON'T LOOK SO GOOD.
YEAH. THAT'S BECAUSE YOU'RE SENSING MY FEAR.

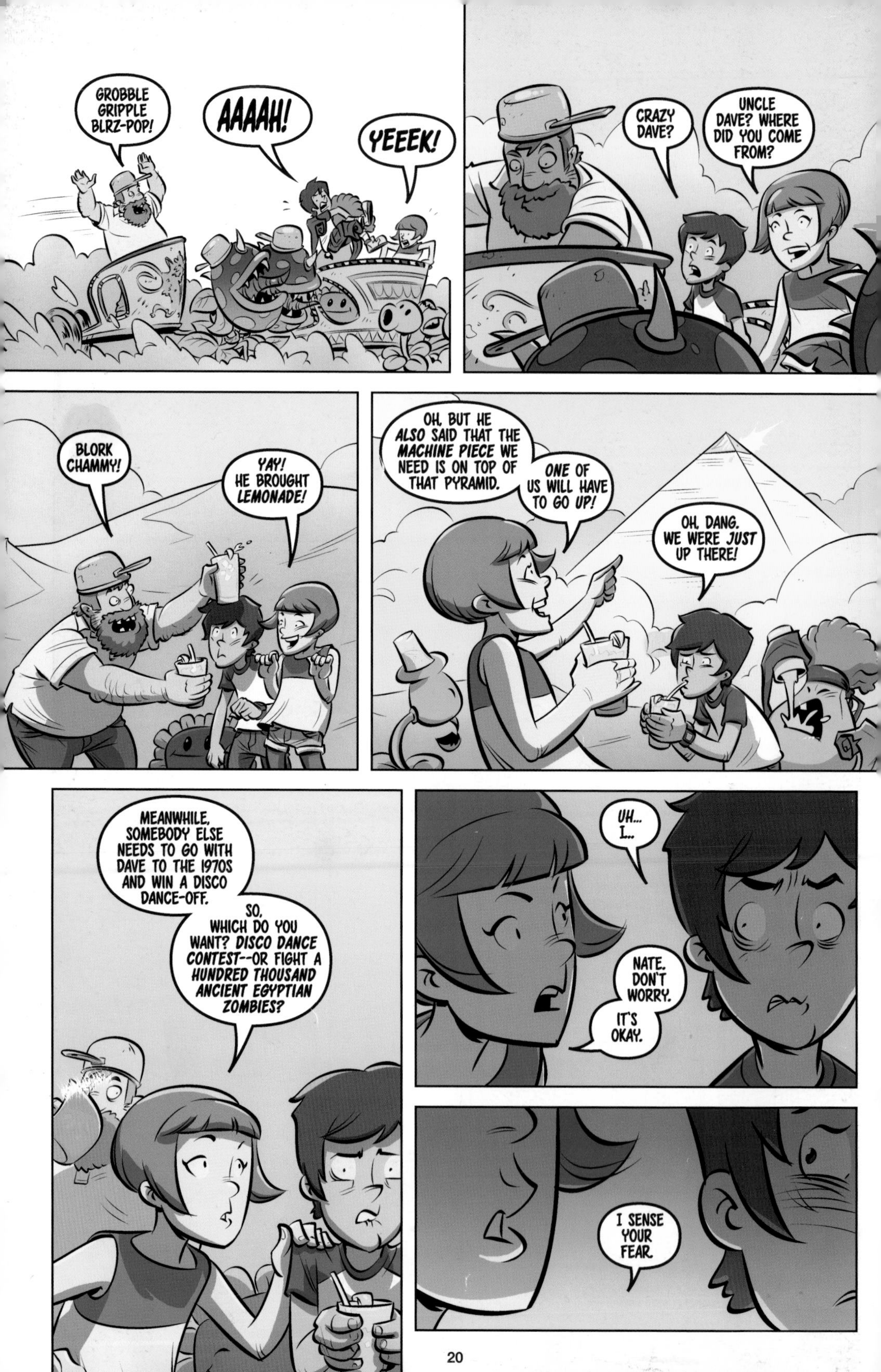
GROBBLE GRIPPLE BLRZ-POP!
AAAAH!
YEEEK!
CRAZY DAVE?
UNCLE DAVE? WHERE DID YOU COME FROM?
BLORK CHAMMY!
YAY! HE BROUGHT LEMONADE!
OH, BUT HE ALSO SAID THAT THE MACHINE PIECE WE NEED IS ON TOP OF THAT PYRAMID.
ONE OF US WILL HAVE TO GO UP!
OH, DANG. WE WERE JUST UP THERE!
MEANWHILE, SOMEBODY ELSE NEEDS TO GO WITH DAVE TO THE 1970S AND WIN A DISCO DANCE-OFF.
SO, WHICH DO YOU WANT? DISCO DANCE CONTEST--OR FIGHT A HUNDRED THOUSAND ANCIENT EGYPTIAN ZOMBIES?
UH... I...
NATE. DON'T WORRY.
IT'S OKAY.
I SENSE YOUR FEAR.

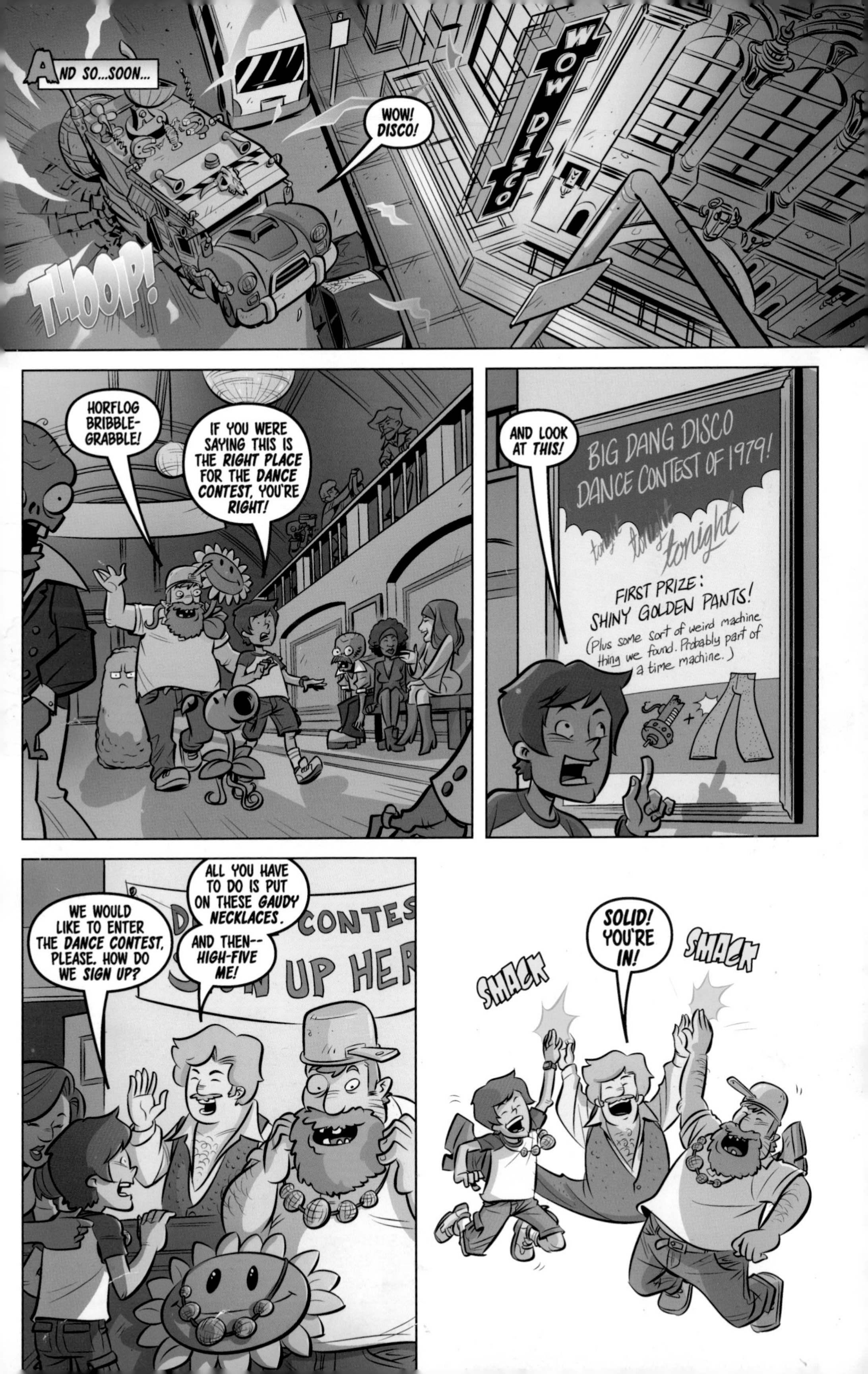

AND SO...SOON...
THOOIP!
WOW! DISCO!
WOW DISCO
HORFLOG BRIBBLE-GRABBLE!
IF YOU WERE SAYING THIS IS THE RIGHT PLACE FOR THE DANCE CONTEST, YOU'RE RIGHT!
AND LOOK AT THIS!
BIG DANG DISCO DANCE CONTEST OF 1979!
tonight tonight tonight
FIRST PRIZE: SHINY GOLDEN PANTS!
(Plus some sort of weird machine thing we found. Probably part of a time machine.)
WE WOULD LIKE TO ENTER THE DANCE CONTEST, PLEASE. HOW DO WE SIGN UP?
ALL YOU HAVE TO DO IS PUT ON THESE GAUDY NECKLACES.
AND THEN--HIGH-FIVE ME!
SMACK
SOLID! YOU'RE IN!
SMACK

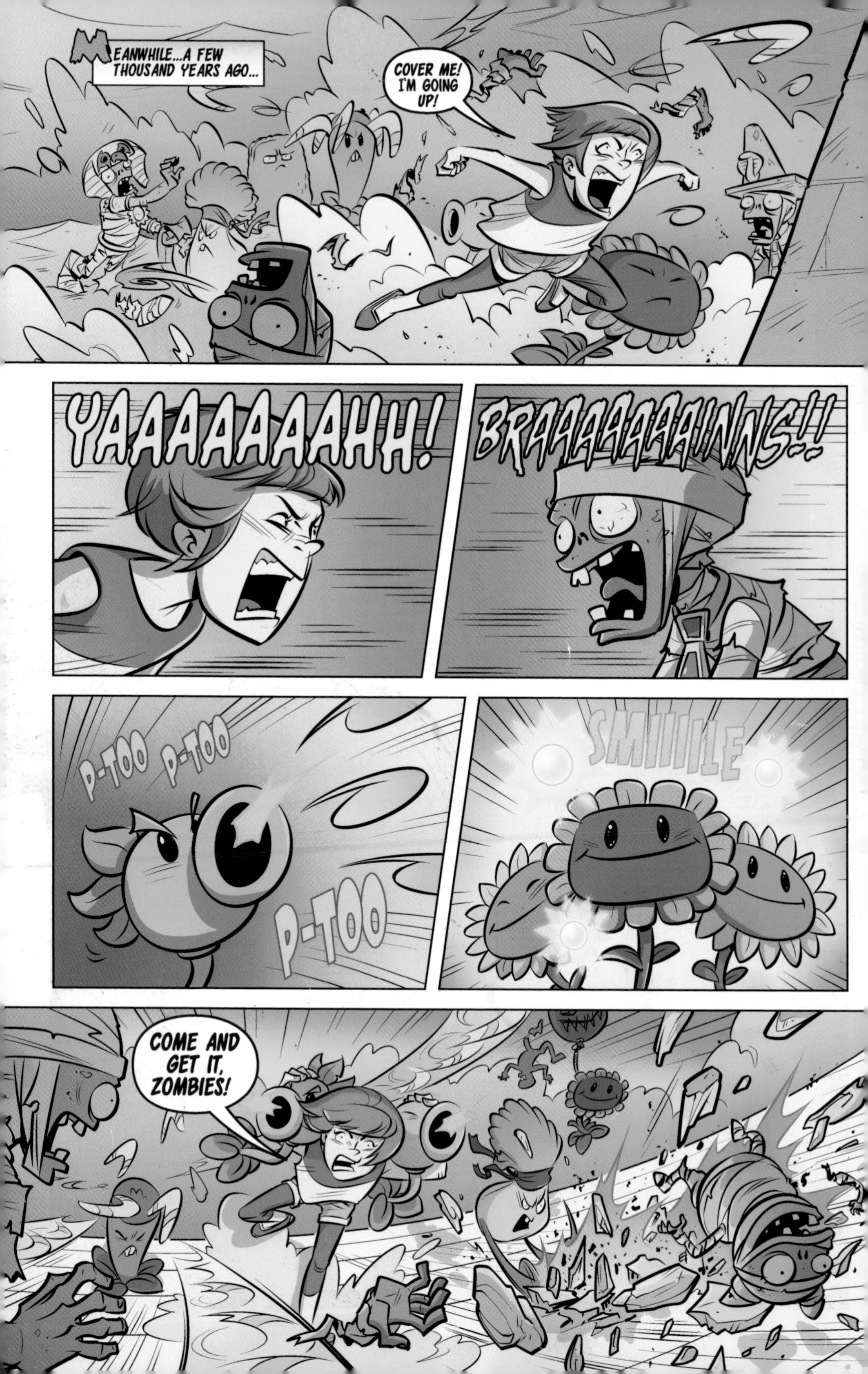
MEANWHILE...A FEW THOUSAND YEARS AGO...
COVER ME! I'M GOING UP!
YAAAAAAAHH!
BRAAAAAAAAINNS!!
P-TOO P-TOO
P-TOO
SMIIIILE
COME AND GET IT, ZOMBIES!

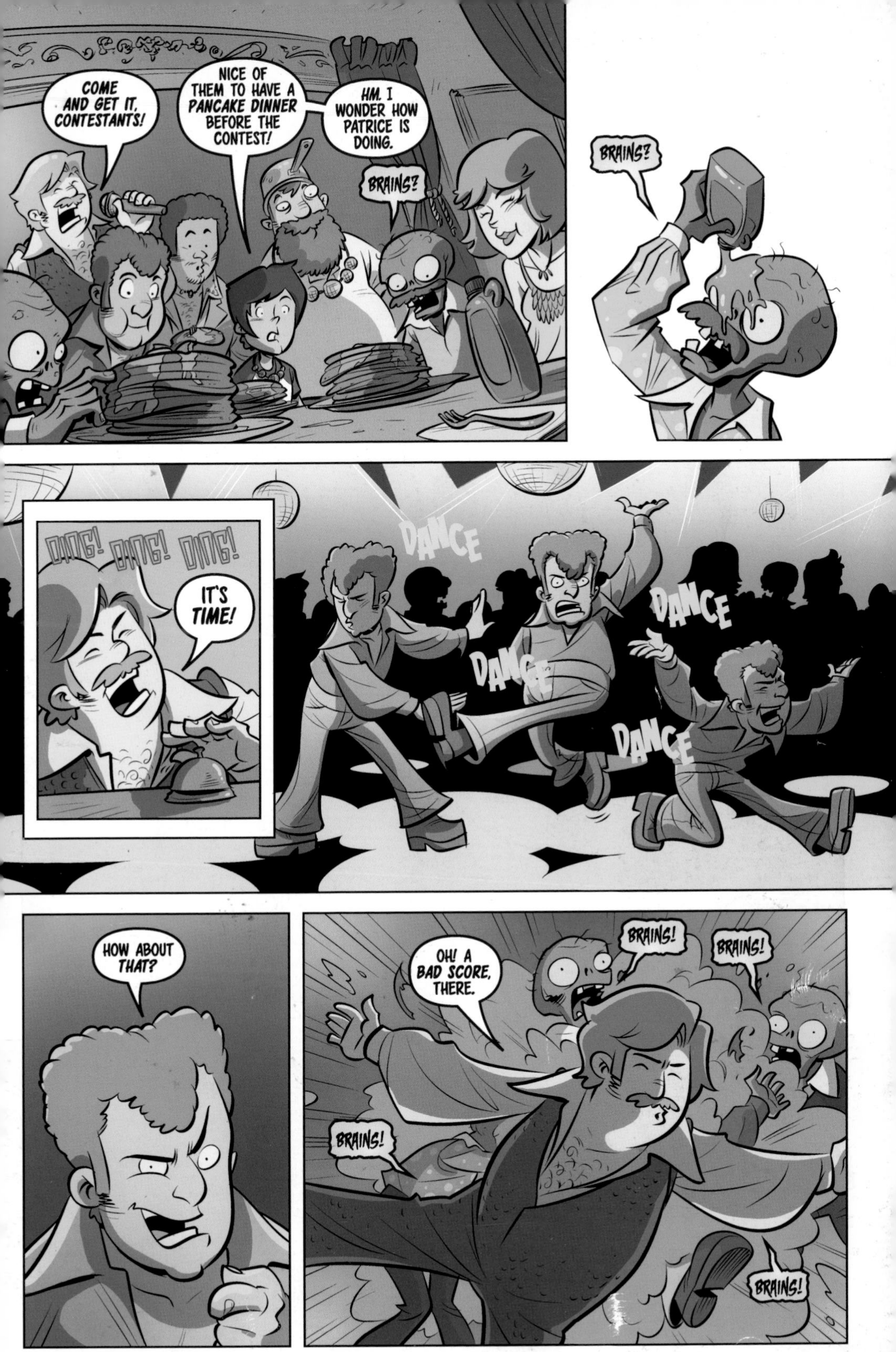
COME AND GET IT, CONTESTANTS!
NICE OF THEM TO HAVE A PANCAKE DINNER BEFORE THE CONTEST!
HM. I WONDER HOW PATRICE IS DOING.
BRAINS?
BRAINS?
DING! DING! DING!
IT'S TIME!
DANCE
DANCE
DANCE
DANCE
HOW ABOUT THAT?
OH! A BAD SCORE, THERE.
BRAINS!
BRAINS!
BRAINS!
BRAINS!

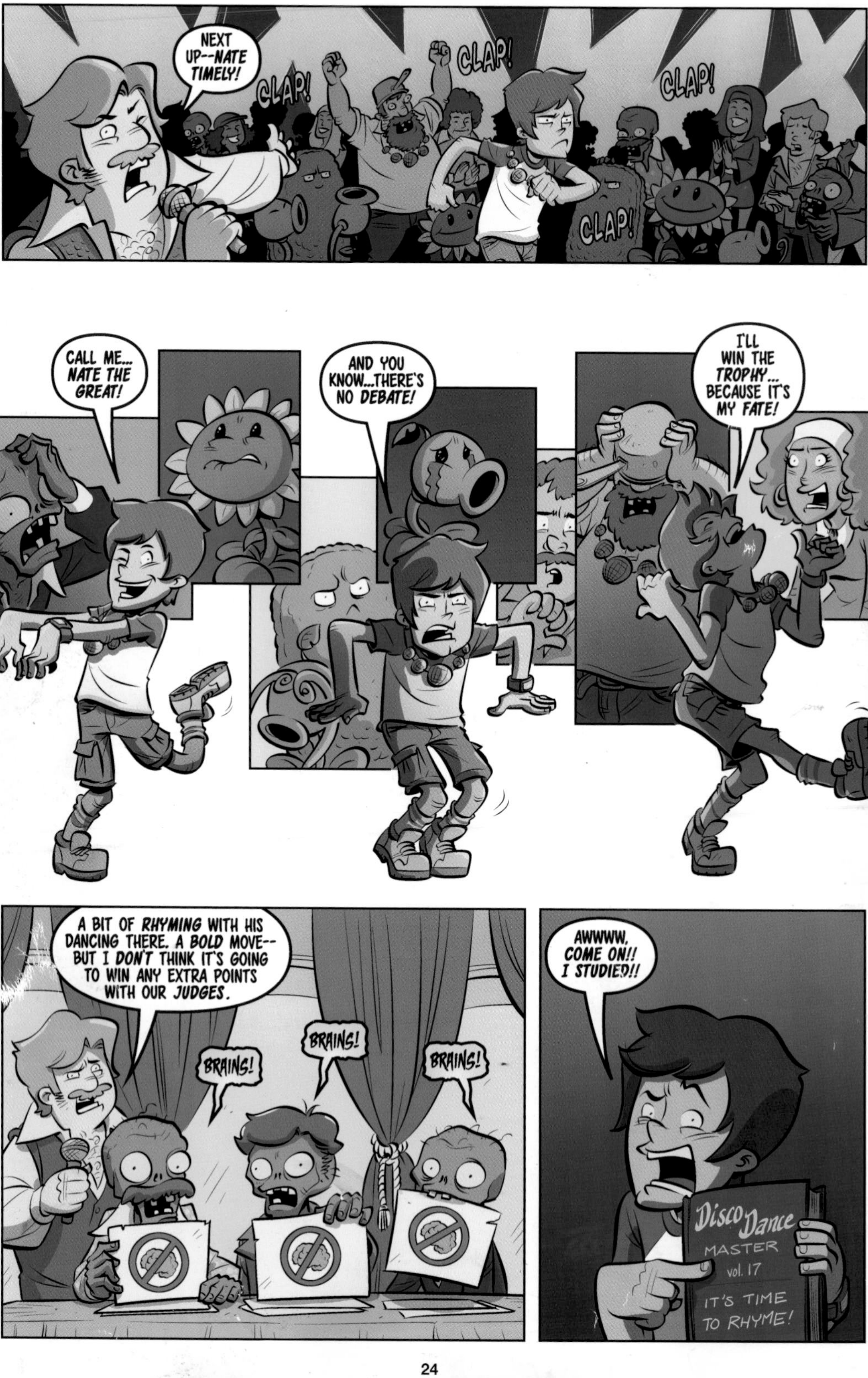

NEXT UP--NATE TIMELY!
CLAP!
CLAP!
CLAP!
CLAP!
CALL ME... NATE THE GREAT!
AND YOU KNOW...THERE'S NO DEBATE!
I'LL WIN THE TROPHY... BECAUSE IT'S MY FATE!
A BIT OF RHYMING WITH HIS DANCING THERE. A BOLD MOVE--BUT I DON'T THINK IT'S GOING TO WIN ANY EXTRA POINTS WITH OUR JUDGES.
BRAINS!
BRAINS!
BRAINS!
AWWWW, COME ON!! I STUDIED!!
Disco Dance MASTER vol. 17
IT'S TIME TO RHYME!

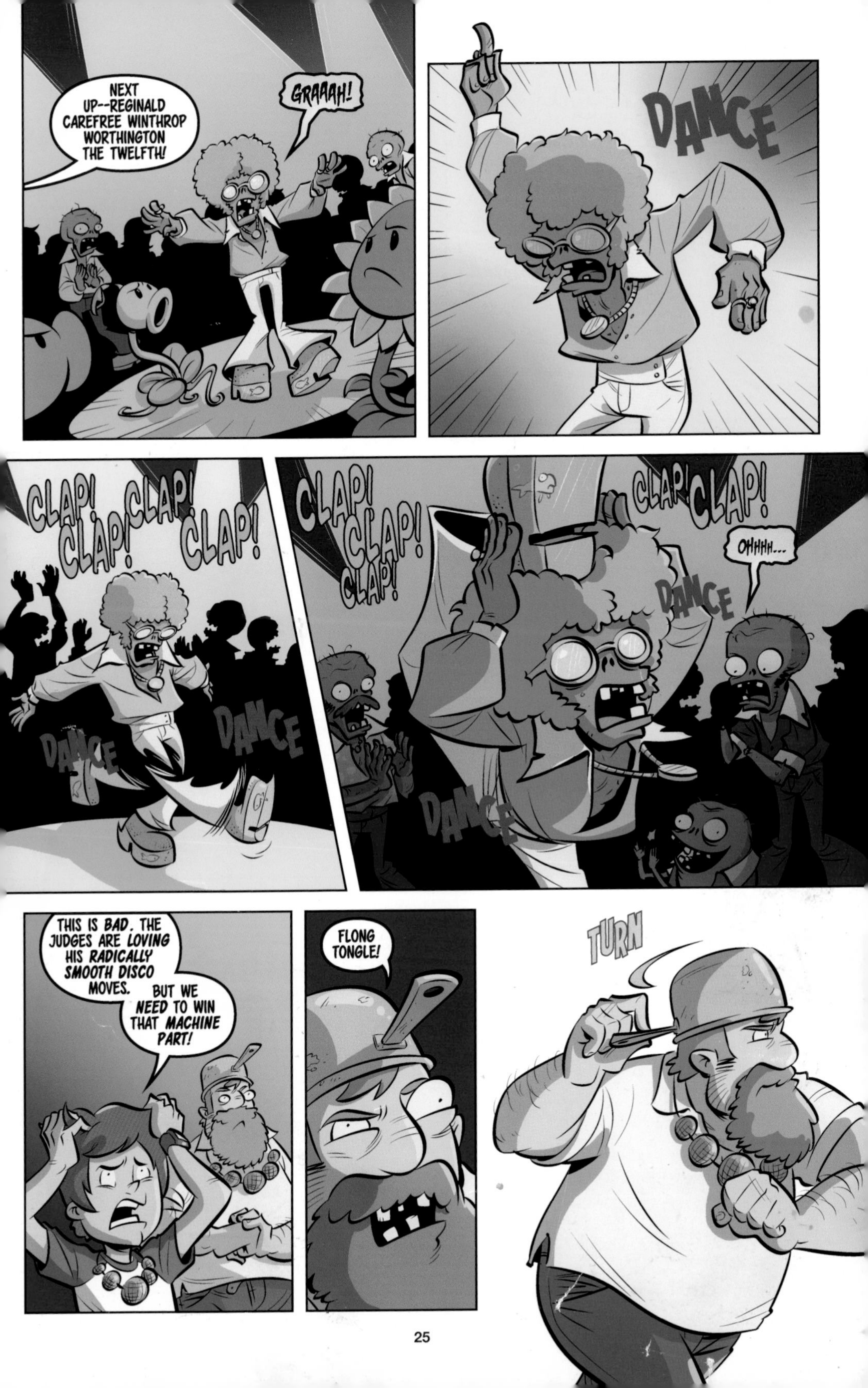
NEXT UP--REGINALD CAREFREE WINTHROP WORTHINGTON THE TWELFTH!
GRAAAAH!
DANCE
CLAP! CLAP! CLAP! CLAP!
DANCE
DANCE
CLAP! CLAP! CLAP!
CLAP! CLAP!
OHHHH...
DANCE
DANCE
THIS IS *BAD*. THE JUDGES ARE *LOVING* HIS *RADICALLY SMOOTH DISCO* MOVES.
BUT WE *NEED* TO WIN THAT *MACHINE* PART!
FLONG TONGLE!
TURN

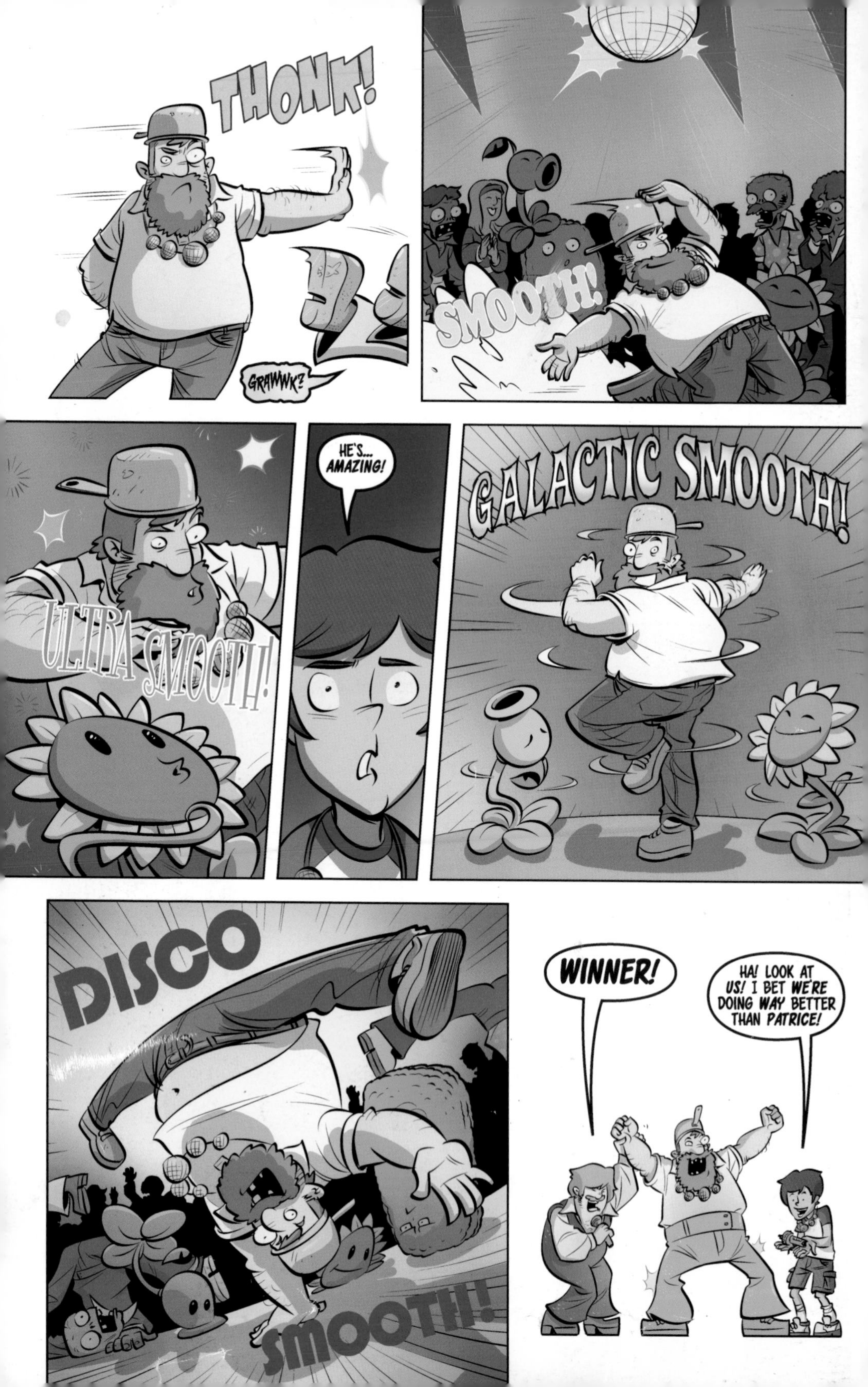
THONK!
GRAWNK?
SMOOTH!
ULTRA SMOOTH!
HE'S... AMAZING!
GALACTIC SMOOTH!
DISCO
SMOOTH!
WINNER!
HA! LOOK AT US! I BET WE'RE DOING WAY BETTER THAN PATRICE!

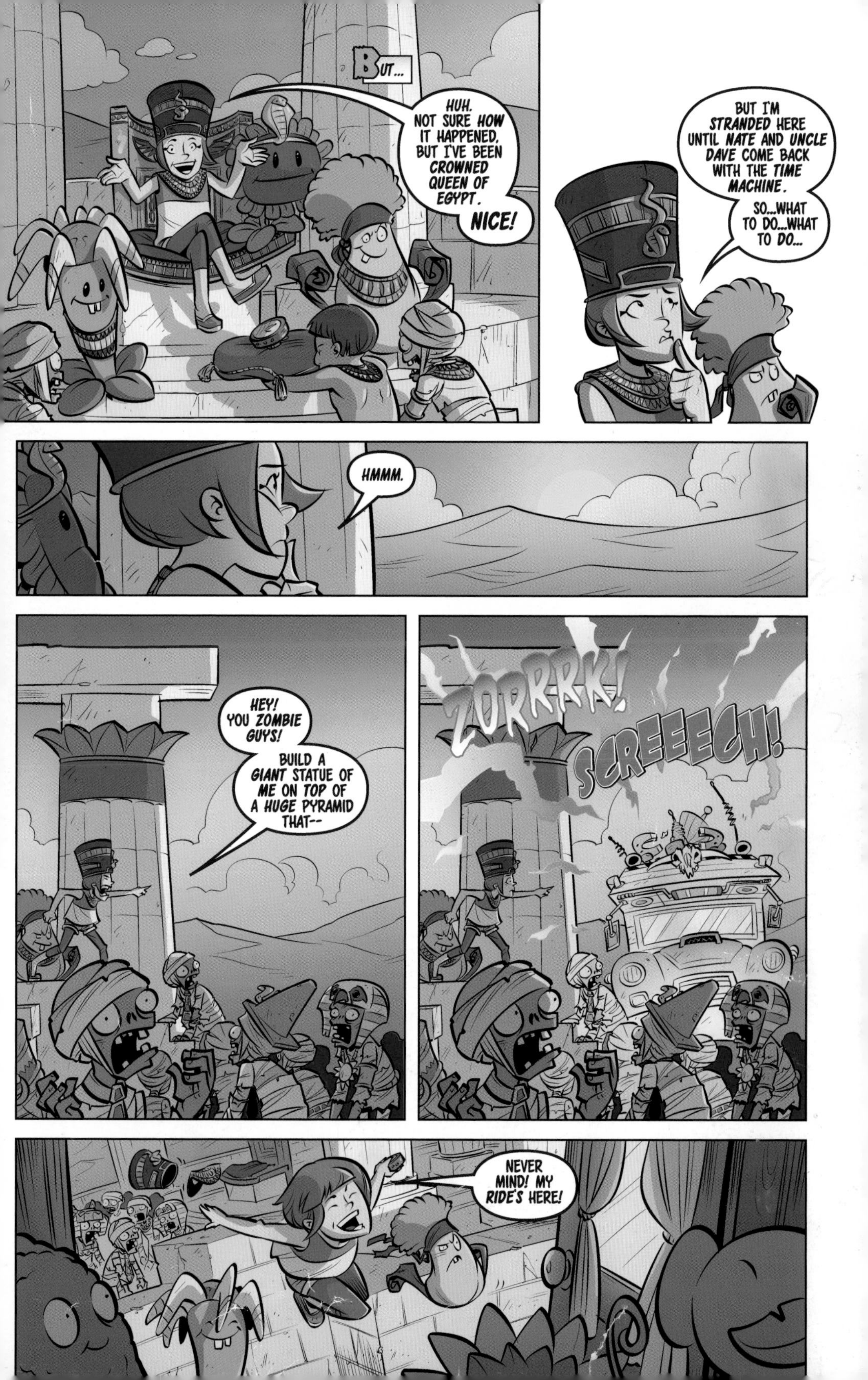
BUT...
HUH. NOT SURE HOW IT HAPPENED, BUT I'VE BEEN CROWNED QUEEN OF EGYPT.
NICE!
BUT I'M STRANDED HERE UNTIL NATE AND UNCLE DAVE COME BACK WITH THE TIME MACHINE.
SO...WHAT TO DO...WHAT TO DO...
HMMM.
HEY! YOU ZOMBIE GUYS!
BUILD A GIANT STATUE OF ME ON TOP OF A HUGE PYRAMID THAT--
ZORRRK!
SCREEECH!
NEVER MIND! MY RIDE'S HERE!

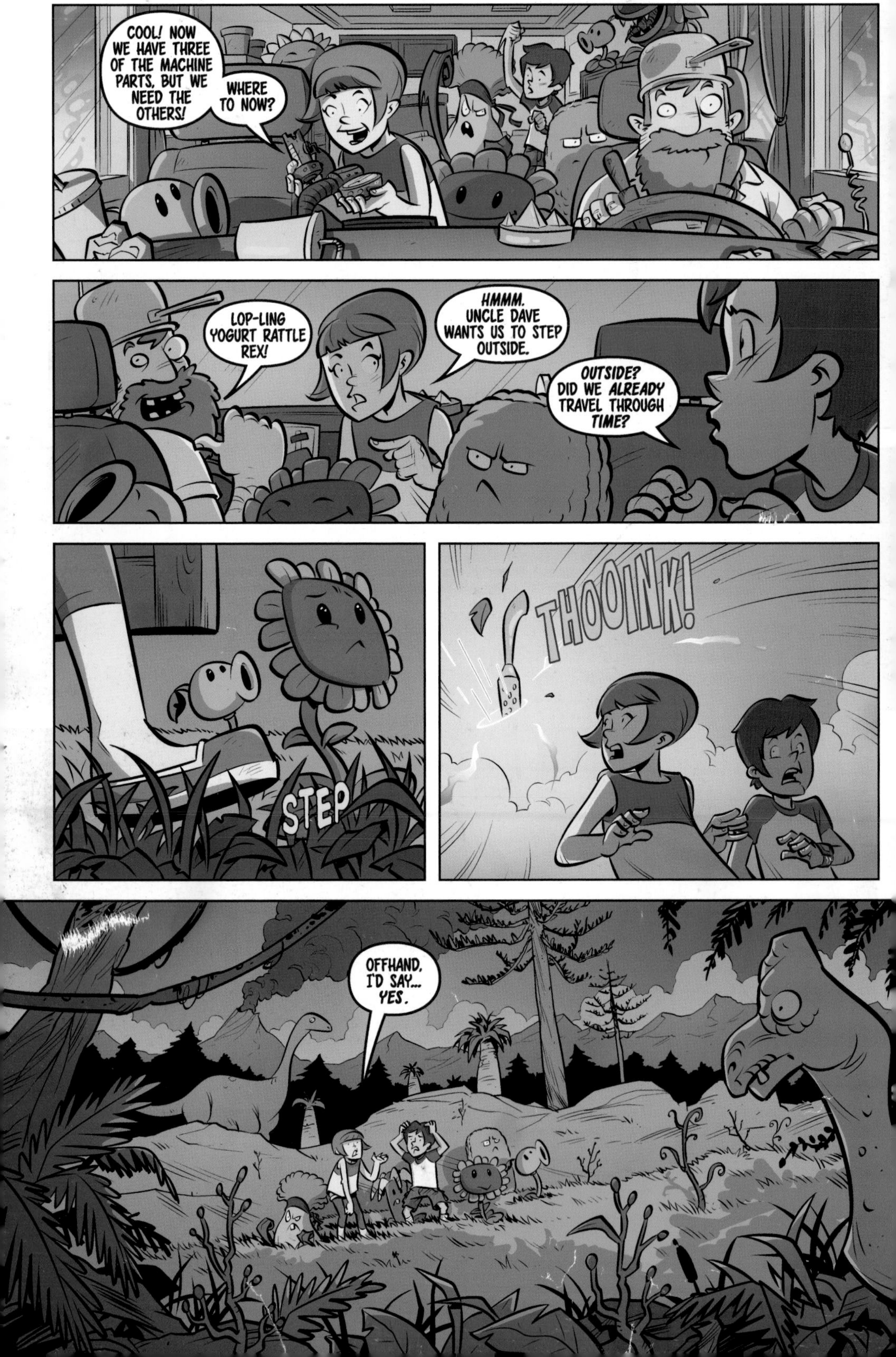
COOL! NOW WE HAVE THREE OF THE MACHINE PARTS, BUT WE NEED THE OTHERS!
WHERE TO NOW?
LOP-LING YOGURT RATTLE REX!
HMMM. UNCLE DAVE WANTS US TO STEP OUTSIDE.
OUTSIDE? DID WE ALREADY TRAVEL THROUGH TIME?
STEP
THOOINK!
OFFHAND, I'D SAY... YES.

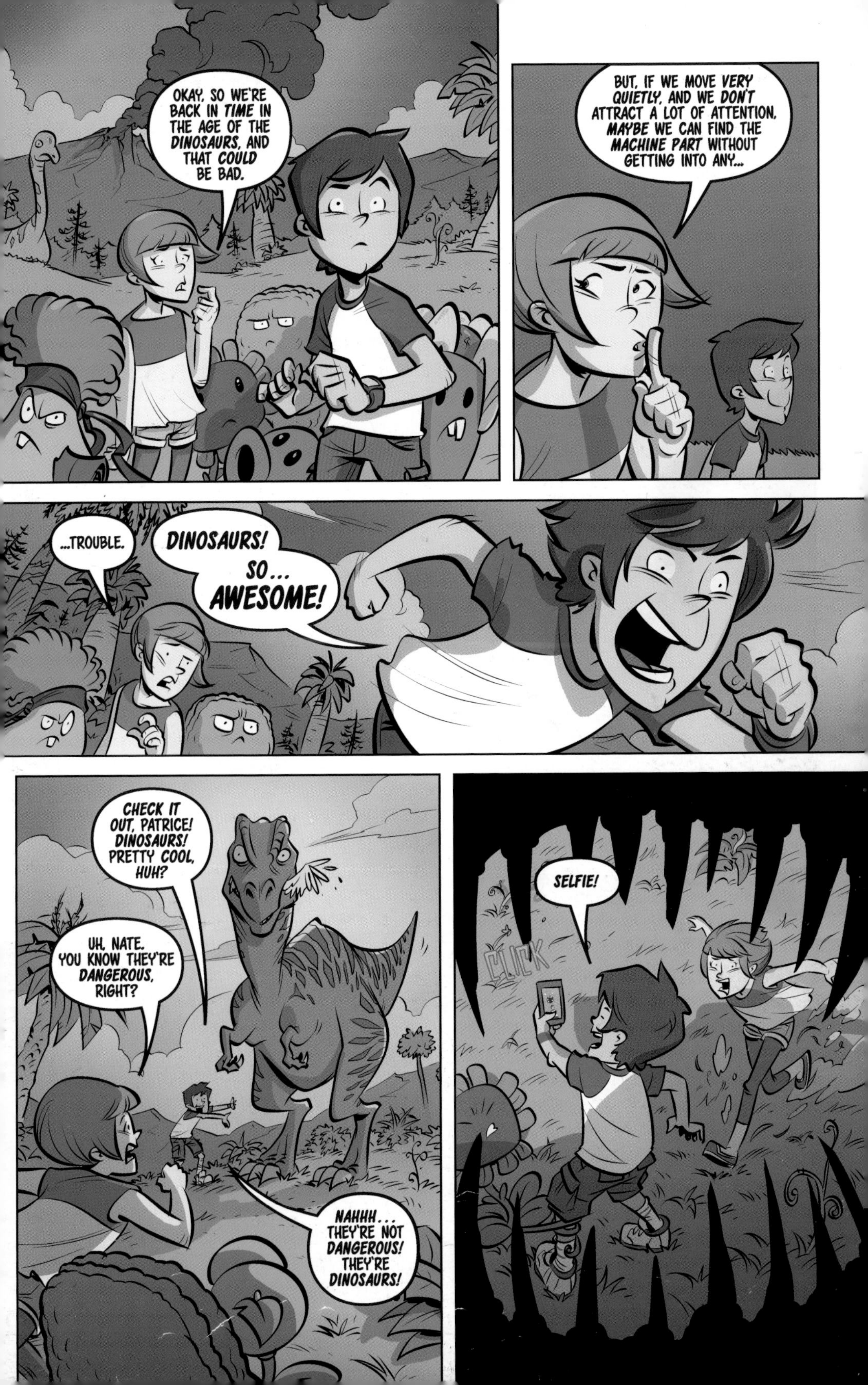
OKAY, SO WE'RE BACK IN TIME IN THE AGE OF THE DINOSAURS, AND THAT COULD BE BAD.
BUT, IF WE MOVE VERY QUIETLY, AND WE DON'T ATTRACT A LOT OF ATTENTION, MAYBE WE CAN FIND THE MACHINE PART WITHOUT GETTING INTO ANY...
...TROUBLE.
DINOSAURS! SO... AWESOME!
CHECK IT OUT, PATRICE! DINOSAURS! PRETTY COOL, HUH?
UH, NATE. YOU KNOW THEY'RE DANGEROUS, RIGHT?
NAHHH... THEY'RE NOT DANGEROUS! THEY'RE DINOSAURS!
CLICK
SELFIE!

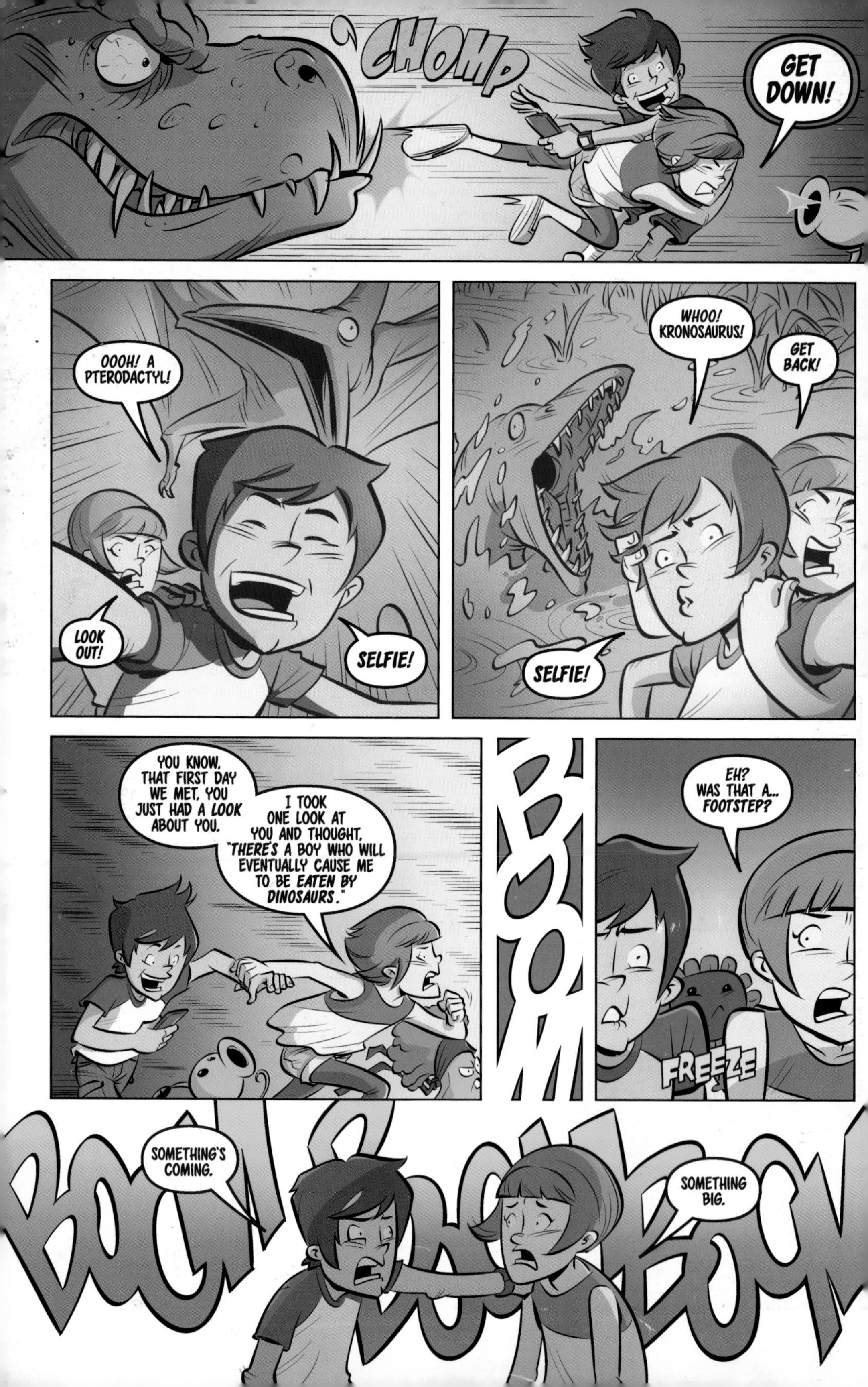
CHOMP
GET DOWN!
OOOH! A PTERODACTYL!
LOOK OUT!
SELFIE!
WHOO! KRONOSAURUS!
GET BACK!
SELFIE!
YOU KNOW, THAT FIRST DAY WE MET, YOU JUST HAD A LOOK ABOUT YOU.
I TOOK ONE LOOK AT YOU AND THOUGHT, "THERE'S A BOY WHO WILL EVENTUALLY CAUSE ME TO BE EATEN BY DINOSAURS."
BOOM
EH? WAS THAT A... FOOTSTEP?
FREEZE
SOMETHING'S COMING.
SOMETHING BIG.
BOOM BOOM BOOM

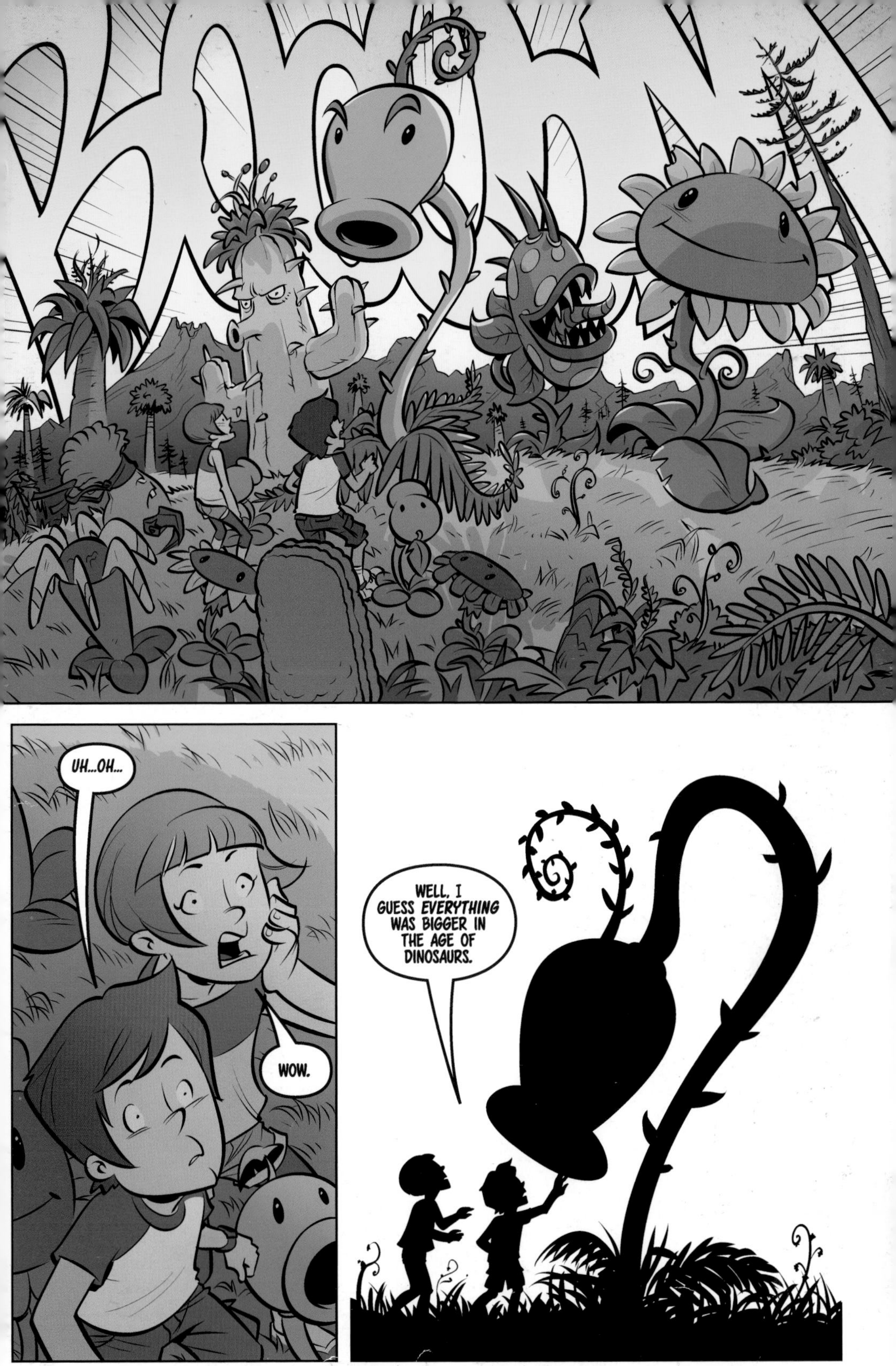
UH...OH...
WOW.
WELL, I GUESS EVERYTHING WAS BIGGER IN THE AGE OF DINOSAURS.

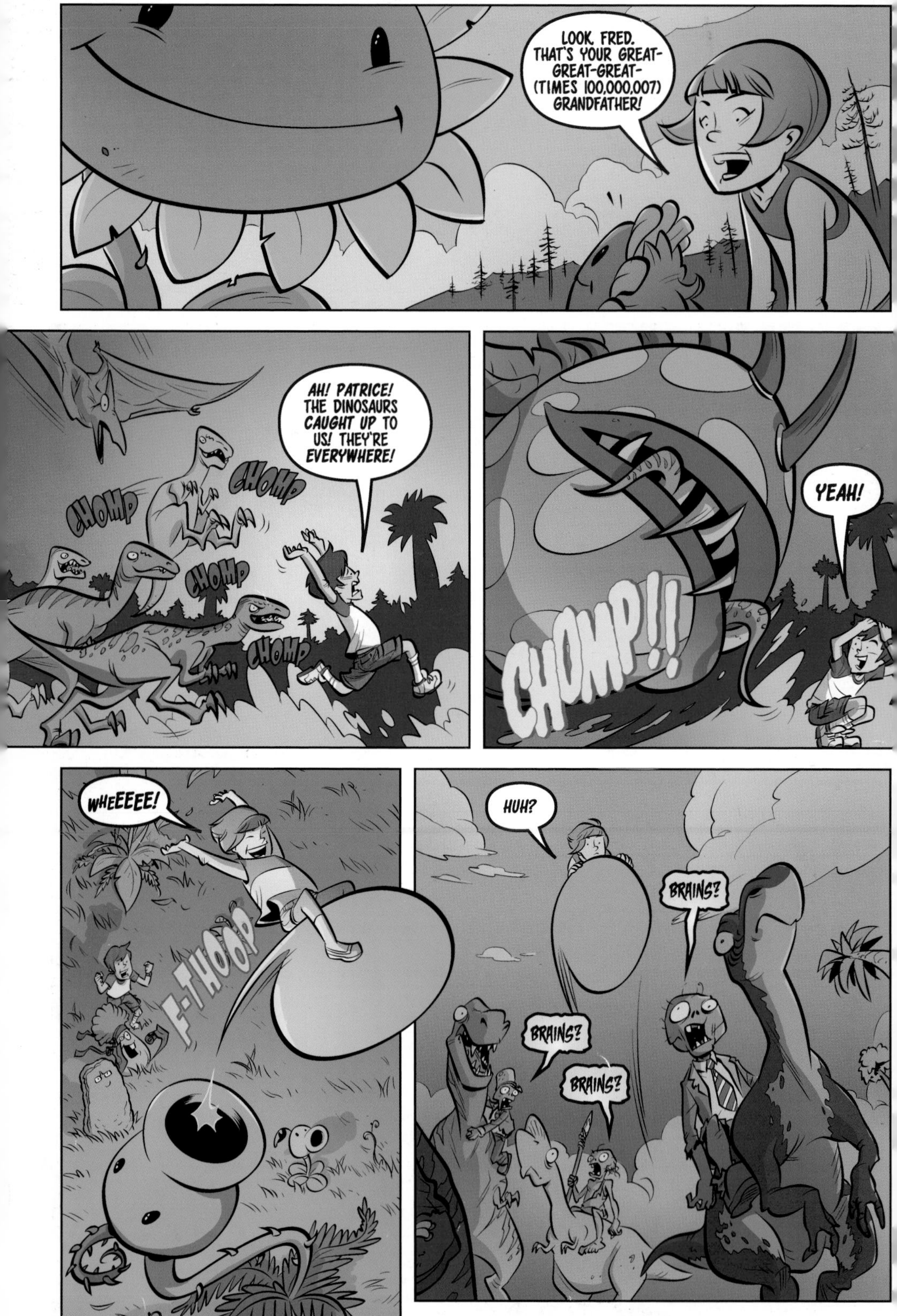
LOOK, FRED. THAT'S YOUR GREAT-GREAT-GREAT-(TIMES 100,000,007) GRANDFATHER!
AH! PATRICE! THE DINOSAURS CAUGHT UP TO US! THEY'RE EVERYWHERE!
CHOMP
CHOMP
CHOMP
CHOMP
YEAH!
CHOMP!!!
WHEEEEE!
F-THOOP
HUH?
BRAINS?
BRAINS?
BRAINS?

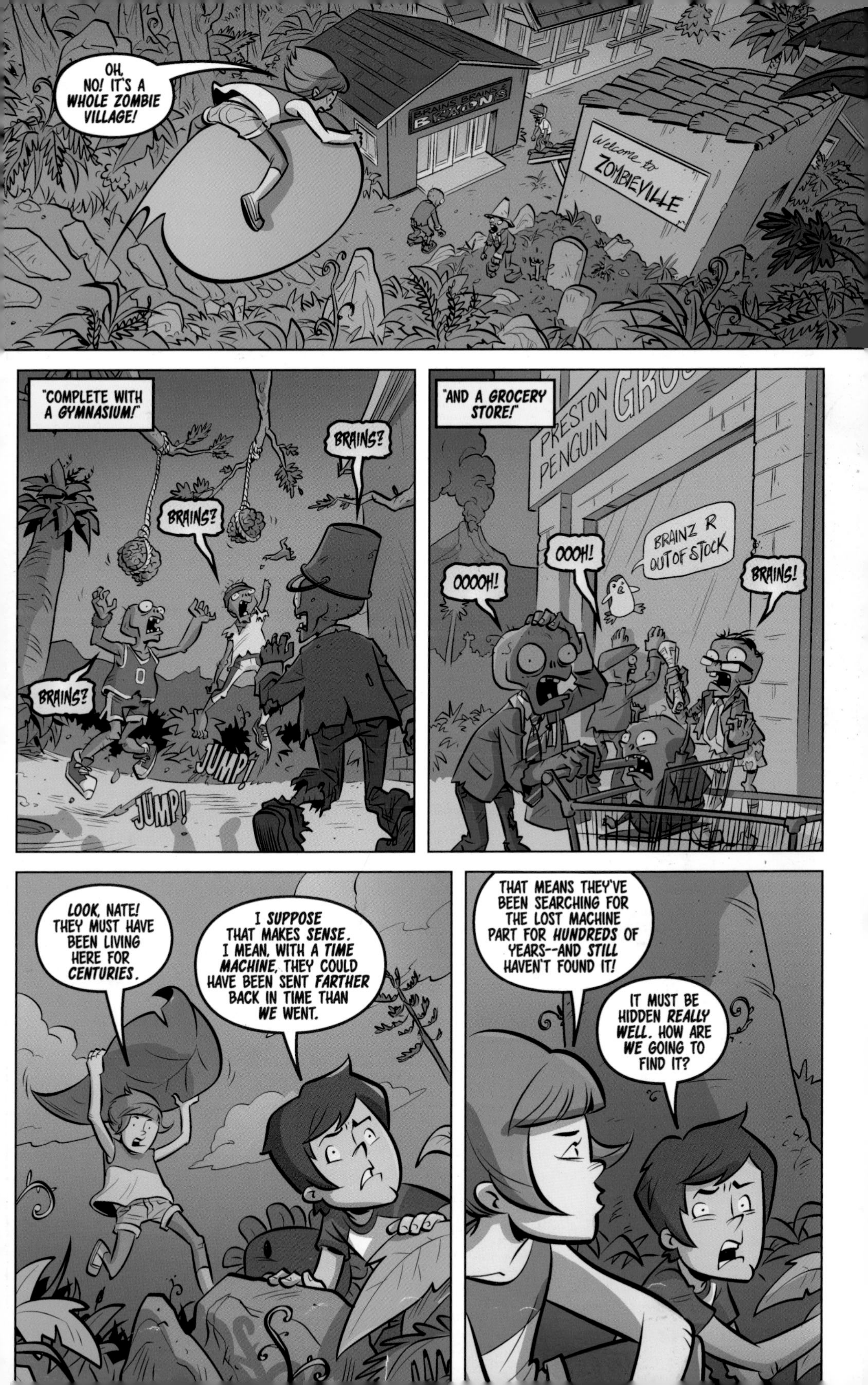

OH, NO! IT'S A WHOLE ZOMBIE VILLAGE!
BRAINS BRAINS & BRAINS
Welcome to ZOMBIEVILLE
"COMPLETE WITH A GYMNASIUM!"
BRAINS?
BRAINS?
BRAINS?
JUMP!
JUMP!
"AND A GROCERY STORE!"
PRESTON PENGUIN GRO
BRAINZ R OUT OF STOCK
OOOOH!
OOOH!
BRAINS!
LOOK, NATE! THEY MUST HAVE BEEN LIVING HERE FOR CENTURIES.
I SUPPOSE THAT MAKES SENSE. I MEAN, WITH A TIME MACHINE, THEY COULD HAVE BEEN SENT FARTHER BACK IN TIME THAN WE WENT.
THAT MEANS THEY'VE BEEN SEARCHING FOR THE LOST MACHINE PART FOR HUNDREDS OF YEARS--AND STILL HAVEN'T FOUND IT!
IT MUST BE HIDDEN REALLY WELL. HOW ARE WE GOING TO FIND IT?

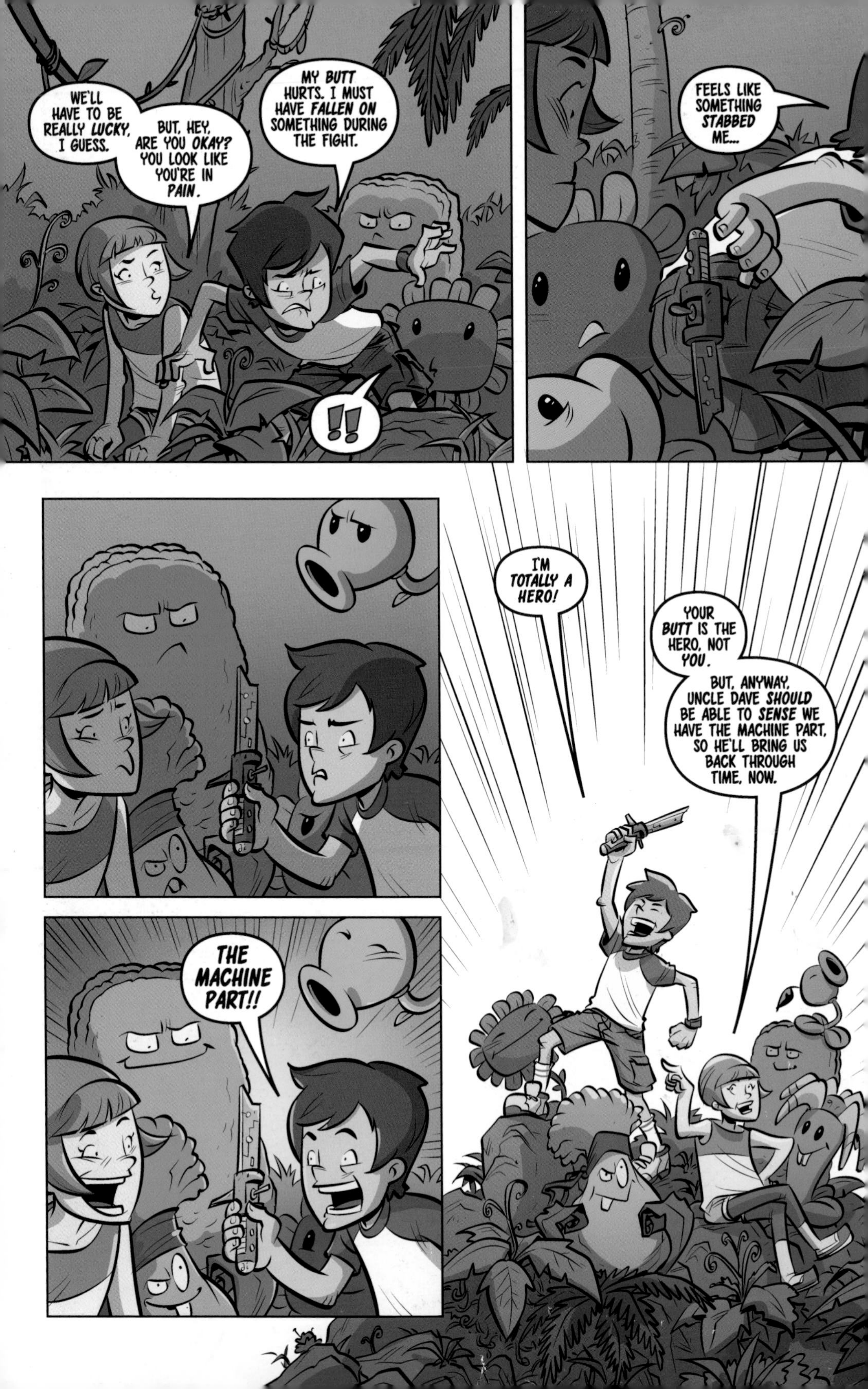
WE'LL HAVE TO BE REALLY LUCKY, I GUESS.
BUT, HEY, ARE YOU OKAY? YOU LOOK LIKE YOU'RE IN PAIN.
MY BUTT HURTS. I MUST HAVE FALLEN ON SOMETHING DURING THE FIGHT.
!!
FEELS LIKE SOMETHING STABBED ME...
THE MACHINE PART!!
I'M TOTALLY A HERO!
YOUR BUTT IS THE HERO, NOT YOU.
BUT, ANYWAY, UNCLE DAVE SHOULD BE ABLE TO SENSE WE HAVE THE MACHINE PART, SO HE'LL BRING US BACK THROUGH TIME, NOW.

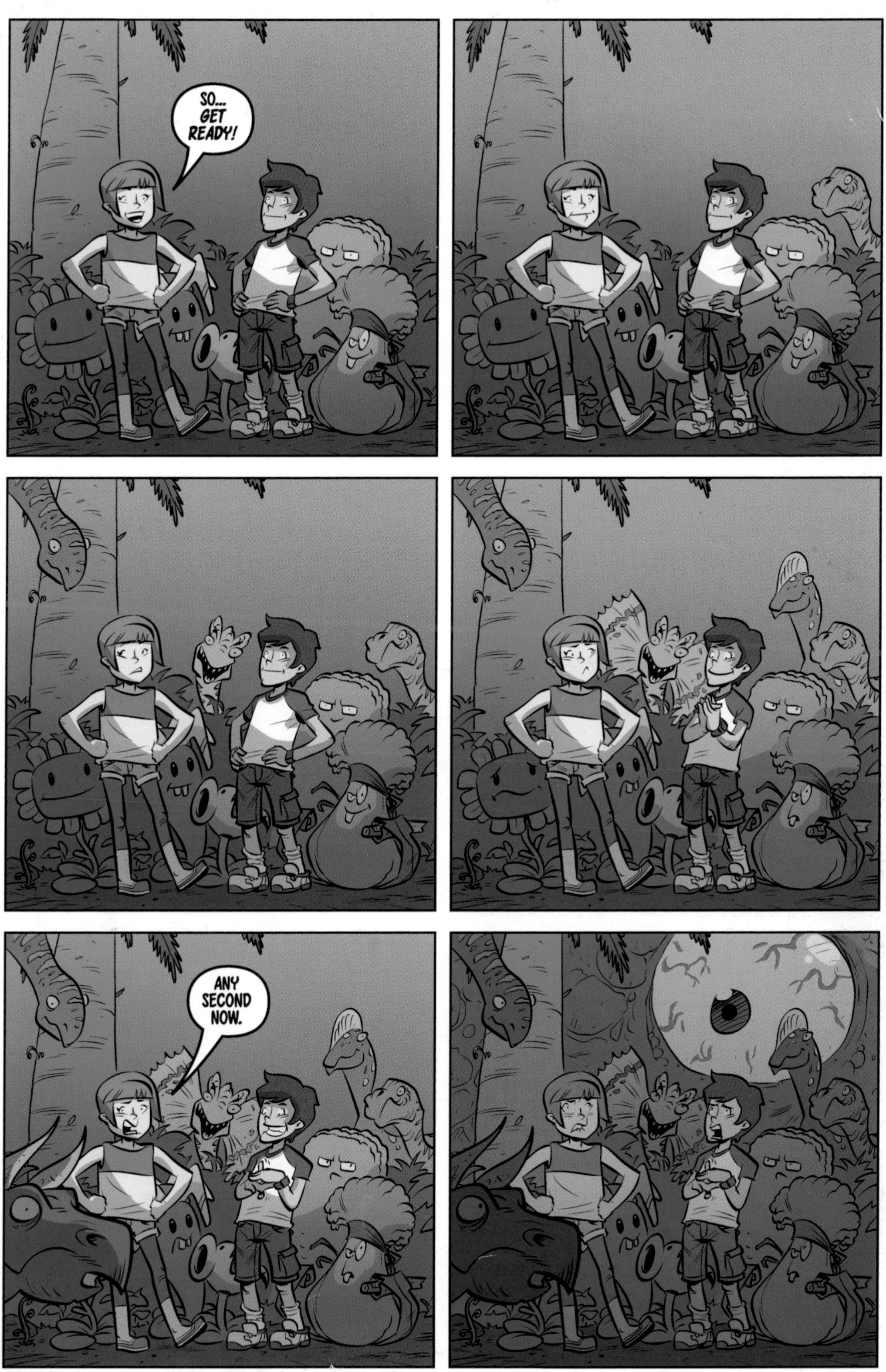
SO... GET READY!
ANY SECOND NOW.

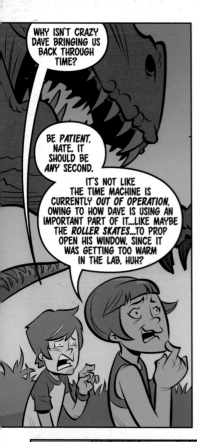

WHY ISN'T CRAZY DAVE BRINGING US BACK THROUGH TIME?

BE PATIENT, NATE. IT SHOULD BE ANY SECOND.

IT'S NOT LIKE THE TIME MACHINE IS CURRENTLY *OUT OF OPERATION*, OWING TO HOW DAVE IS USING AN IMPORTANT PART OF IT...LIKE MAYBE THE *ROLLER SKATES*...TO PROP OPEN HIS WINDOW, SINCE IT WAS GETTING TOO WARM IN THE LAB, HUH?

EANWHILE, MILLIONS OF YEARS IN THE FUTURE...

LA, LA, LA! GARBLE-GRABBLE LA!

OH, THAT'S *TOTALLY* HAPPENING.

OKAY, SO YOU AND I HAVE TO SURVIVE *LONG ENOUGH* FOR DAVE TO REMEMBER THAT HE SENT US BACK TO THE *AGE OF THE DINOSAURS* IN AN ATTEMPT TO SAVE *THE WORLD.*

YOU KNOW, THAT'S SOMETHING THAT *MOST* OF US, QUITE FRANKLY, WOULD *REMEMBER.*

WELL, *WE* NEED TO REMEMBER TO *FIGHT!*

FIGHT? I THOUGHT WE WERE GOING TO RUN.

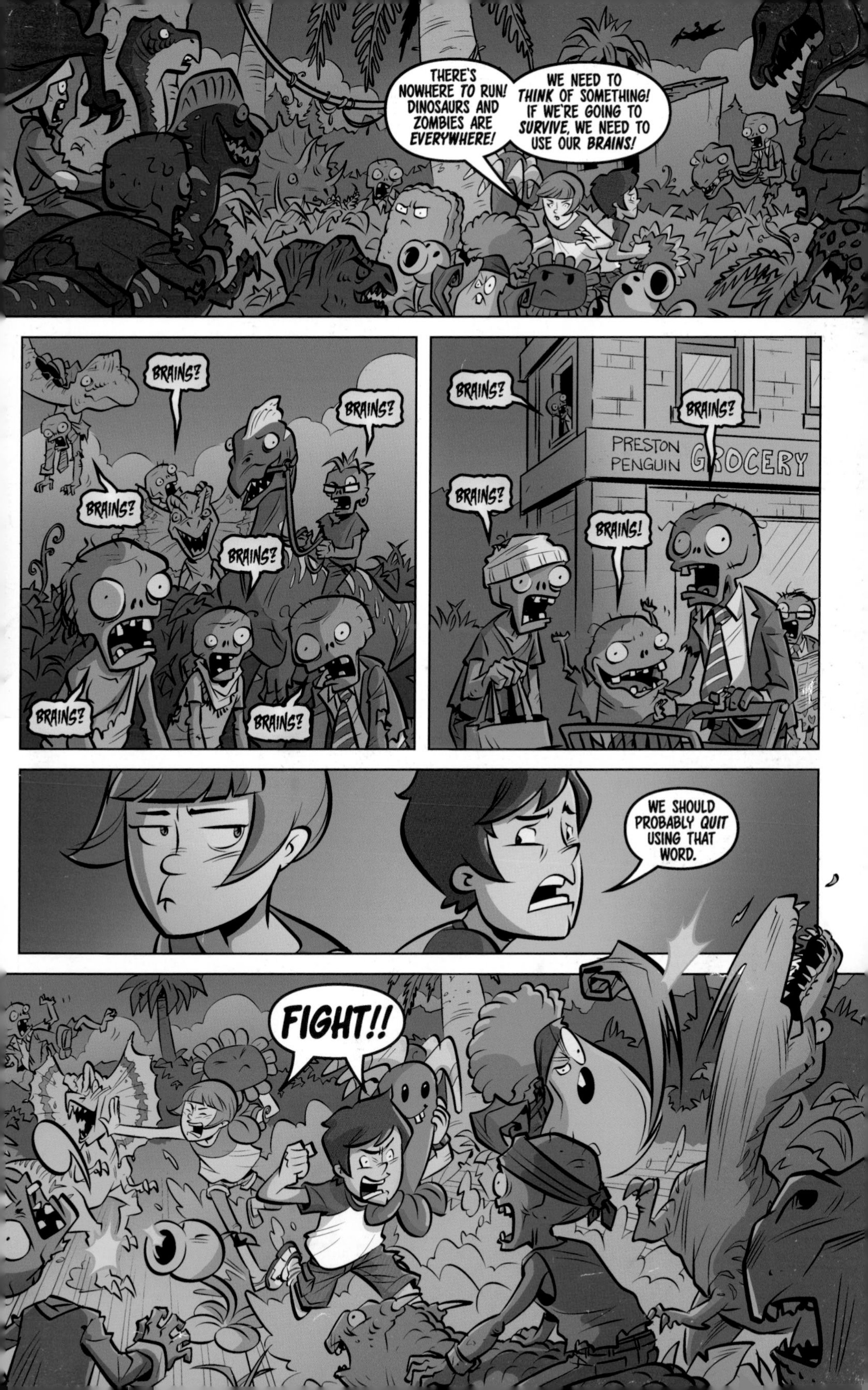
THERE'S NOWHERE TO RUN! DINOSAURS AND ZOMBIES ARE EVERYWHERE!
WE NEED TO THINK OF SOMETHING! IF WE'RE GOING TO SURVIVE, WE NEED TO USE OUR BRAINS!
BRAINS?
BRAINS?
BRAINS?
BRAINS?
BRAINS?
BRAINS?
BRAINS?
BRAINS?
PRESTON PENGUIN GROCERY
BRAINS?
BRAINS?
BRAINS!
WE SHOULD PROBABLY QUIT USING THAT WORD.
FIGHT!!

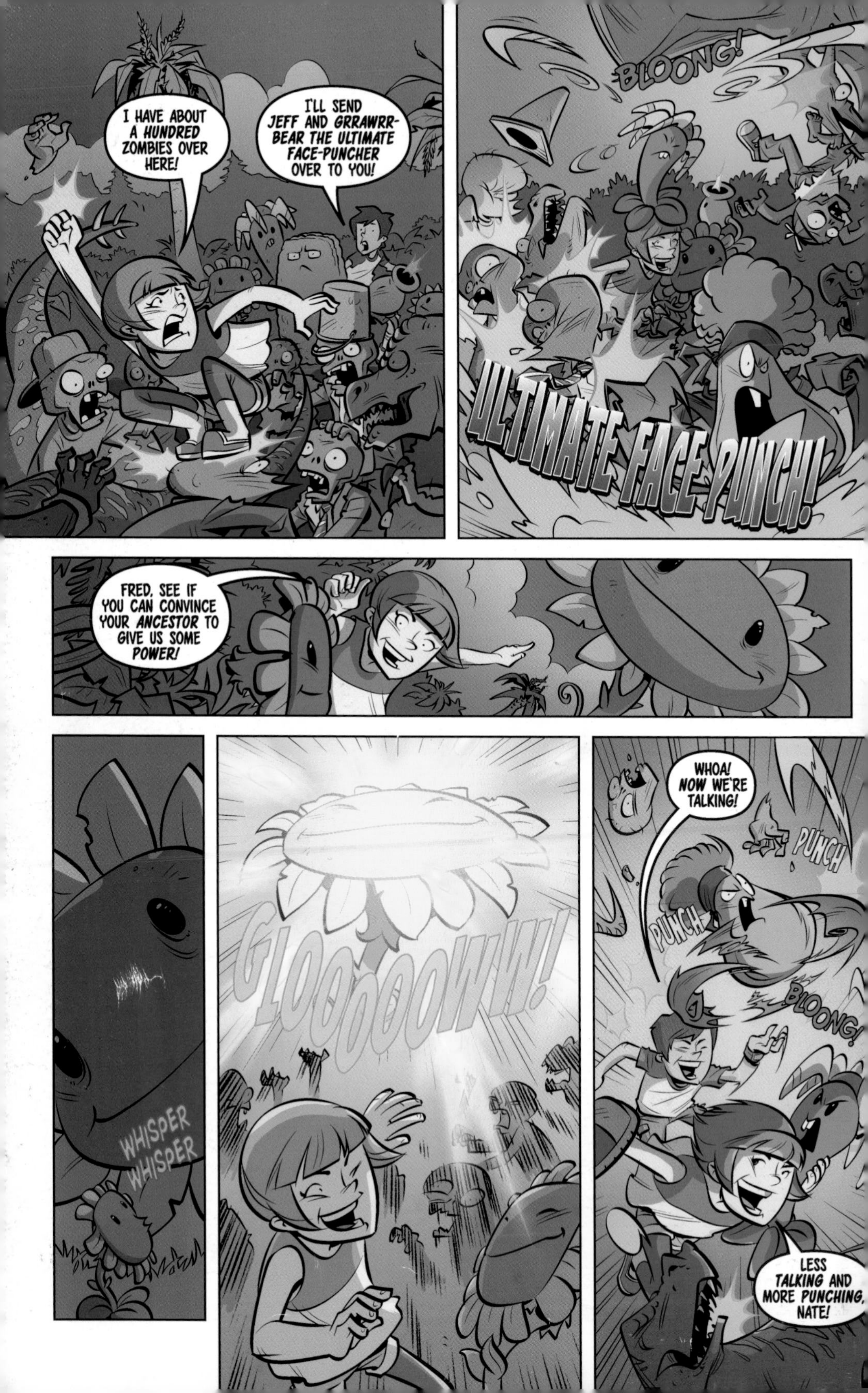

I HAVE ABOUT A HUNDRED ZOMBIES OVER HERE!
I'LL SEND JEFF AND GRRAWRR-BEAR THE ULTIMATE FACE-PUNCHER OVER TO YOU!
BLOONG!
ULTIMATE FACE PUNCH!
FRED, SEE IF YOU CAN CONVINCE YOUR ANCESTOR TO GIVE US SOME POWER!
WHISPER WHISPER
GLOOOOOWW!
WHOA! NOW WE'RE TALKING!
PUNCH
PUNCH
BLOONG!
LESS TALKING AND MORE PUNCHING, NATE!

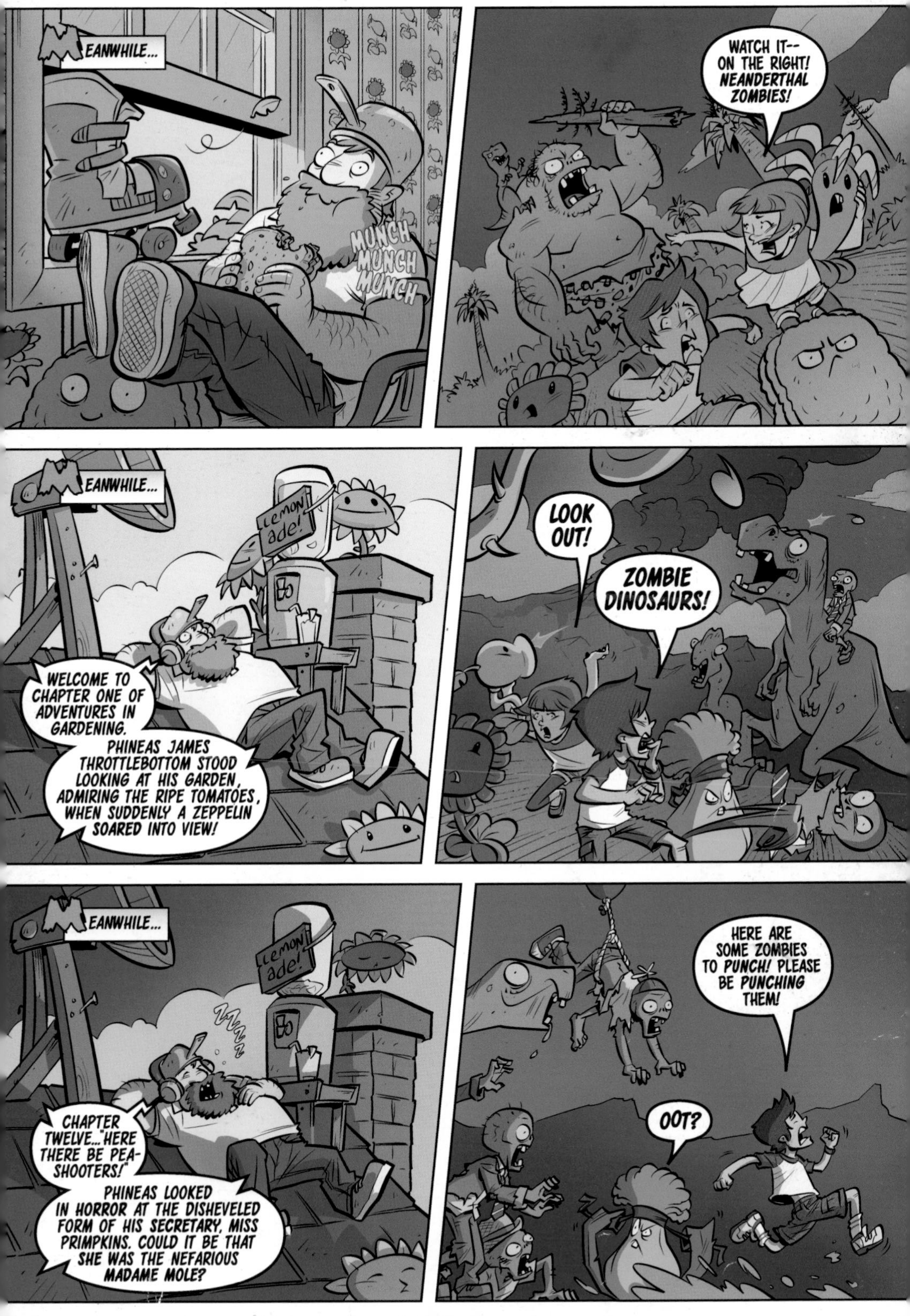
MEANWHILE...
MUNCH MUNCH MUNCH
WATCH IT-- ON THE RIGHT! NEANDERTHAL ZOMBIES!
MEANWHILE...
LEMON ade!
WELCOME TO CHAPTER ONE OF ADVENTURES IN GARDENING.
PHINEAS JAMES THROTTLEBOTTOM STOOD LOOKING AT HIS GARDEN, ADMIRING THE RIPE TOMATOES, WHEN SUDDENLY A ZEPPELIN SOARED INTO VIEW!
LOOK OUT!
ZOMBIE DINOSAURS!
MEANWHILE...
LEMON ade!
ZZZZ
CHAPTER TWELVE..."HERE THERE BE PEA-SHOOTERS!"
PHINEAS LOOKED IN HORROR AT THE DISHEVELED FORM OF HIS SECRETARY, MISS PRIMPKINS. COULD IT BE THAT SHE WAS THE NEFARIOUS MADAME MOLE?
HERE ARE SOME ZOMBIES TO PUNCH! PLEASE BE PUNCHING THEM!
OOT?

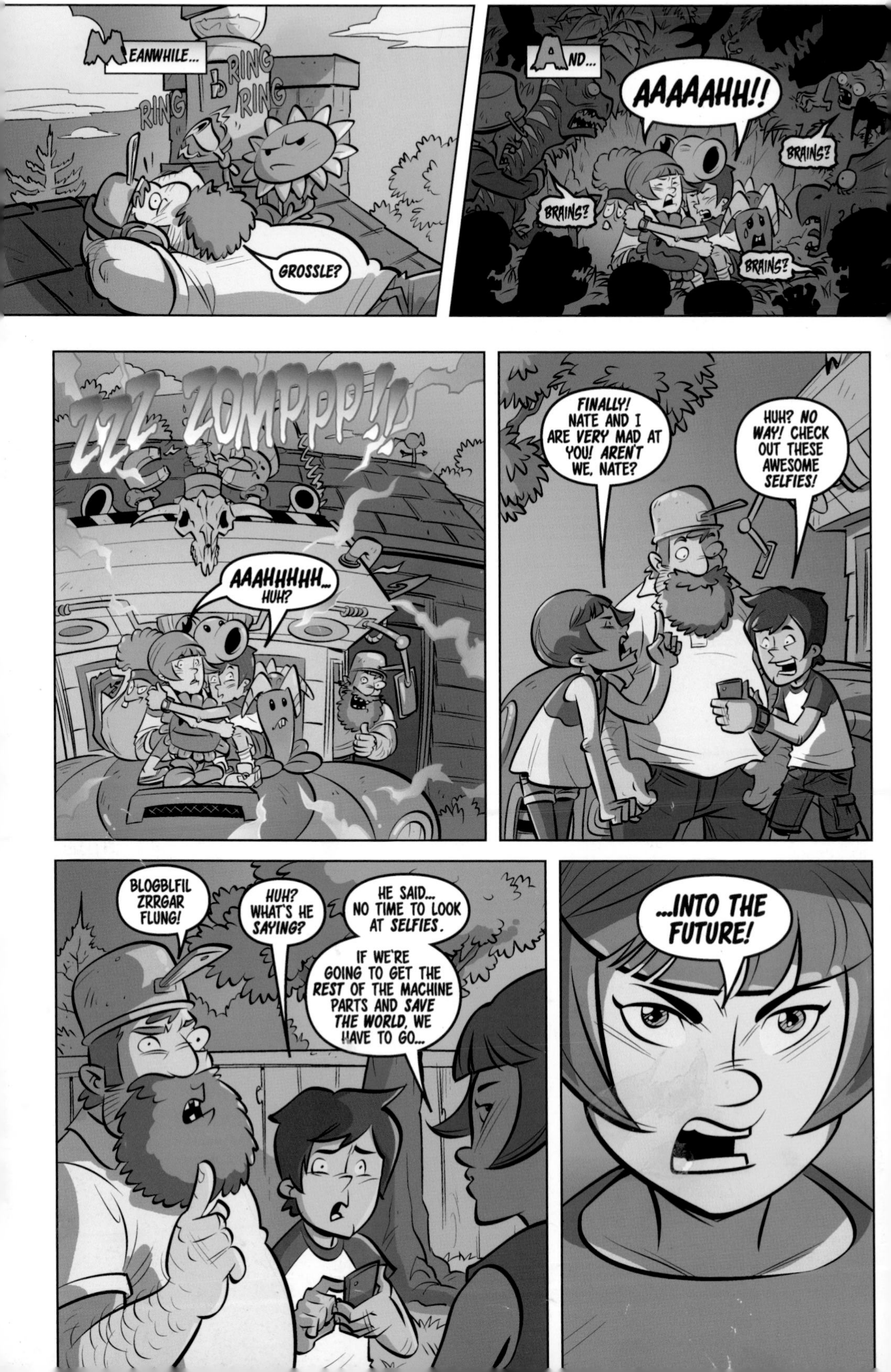
MEANWHILE...
RING
BRING
RING
GROSSLE?
AND...
AAAAAHH!!
BRAINS?
BRAINS?
BRAINS?
ZZZ ZOMPPP!!!
AAAHHHHH... HUH?
FINALLY! NATE AND I ARE VERY MAD AT YOU! AREN'T WE, NATE?
HUH? NO WAY! CHECK OUT THESE AWESOME SELFIES!
BLOGBLFIL ZRRGAR FLUNG!
HUH? WHAT'S HE SAYING?
HE SAID... NO TIME TO LOOK AT SELFIES.
IF WE'RE GOING TO GET THE REST OF THE MACHINE PARTS AND SAVE THE WORLD, WE HAVE TO GO...
...INTO THE FUTURE!

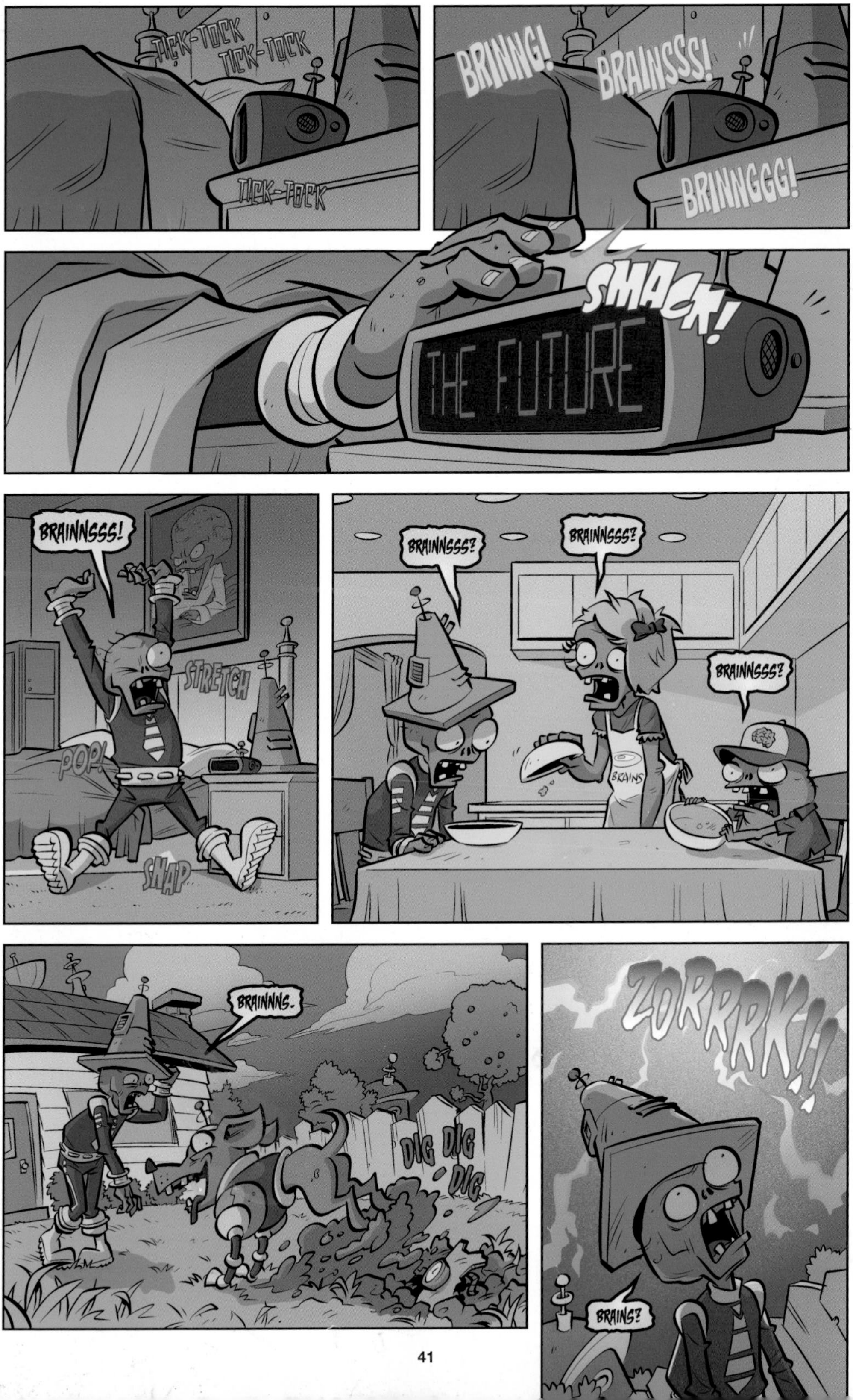
TICK-TOCK
TICK-TOCK
TICK-TOCK
BRINNG!
BRAINSSS!
BRINNGGG!
SMACK!
THE FUTURE
BRAINNSSS!
STRETCH
POP!
SNAP
BRAINNSSS?
BRAINNSSS?
BRAINNSSS?
BRAINS
BRAINNNS.
DIG DIG
DIG
ZORRRK!!
BRAINS?

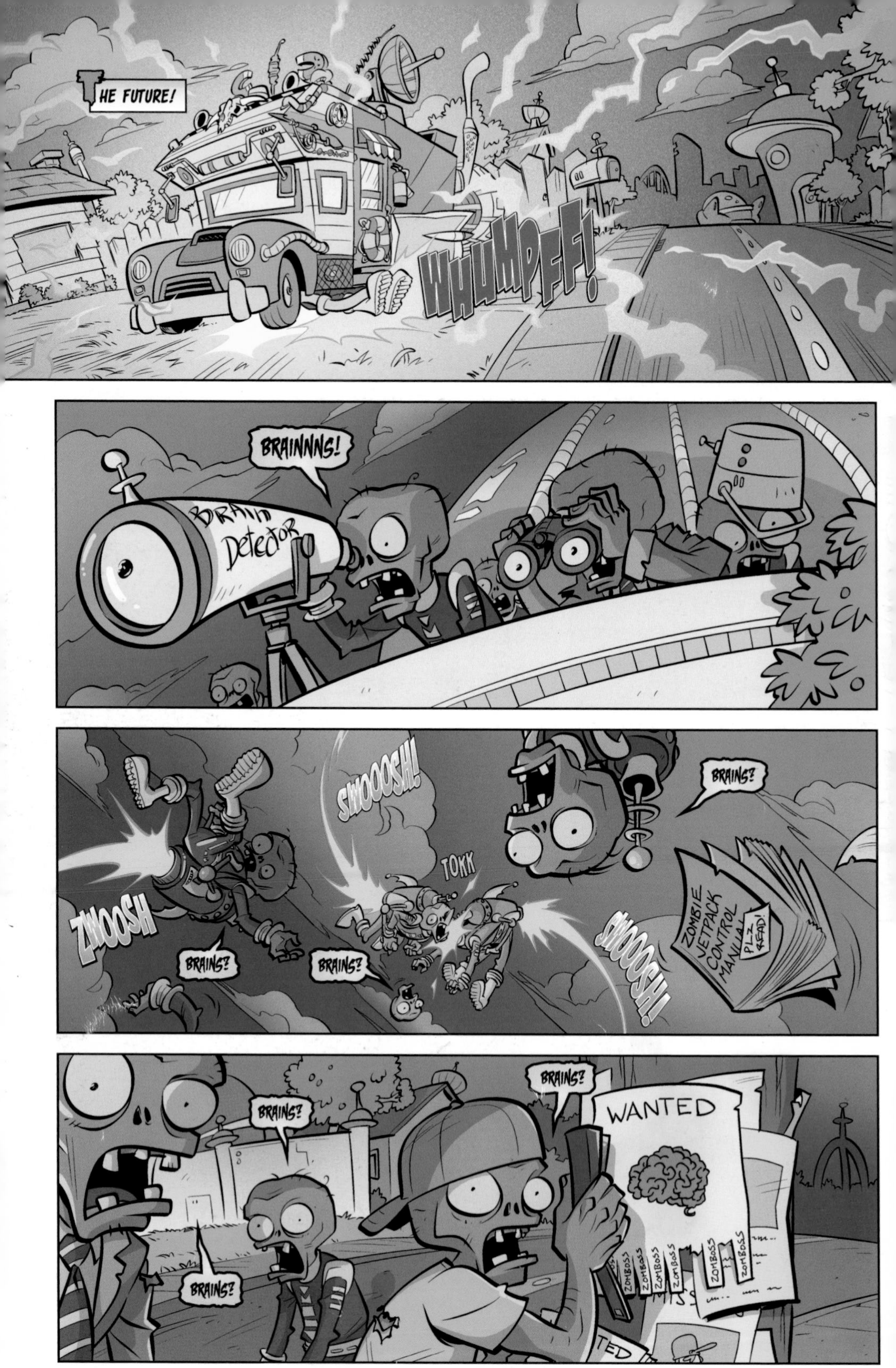
THE FUTURE!
WHUMPFF!
BRAINNNS!
BRAIN DETECTOR
SWOOOSH!
BRAINS?
ZWOOSH
BRAINS?
BRAINS?
TOKK
SWOOOSH!
ZOMBIE JETPACK CONTROL MANUAL
PLZ READ!
BRAINS?
BRAINS?
BRAINS?
WANTED
ZOMBOSS ZOMBOSS ZOMBOSS ZOMBOSS ZOMBOSS ZOMBOSS ZOMBOSS

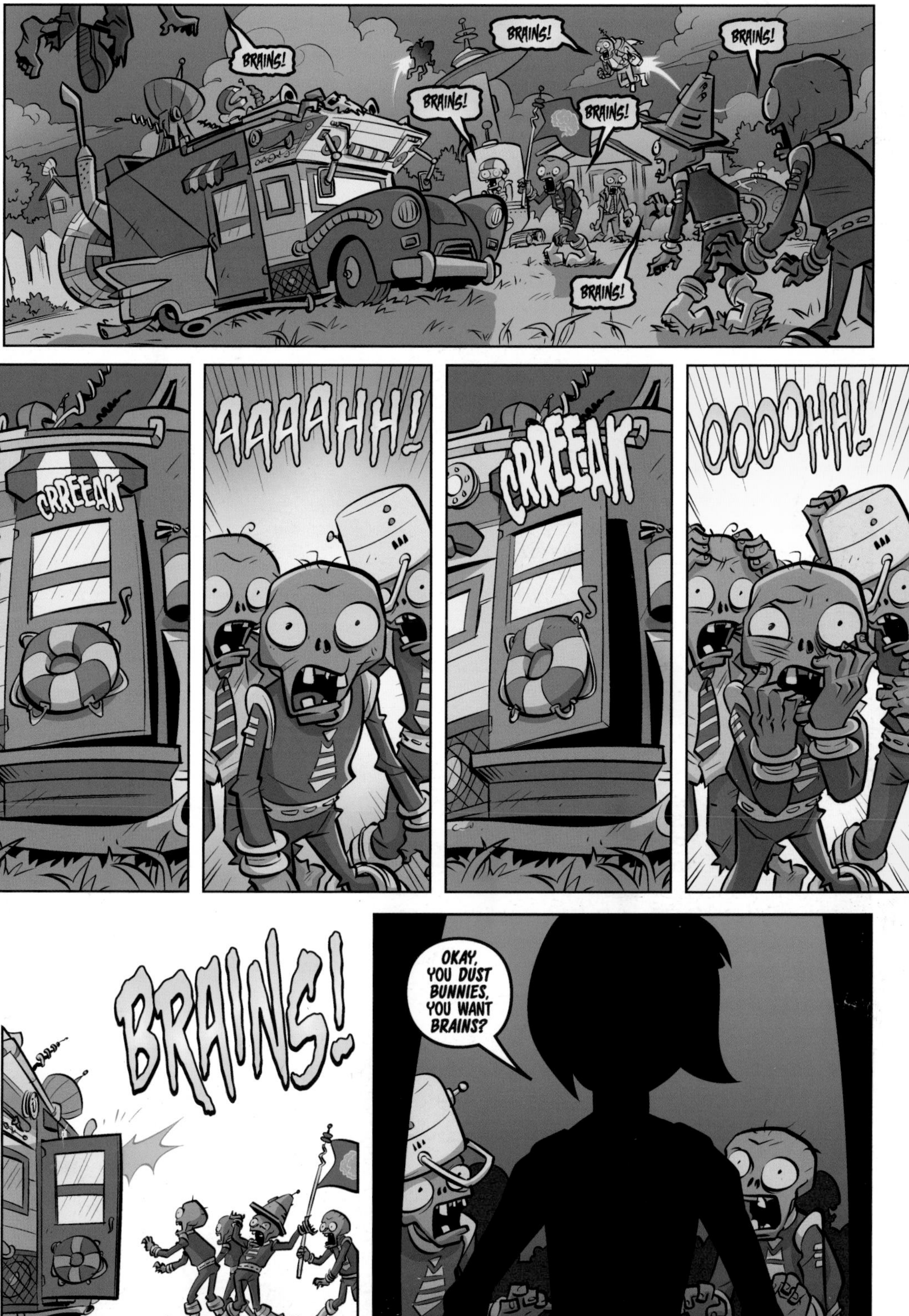
BRAINS!
BRAINS!
BRAINS!
BRAINS!
BRAINS!
BRAINS!
CRREEAK
AAAAHH!
CRREEAK
OOOOHH!
BRAINS!
OKAY, YOU DUST BUNNIES, YOU WANT BRAINS?

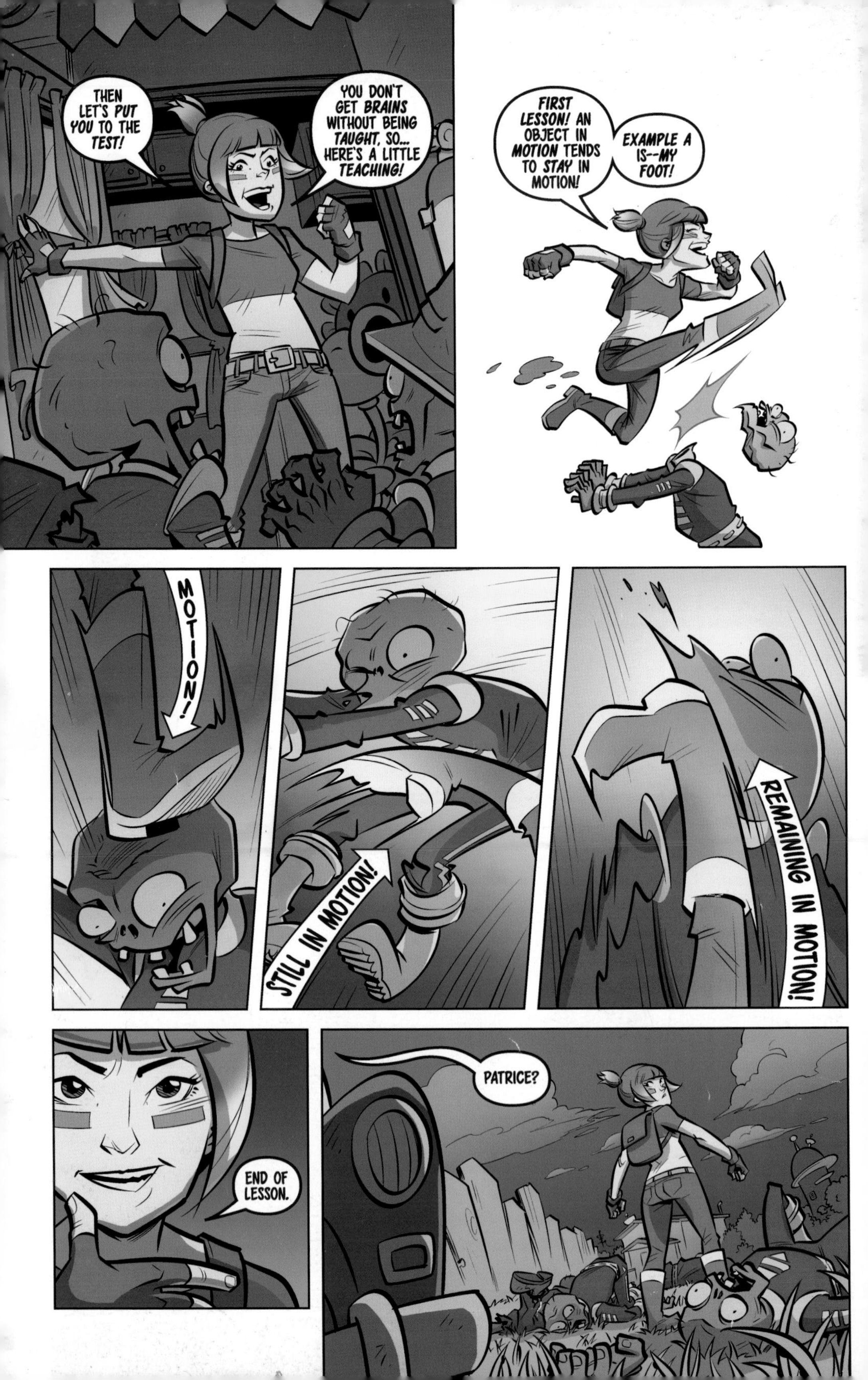
THEN LET'S PUT YOU TO THE TEST!
YOU DON'T GET BRAINS WITHOUT BEING TAUGHT, SO... HERE'S A LITTLE TEACHING!
FIRST LESSON! AN OBJECT IN MOTION TENDS TO STAY IN MOTION!
EXAMPLE A IS--MY FOOT!
MOTION!
STILL IN MOTION!
REMAINING IN MOTION!
END OF LESSON.
PATRICE?

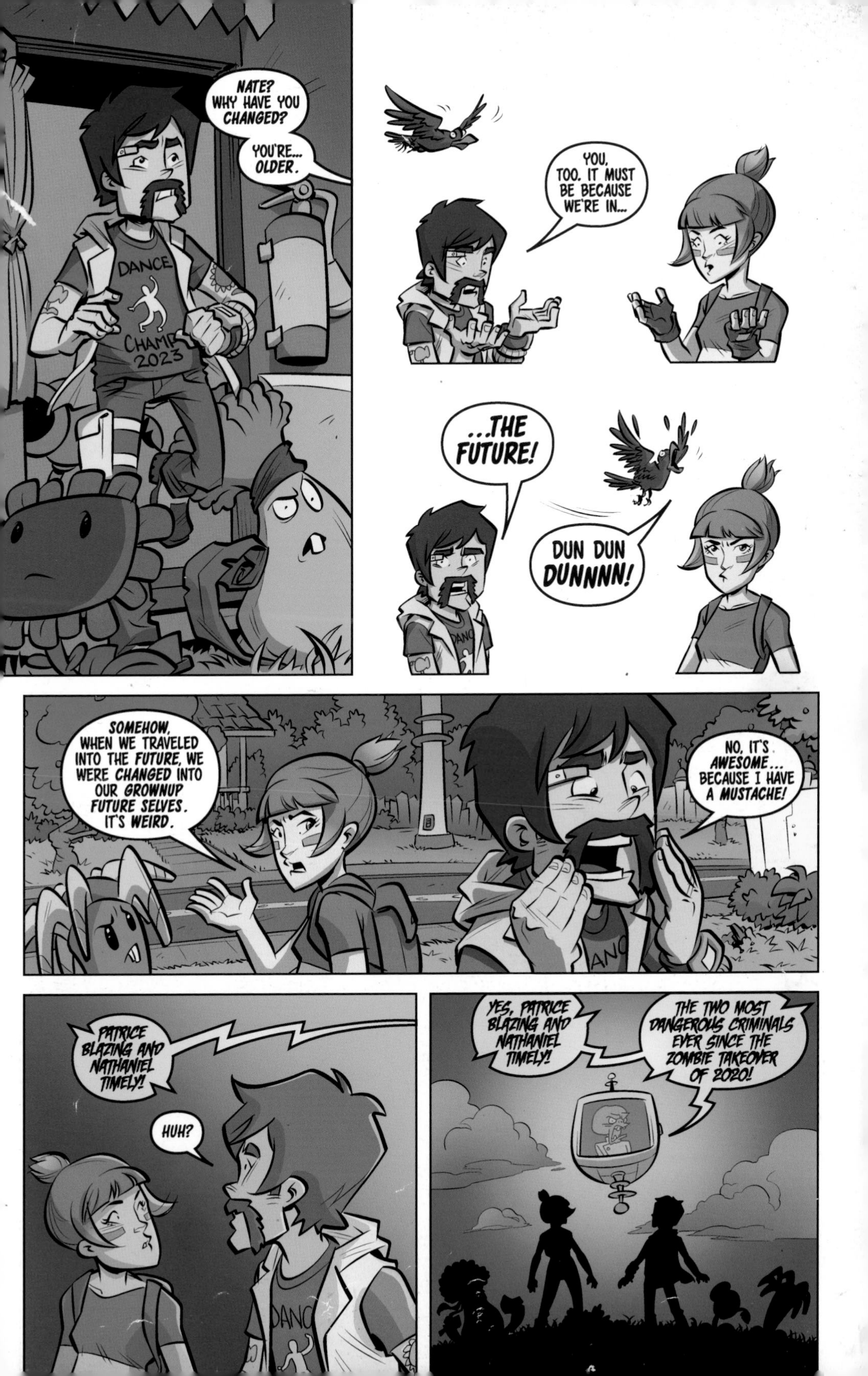
NATE? WHY HAVE YOU CHANGED?
YOU'RE... OLDER.
DANCE CHAMP 2023
YOU, TOO. IT MUST BE BECAUSE WE'RE IN...
...THE FUTURE!
DUN DUN DUNNNN!
SOMEHOW, WHEN WE TRAVELED INTO THE FUTURE, WE WERE CHANGED INTO OUR GROWNUP FUTURE SELVES. IT'S WEIRD.
NO, IT'S AWESOME... BECAUSE I HAVE A MUSTACHE!
PATRICE BLAZING AND NATHANIEL TIMELY!
HUH?
YES, PATRICE BLAZING AND NATHANIEL TIMELY!
THE TWO MOST DANGEROUS CRIMINALS EVER SINCE THE ZOMBIE TAKEOVER OF 2020!

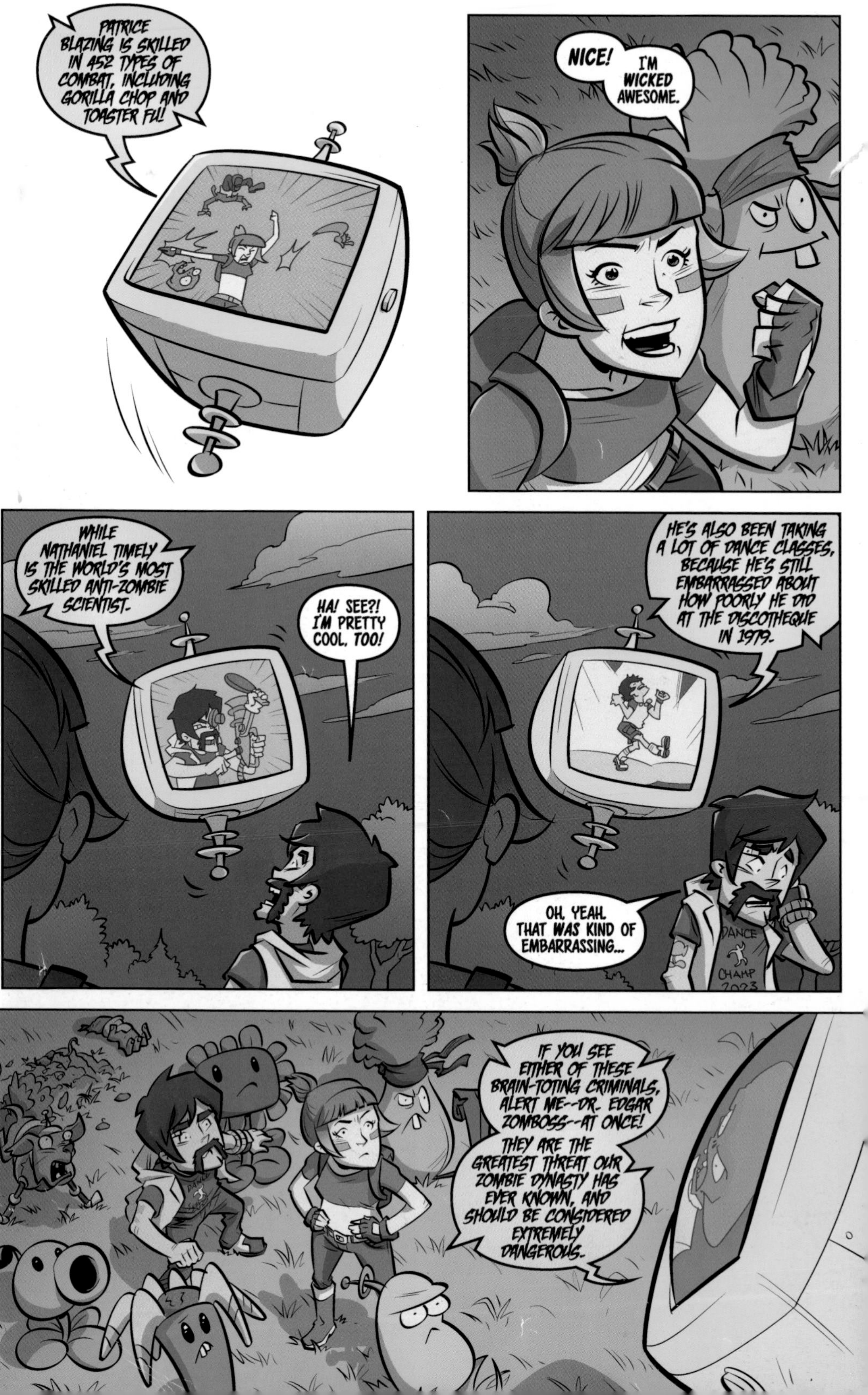
PATRICE BLAZING IS SKILLED IN 452 TYPES OF COMBAT, INCLUDING GORILLA CHOP AND TOASTER FU!
NICE!
I'M WICKED AWESOME.
WHILE NATHANIEL TIMELY IS THE WORLD'S MOST SKILLED ANTI-ZOMBIE SCIENTIST.
HA! SEE?! I'M PRETTY COOL, TOO!
HE'S ALSO BEEN TAKING A LOT OF DANCE CLASSES, BECAUSE HE'S STILL EMBARRASSED ABOUT HOW POORLY HE DID AT THE DISCOTHEQUE IN 1979.
OH, YEAH. THAT WAS KIND OF EMBARRASSING...
DANCE CHAMP 2023
IF YOU SEE EITHER OF THESE BRAIN-TOTING CRIMINALS, ALERT ME--DR. EDGAR ZOMBOSS--AT ONCE!
THEY ARE THE GREATEST THREAT OUR ZOMBIE DYNASTY HAS EVER KNOWN, AND SHOULD BE CONSIDERED EXTREMELY DANGEROUS.

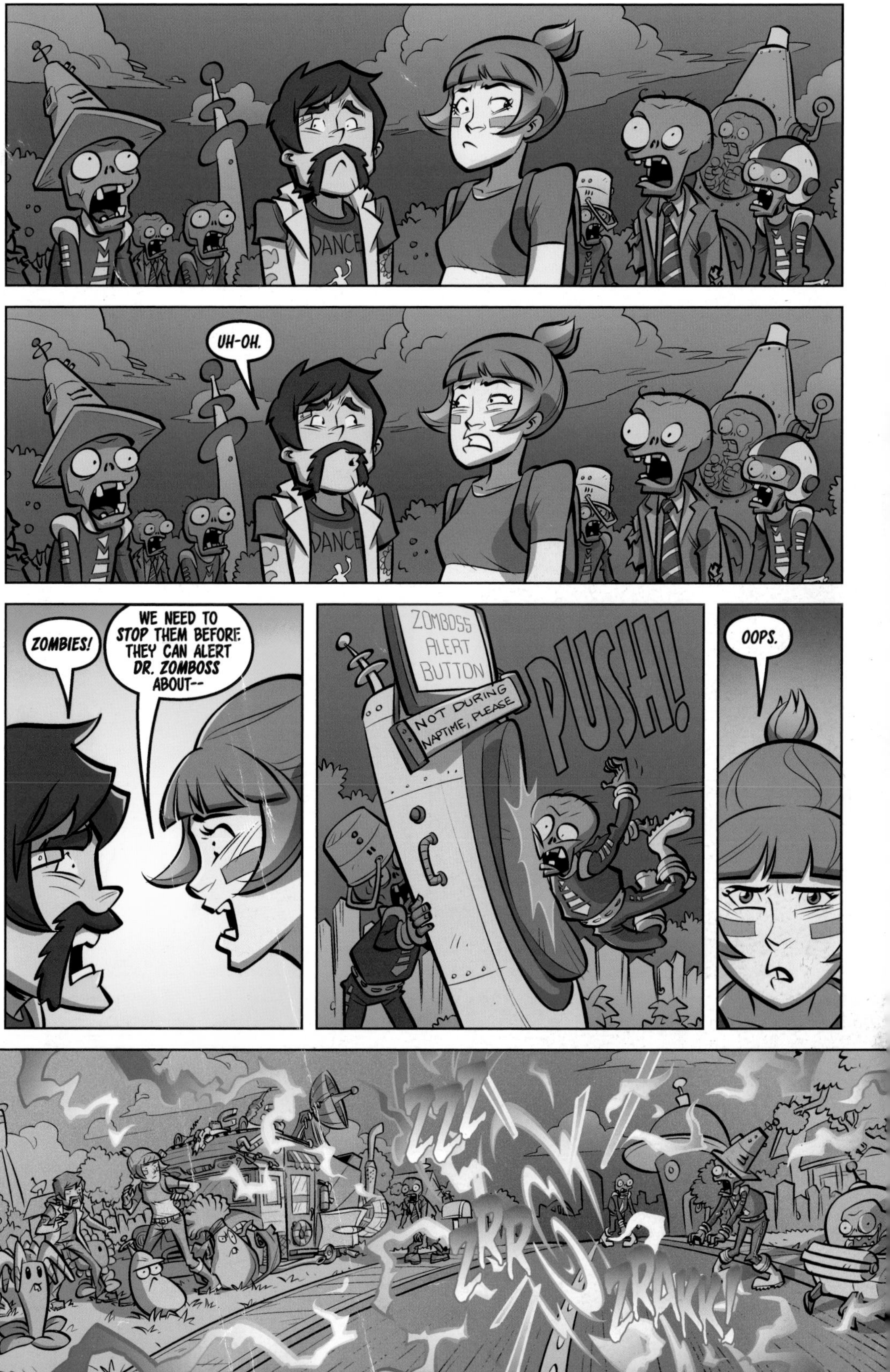

DANCE
UH-OH.
DANCE
ZOMBIES!
WE NEED TO STOP THEM BEFORE THEY CAN ALERT DR. ZOMBOSS ABOUT--
ZOMBOSS ALERT BUTTON
NOT DURING NAPTIME, PLEASE
PUSH!
OOPS.
ZZZ
ZRR
ZRAKK!

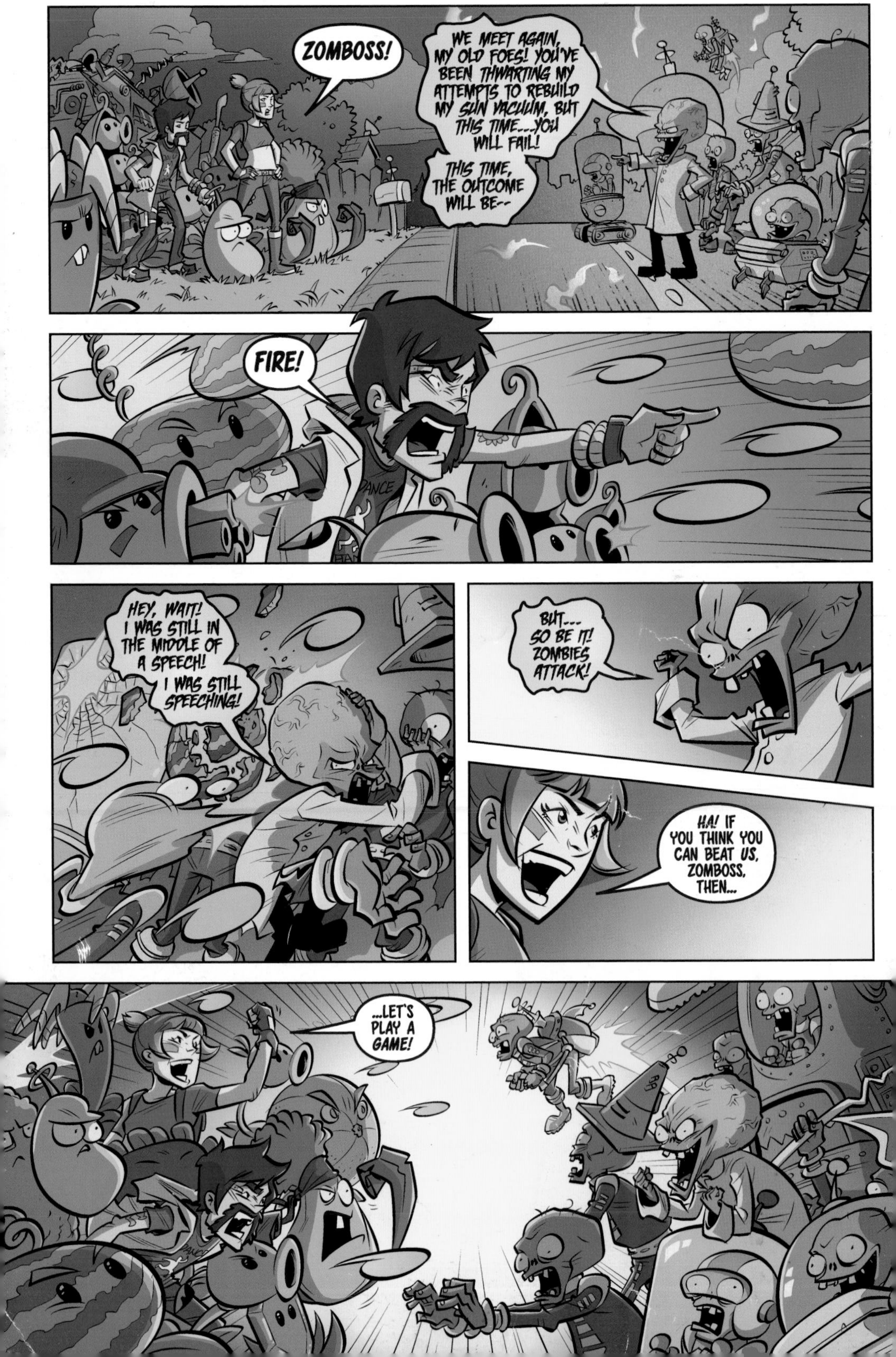
ZOMBOSS!
WE MEET AGAIN, MY OLD FOES! YOU'VE BEEN THWARTING MY ATTEMPTS TO REBUILD MY SUN VACUUM, BUT THIS TIME... YOU WILL FAIL!
THIS TIME, THE OUTCOME WILL BE--
FIRE!
DANCE
HEY, WAIT! I WAS STILL IN THE MIDDLE OF A SPEECH!
I WAS STILL SPEECHING!
BUT... SO BE IT! ZOMBIES ATTACK!
HA! IF YOU THINK YOU CAN BEAT US, ZOMBOSS, THEN...
...LET'S PLAY A GAME!

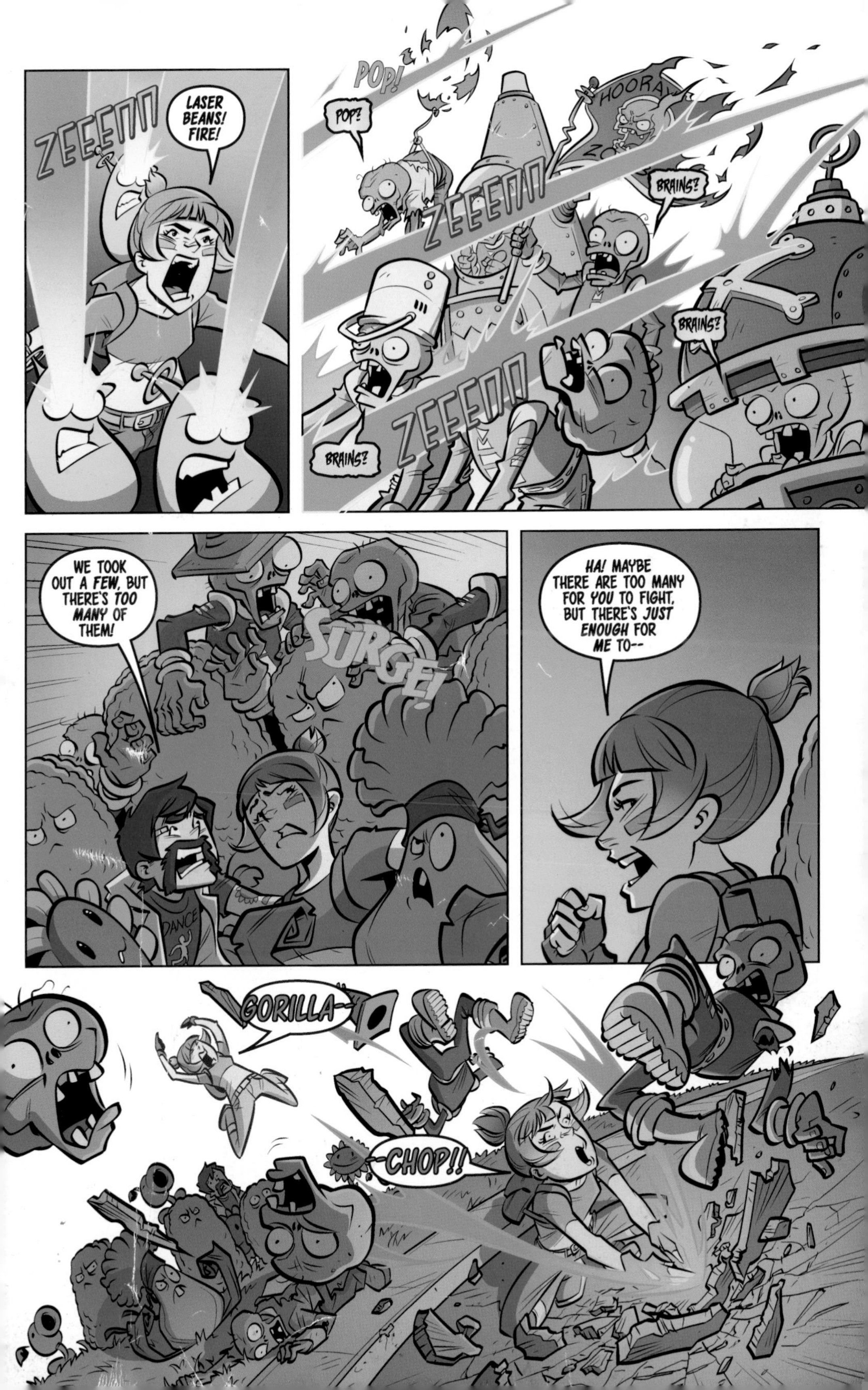
ZEEEMM
LASER BEANS! FIRE!
POP!
POP?
HOORAY
ZEEEMM
BRAINS?
ZEEEMM
BRAINS?
BRAINS?
WE TOOK OUT A FEW, BUT THERE'S TOO MANY OF THEM!
SURGE!
DANCE
HA! MAYBE THERE ARE TOO MANY FOR YOU TO FIGHT, BUT THERE'S JUST ENOUGH FOR ME TO--
GORILLA-
-CHOP!!

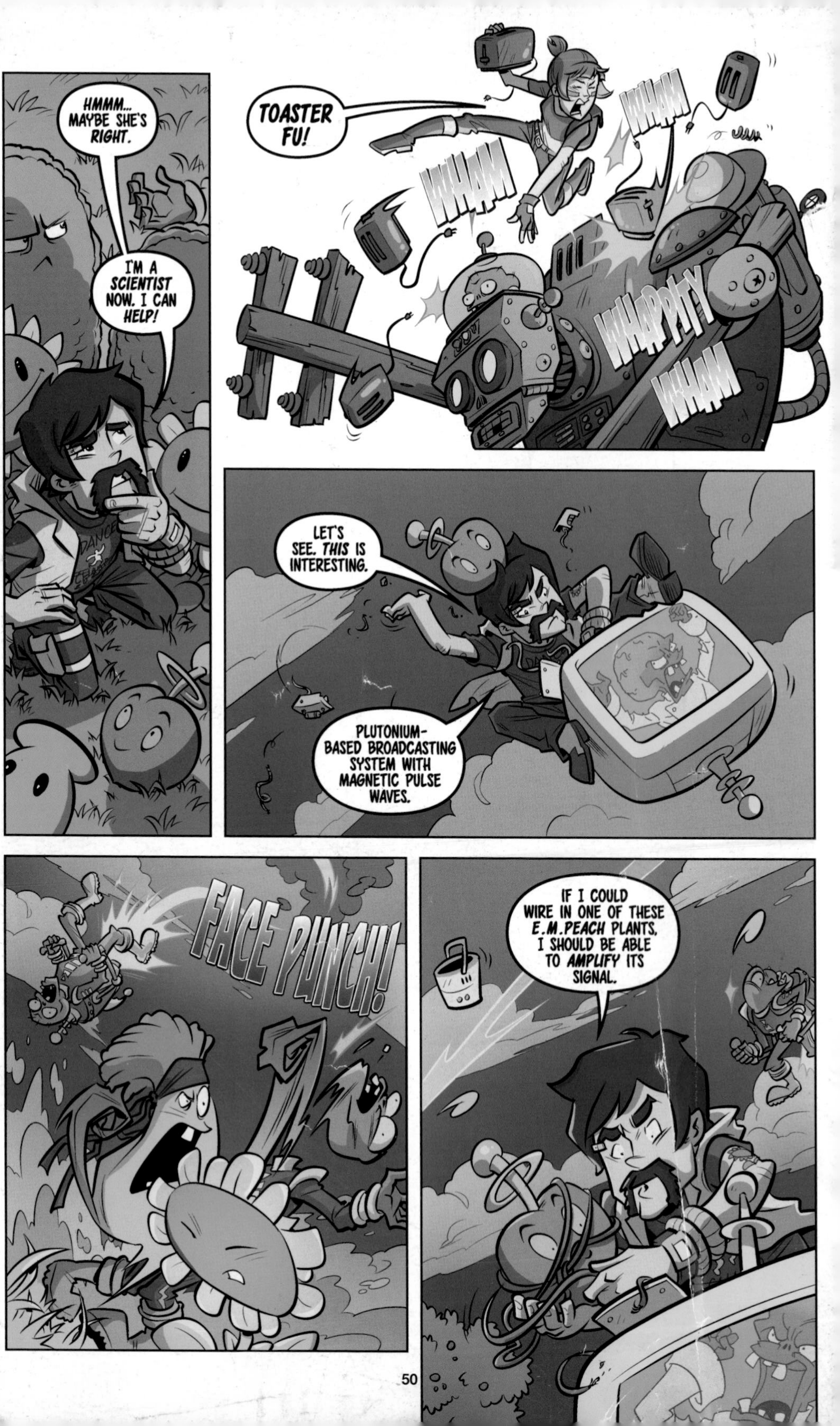
HMMM... MAYBE SHE'S RIGHT.
I'M A SCIENTIST NOW. I CAN HELP!
TOASTER FU!
WHAM
WHAM
WHAPPITY
WHAM
LET'S SEE. THIS IS INTERESTING.
PLUTONIUM-BASED BROADCASTING SYSTEM WITH MAGNETIC PULSE WAVES.
FACE PUNCH!
IF I COULD WIRE IN ONE OF THESE E.M.PEACH PLANTS, I SHOULD BE ABLE TO AMPLIFY ITS SIGNAL.

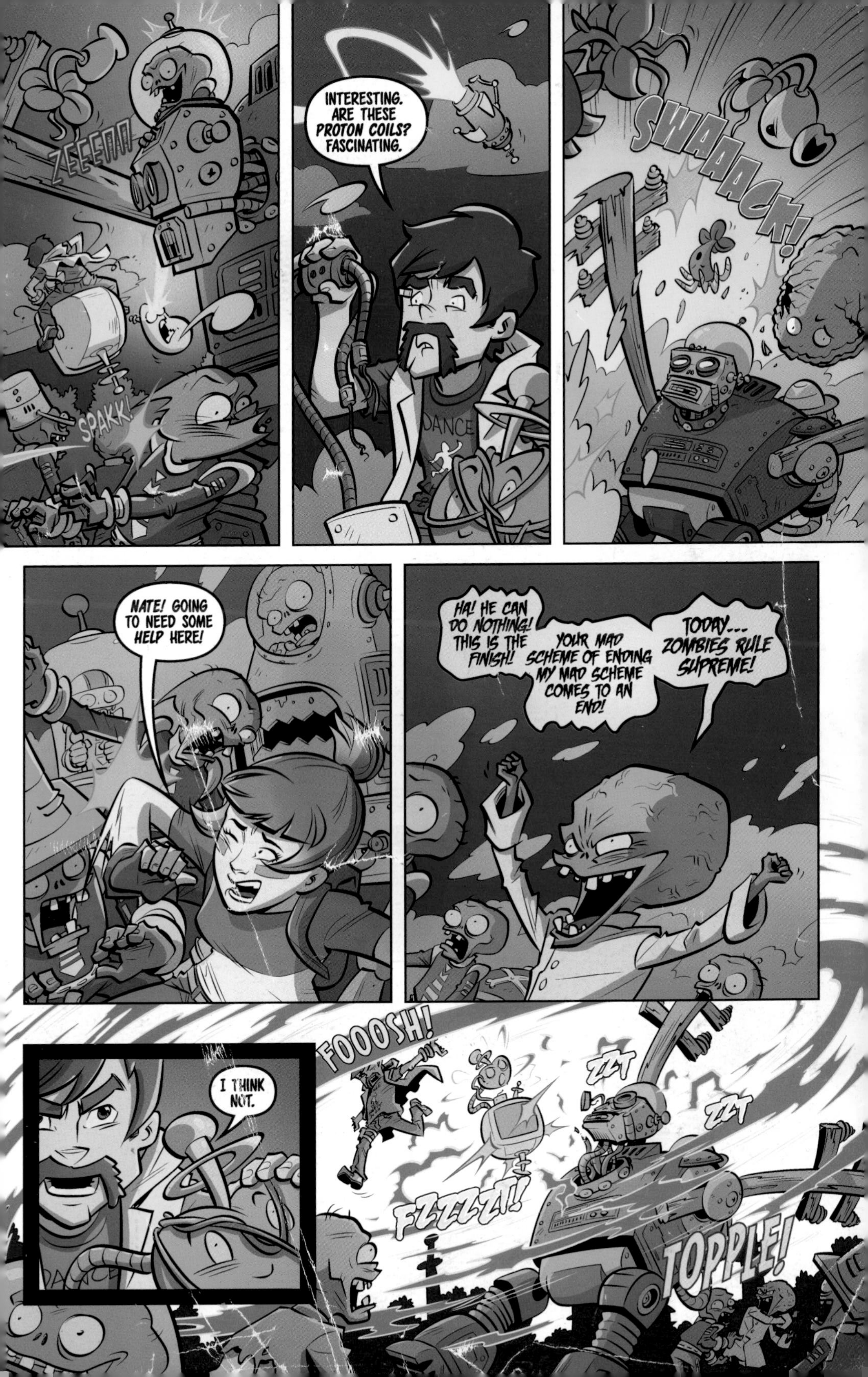
ZEEEMM
SPAKK!
INTERESTING. ARE THESE PROTON COILS? FASCINATING.
DANCE
SWAAACK!
NATE! GOING TO NEED SOME HELP HERE!
HA! HE CAN DO NOTHING! THIS IS THE FINISH!
YOUR MAD SCHEME OF ENDING MY MAD SCHEME COMES TO AN END!
TODAY... ZOMBIES RULE SUPREME!
I THINK NOT.
FOOOSH!
ZZT
ZZT
FZZZZT!
TOPPLE!

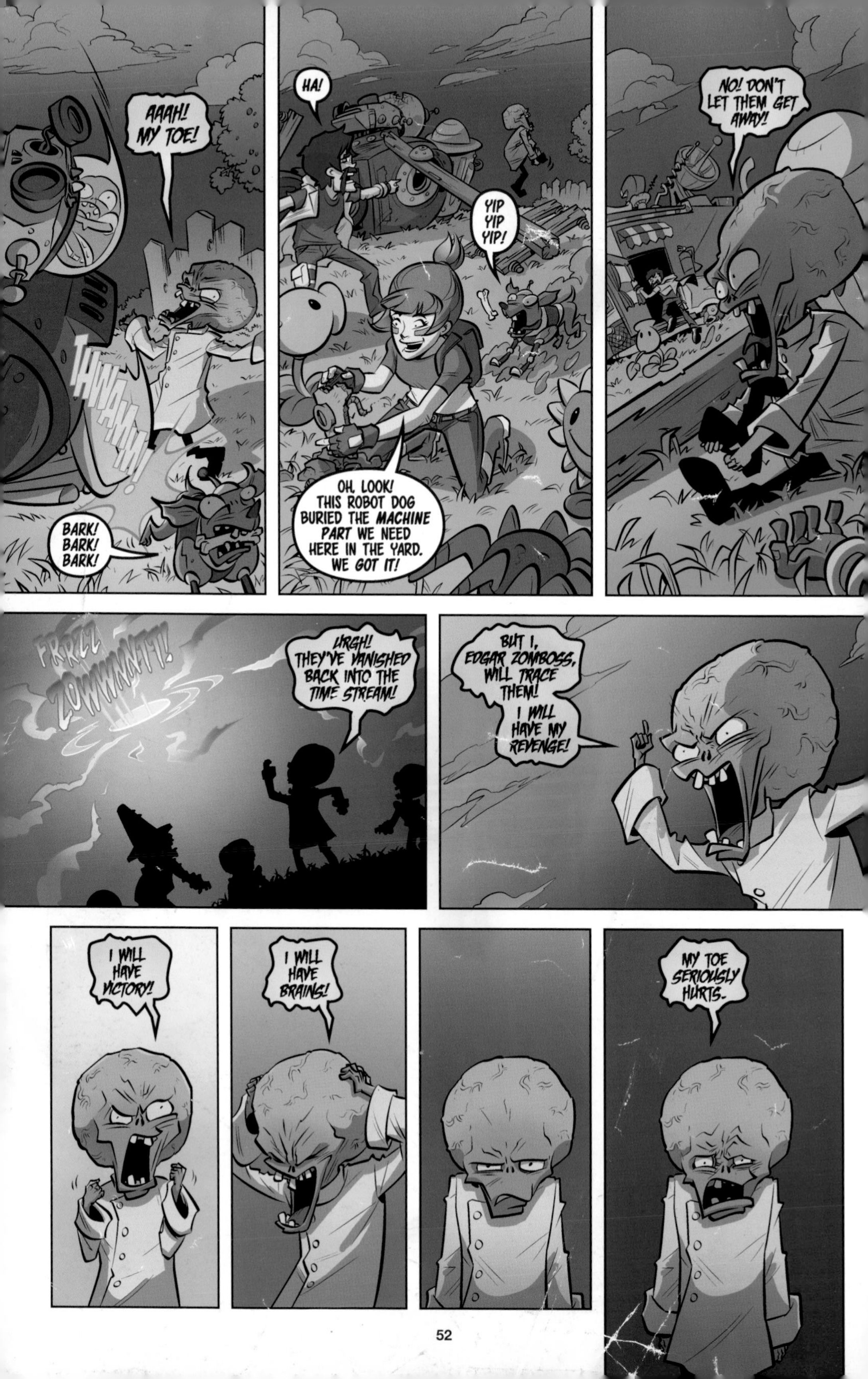
AAAH! MY TOE!
THWAMM!
BARK! BARK! BARK!
HA!
YIP YIP YIP!
OH, LOOK! THIS ROBOT DOG BURIED THE MACHINE PART WE NEED HERE IN THE YARD. WE GOT IT!
NO! DON'T LET THEM GET AWAY!
FRRZZ ZOWWNNTT!
URGH! THEY'VE VANISHED BACK INTO THE TIME STREAM!
BUT I, EDGAR ZOMBOSS, WILL TRACE THEM!
I WILL HAVE MY REVENGE!
I WILL HAVE VICTORY!
I WILL HAVE BRAINS!
MY TOE SERIOUSLY HURTS.

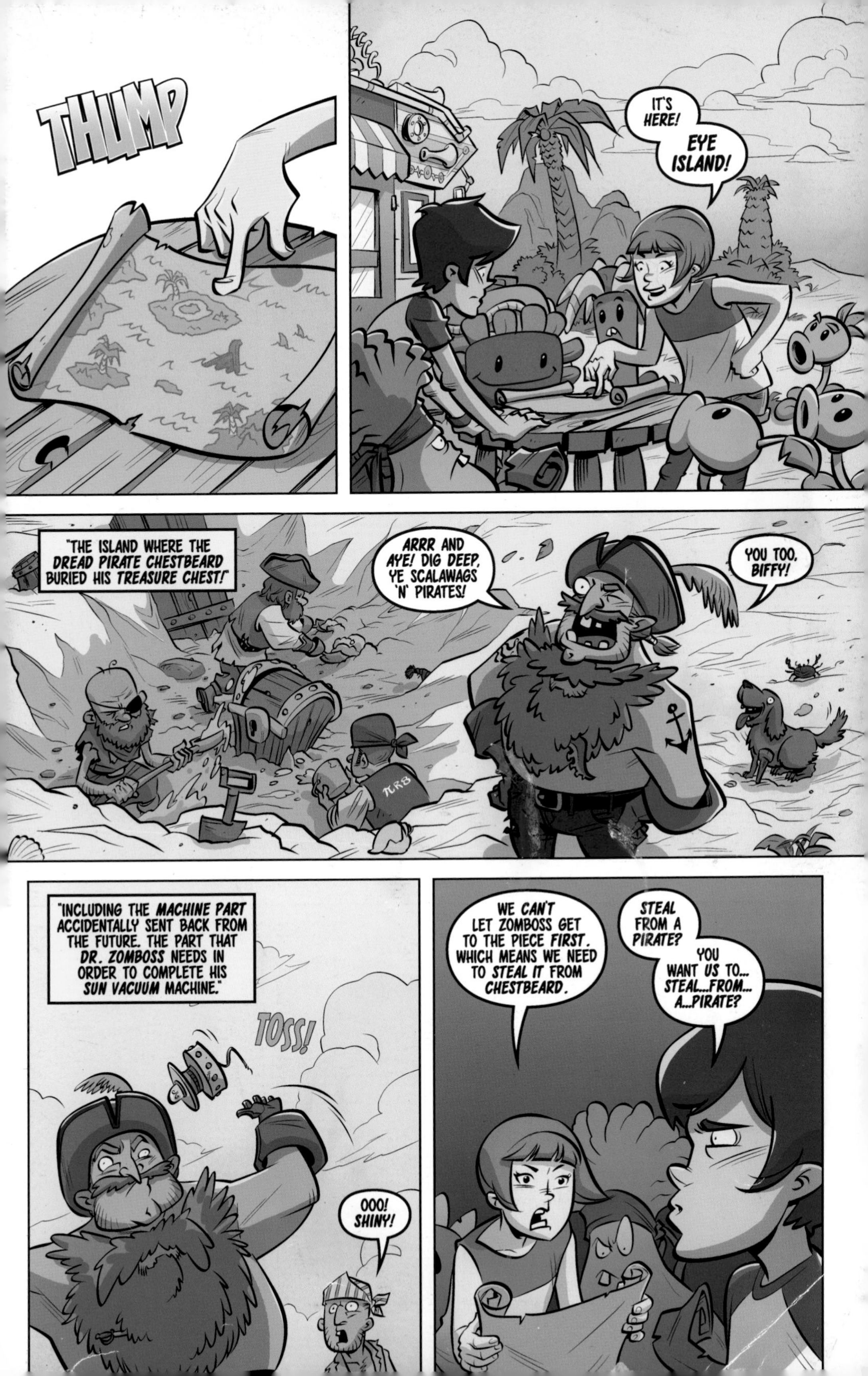
THUMP
IT'S HERE!
EYE ISLAND!
"THE ISLAND WHERE THE DREAD PIRATE CHESTBEARD BURIED HIS TREASURE CHEST!"
ARRR AND AYE! DIG DEEP, YE SCALAWAGS 'N' PIRATES!
YOU TOO, BIFFY!
"INCLUDING THE MACHINE PART ACCIDENTALLY SENT BACK FROM THE FUTURE. THE PART THAT DR. ZOMBOSS NEEDS IN ORDER TO COMPLETE HIS SUN VACUUM MACHINE."
TOSS!
OOO! SHINY!
WE CAN'T LET ZOMBOSS GET TO THE PIECE FIRST. WHICH MEANS WE NEED TO STEAL IT FROM CHESTBEARD.
STEAL FROM A PIRATE?
YOU WANT US TO... STEAL...FROM... A...PIRATE?

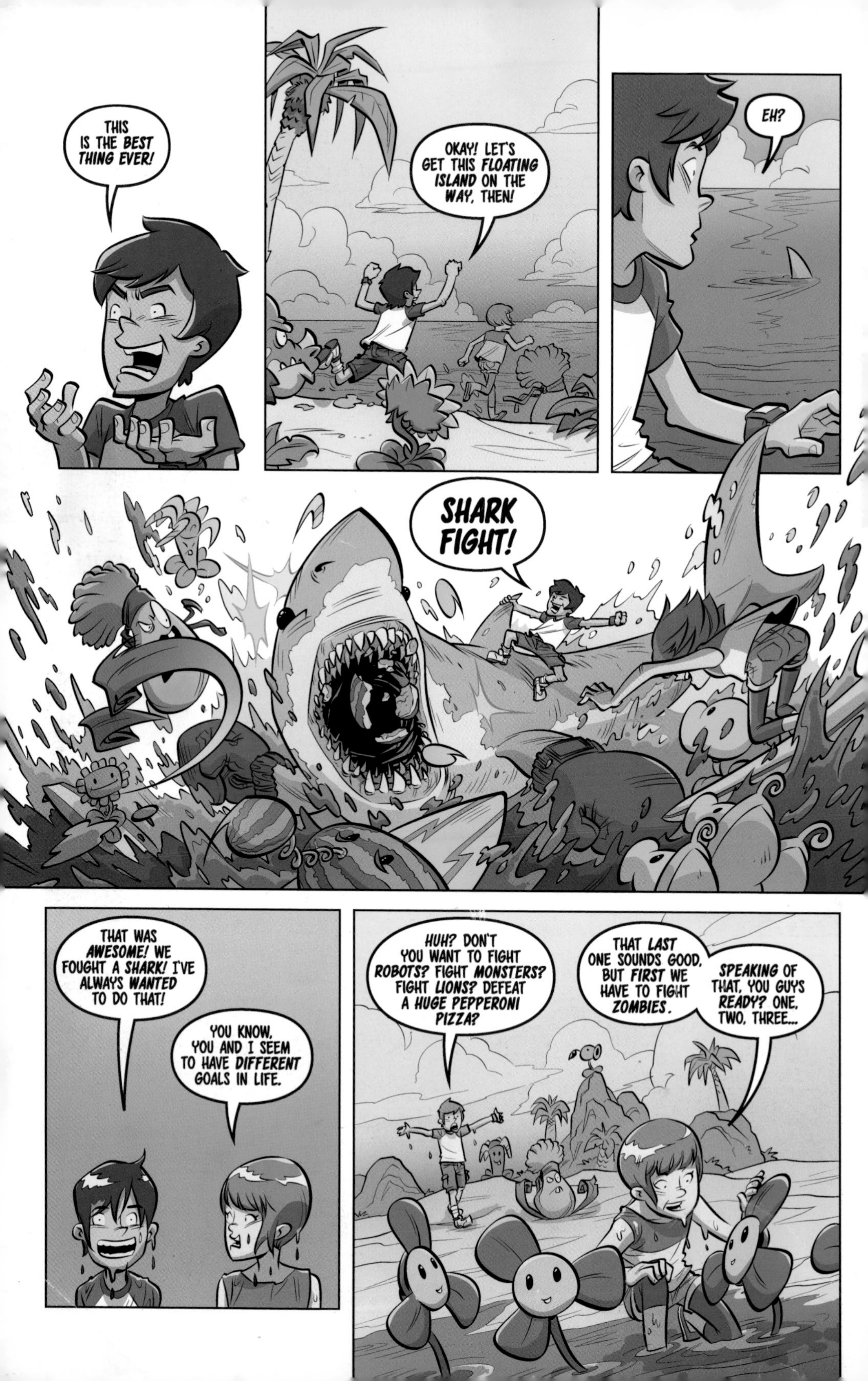
THIS IS THE BEST THING EVER!
OKAY! LET'S GET THIS FLOATING ISLAND ON THE WAY, THEN!
EH?
SHARK FIGHT!
THAT WAS AWESOME! WE FOUGHT A SHARK! I'VE ALWAYS WANTED TO DO THAT!
YOU KNOW, YOU AND I SEEM TO HAVE DIFFERENT GOALS IN LIFE.
HUH? DON'T YOU WANT TO FIGHT ROBOTS? FIGHT MONSTERS? FIGHT LIONS? DEFEAT A HUGE PEPPERONI PIZZA?
THAT LAST ONE SOUNDS GOOD, BUT FIRST WE HAVE TO FIGHT ZOMBIES.
SPEAKING OF THAT, YOU GUYS READY? ONE, TWO, THREE...

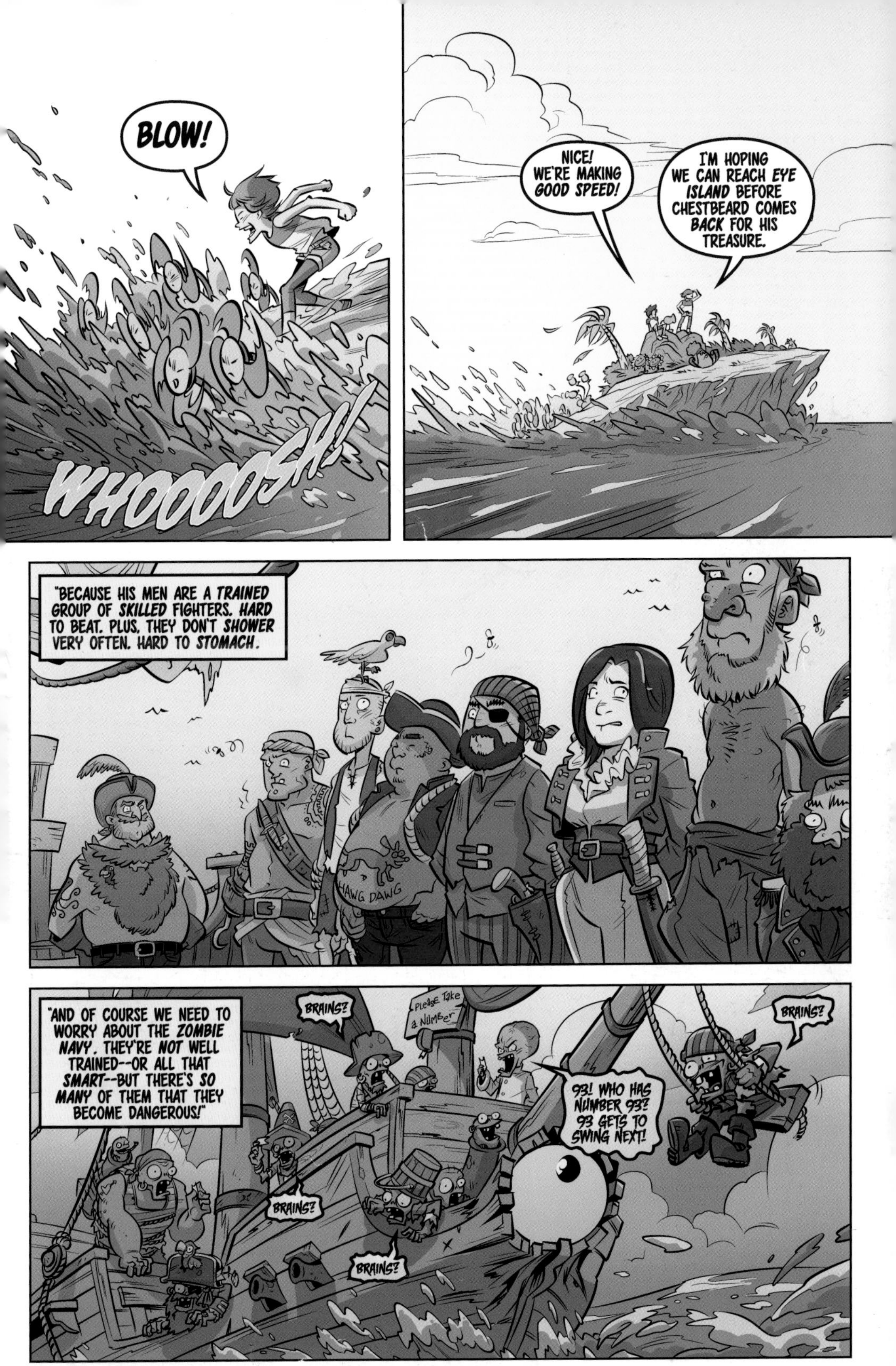
BLOW!
WHOOOOOSH!
NICE! WE'RE MAKING GOOD SPEED!
I'M HOPING WE CAN REACH EYE ISLAND BEFORE CHESTBEARD COMES BACK FOR HIS TREASURE.
"BECAUSE HIS MEN ARE A TRAINED GROUP OF SKILLED FIGHTERS. HARD TO BEAT. PLUS, THEY DON'T SHOWER VERY OFTEN. HARD TO STOMACH.
HAWG DAWG
"AND OF COURSE WE NEED TO WORRY ABOUT THE ZOMBIE NAVY. THEY'RE NOT WELL TRAINED--OR ALL THAT SMART--BUT THERE'S SO MANY OF THEM THAT THEY BECOME DANGEROUS!"
BRAINS?
Please Take a Number
BRAINS?
93! WHO HAS NUMBER 93? 93 GETS TO SWING NEXT!
BRAINS?
BRAINS?

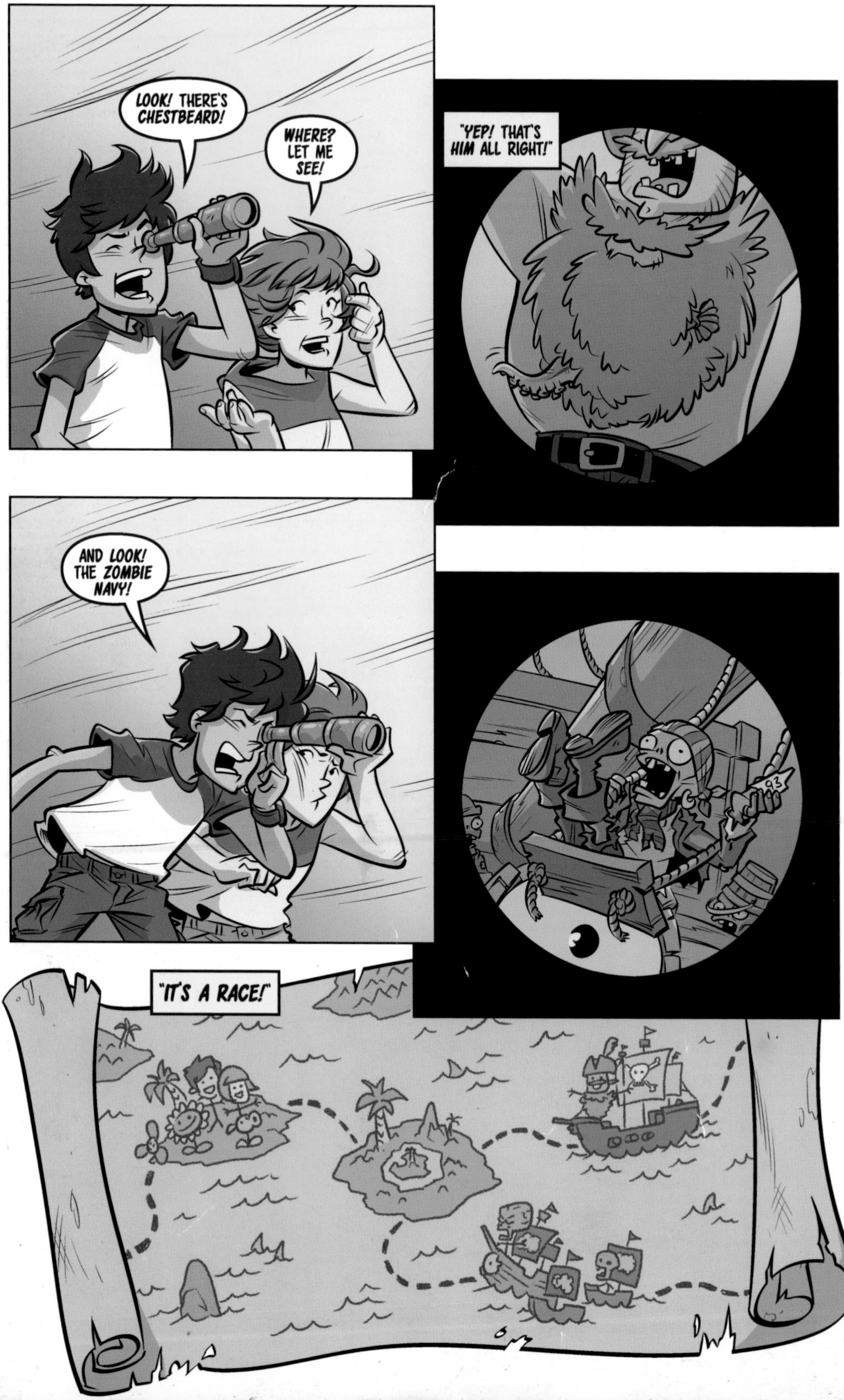
LOOK! THERE'S CHESTBEARD!
WHERE? LET ME SEE!
"YEP! THAT'S HIM ALL RIGHT!"
AND LOOK! THE ZOMBIE NAVY!
"IT'S A RACE!"

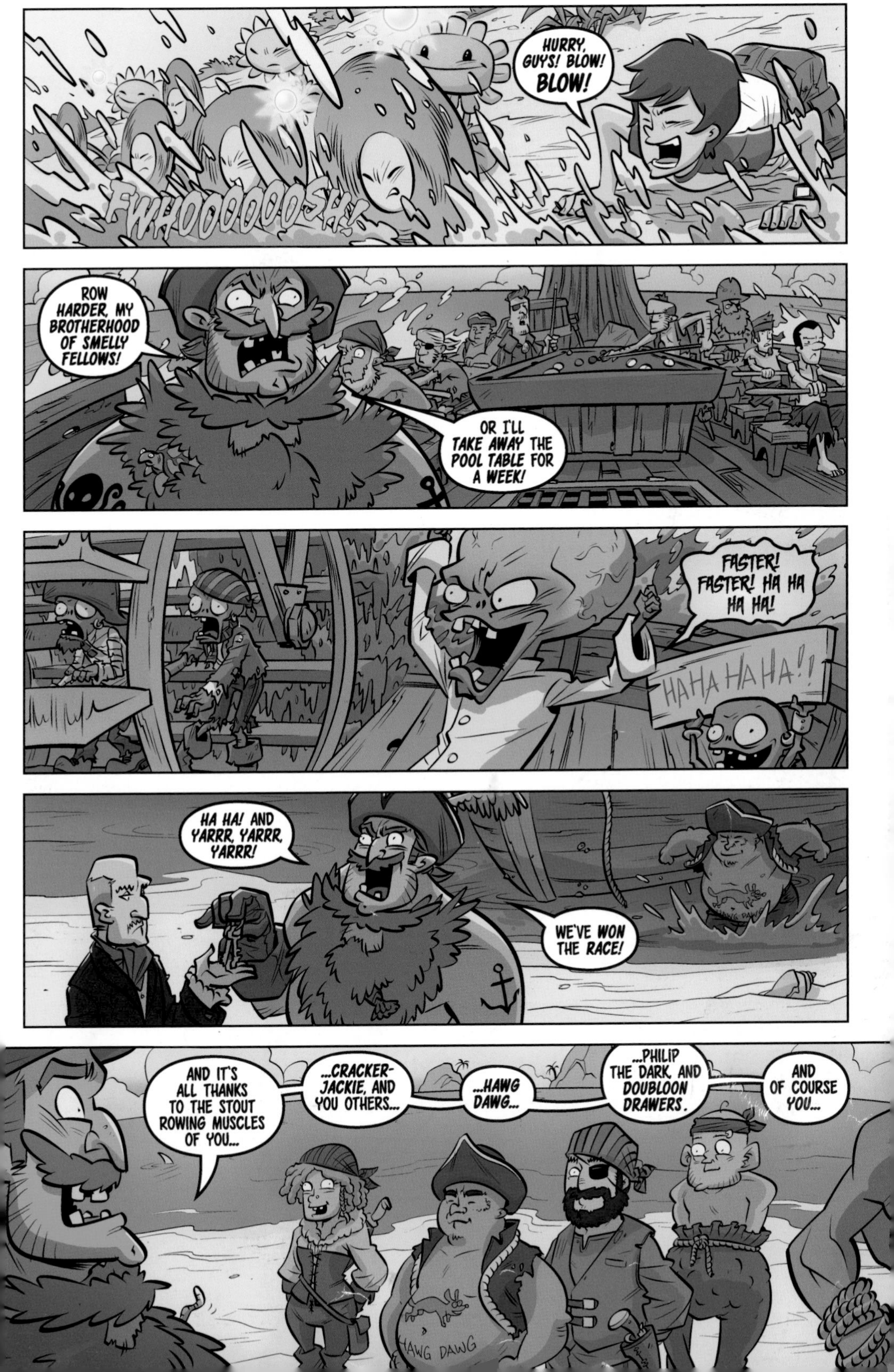
HURRY, GUYS! BLOW! BLOW!
FWHOOOOOOOSH!
ROW HARDER, MY BROTHERHOOD OF SMELLY FELLOWS!
OR I'LL TAKE AWAY THE POOL TABLE FOR A WEEK!
FASTER! FASTER! HA HA HA HA!
HA HA HA HA!!
HA HA! AND YARRR, YARRR, YARRR!
WE'VE WON THE RACE!
HAWG DAWG
AND IT'S ALL THANKS TO THE STOUT ROWING MUSCLES OF YOU...
...CRACKER-JACKIE, AND YOU OTHERS...
...HAWG DAWG...
...PHILIP THE DARK, AND DOUBLOON DRAWERS.
AND OF COURSE YOU...
HAWG DAWG

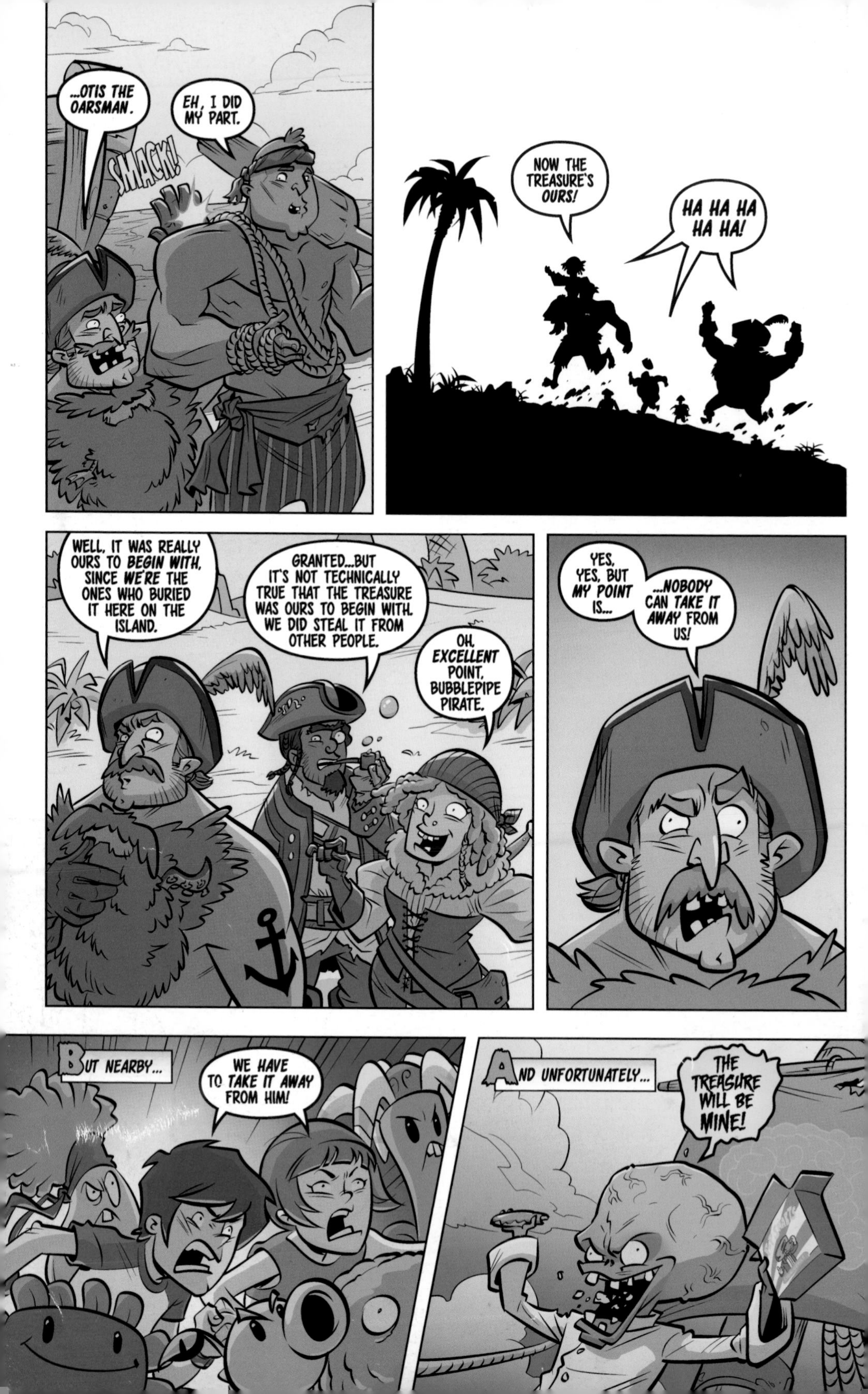
...OTIS THE OARSMAN.
EH, I DID MY PART.
SMACK!
NOW THE TREASURE'S OURS!
HA HA HA HA HA!
WELL, IT WAS REALLY OURS TO BEGIN WITH, SINCE WE'RE THE ONES WHO BURIED IT HERE ON THE ISLAND.
GRANTED...BUT IT'S NOT TECHNICALLY TRUE THAT THE TREASURE WAS OURS TO BEGIN WITH. WE DID STEAL IT FROM OTHER PEOPLE.
OH, EXCELLENT POINT, BUBBLEPIPE PIRATE.
YES, YES, BUT MY POINT IS...
...NOBODY CAN TAKE IT AWAY FROM US!
BUT NEARBY...
WE HAVE TO TAKE IT AWAY FROM HIM!
AND UNFORTUNATELY...
THE TREASURE WILL BE MINE!

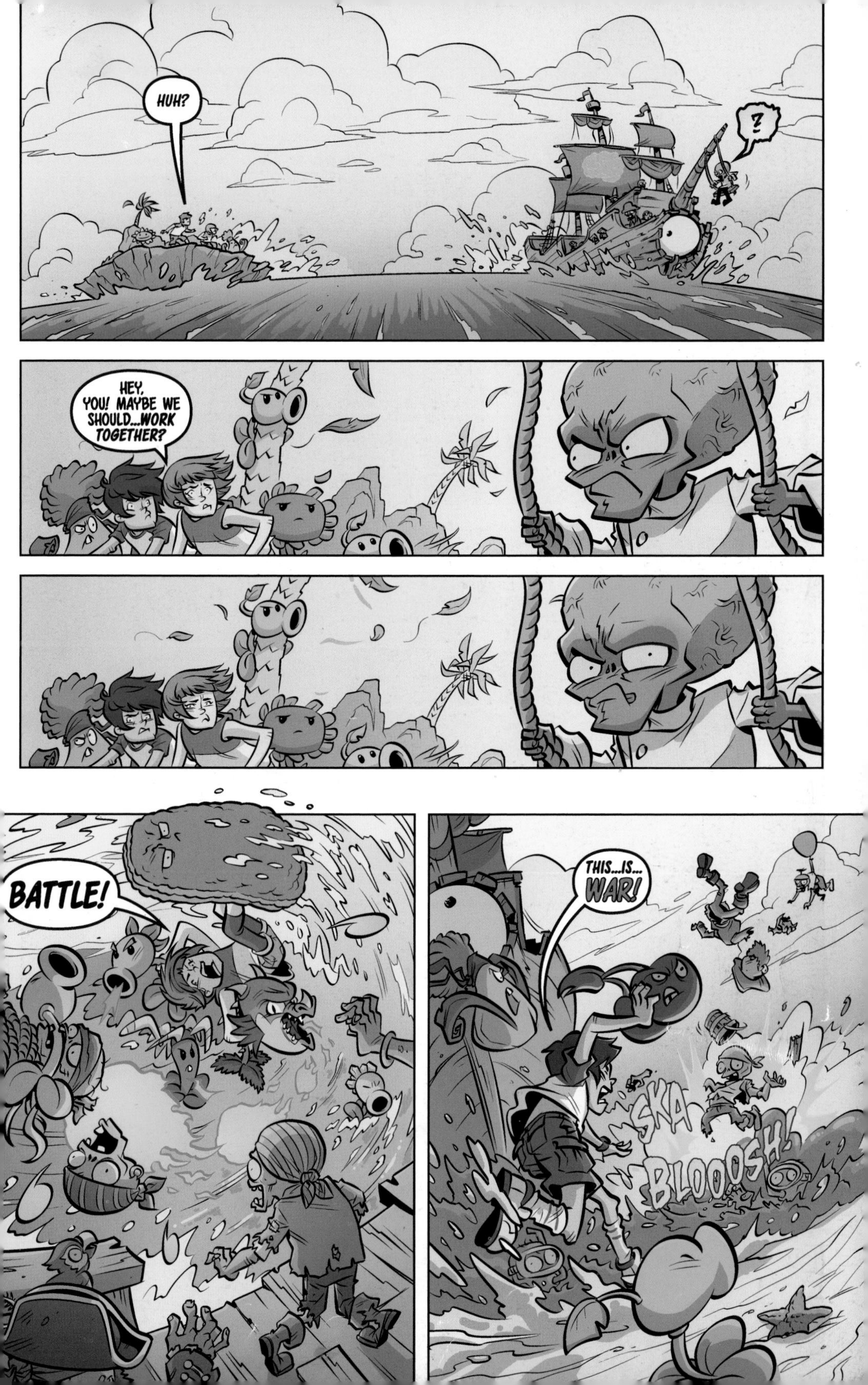
HUH?
?
HEY, YOU! MAYBE WE SHOULD...WORK TOGETHER?
BATTLE!
THIS...IS... WAR!
SKA BLOOOSH!

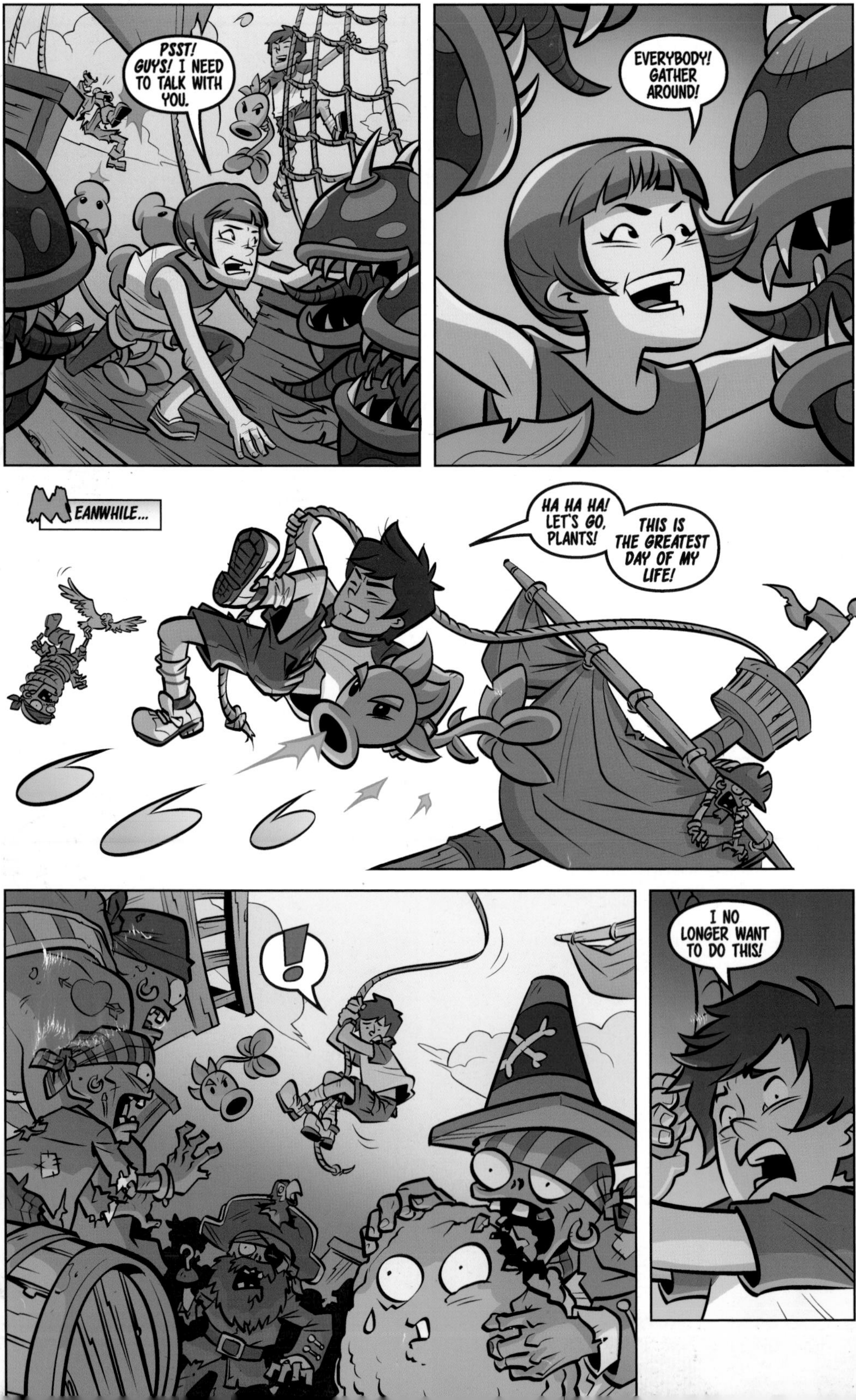

PSST! GUYS! I NEED TO TALK WITH YOU.
EVERYBODY! GATHER AROUND!
MEANWHILE...
HA HA HA! LET'S GO, PLANTS!
THIS IS THE GREATEST DAY OF MY LIFE!
!
I NO LONGER WANT TO DO THIS!

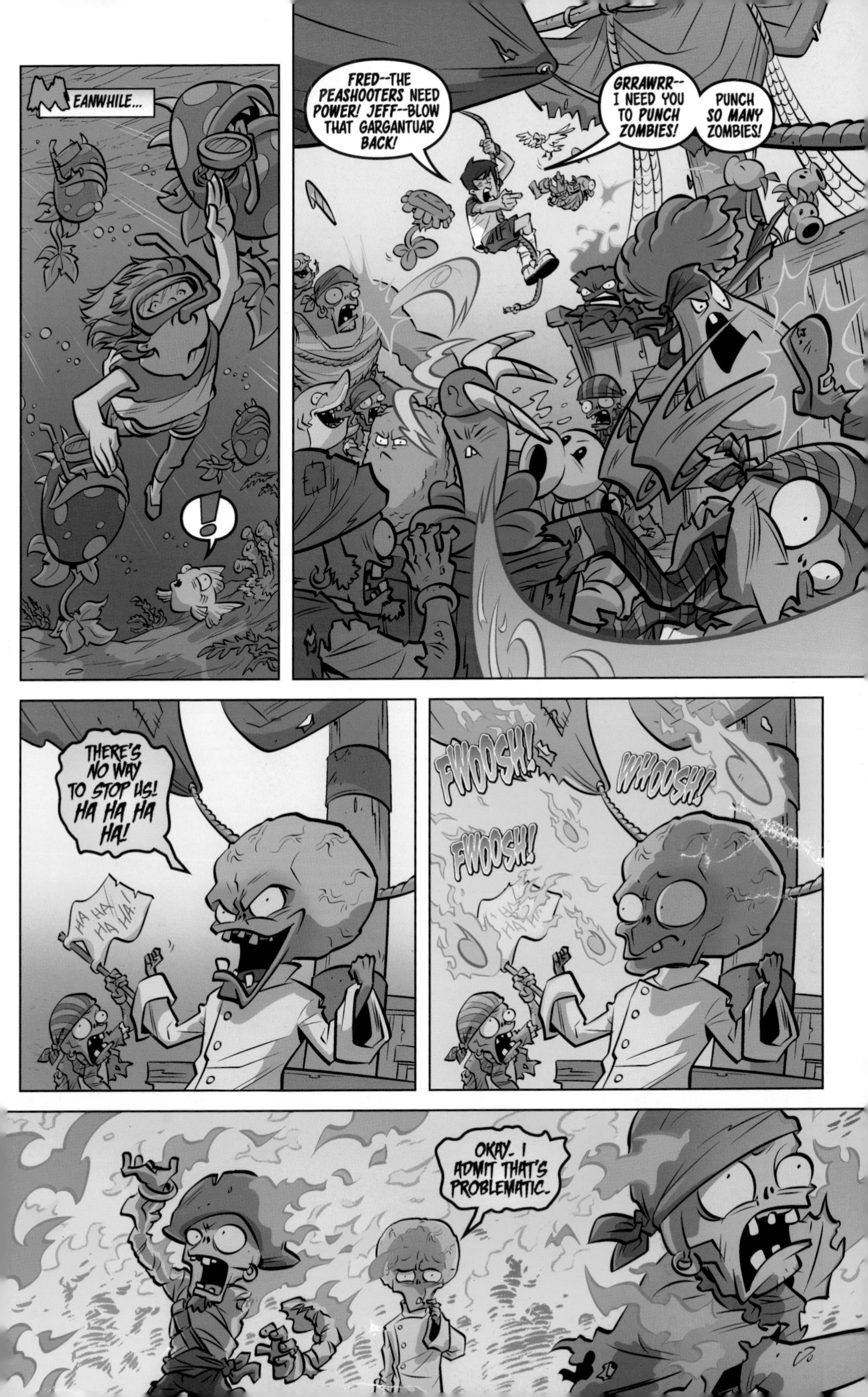

MEANWHILE...
FRED--THE PEASHOOTERS NEED POWER! JEFF--BLOW THAT GARGANTUAR BACK!
GRRAWRR-- I NEED YOU TO PUNCH ZOMBIES!
PUNCH SO MANY ZOMBIES!
THERE'S NO WAY TO STOP US! HA HA HA HA!
HA HA HA HA!
FWOOSH!
WHOOSH!
FWOOSH!
OKAY. I ADMIT THAT'S PROBLEMATIC.

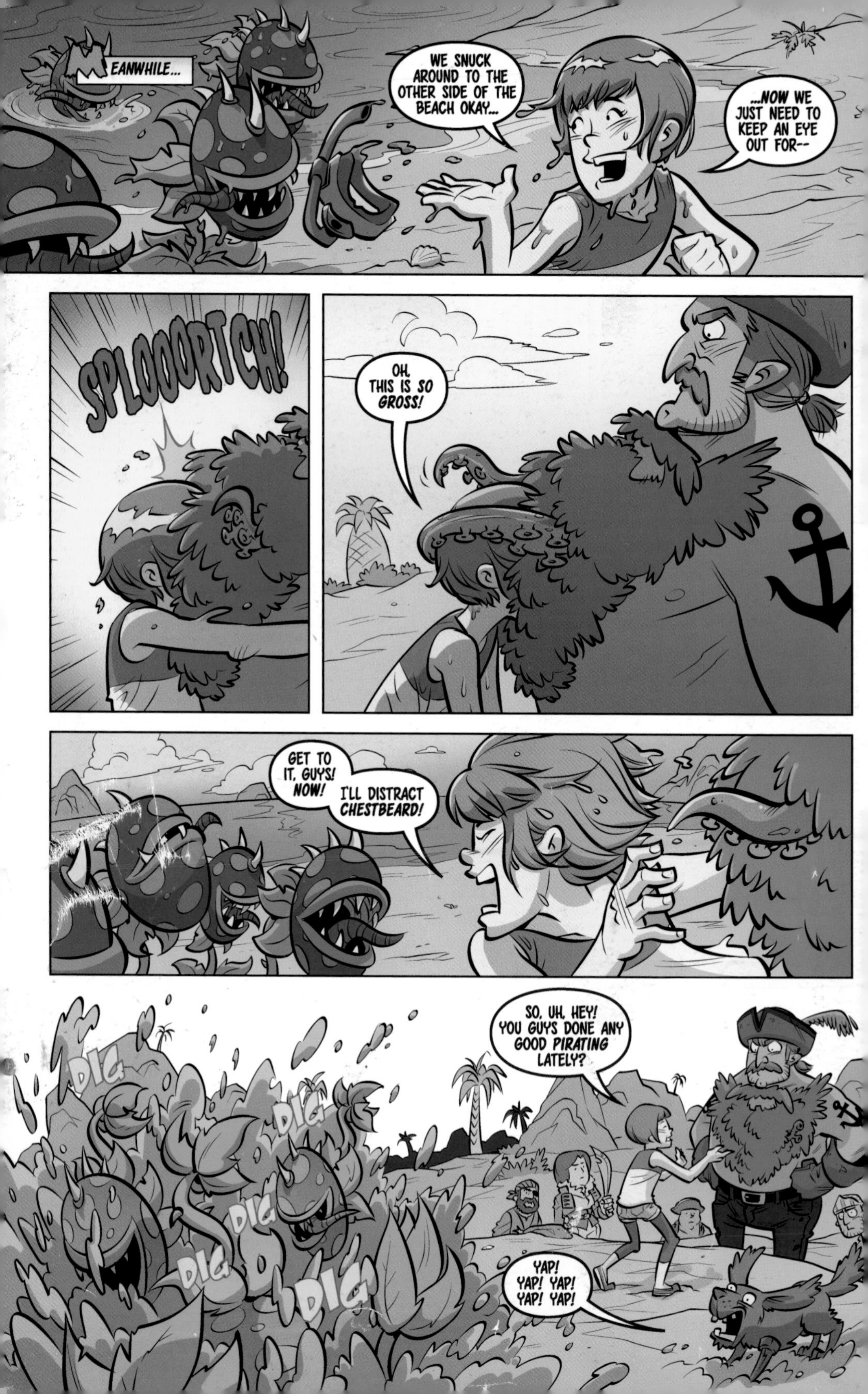
MEANWHILE...
WE SNUCK AROUND TO THE OTHER SIDE OF THE BEACH OKAY...
...NOW WE JUST NEED TO KEEP AN EYE OUT FOR--
SPLOOORTCH!
OH, THIS IS SO GROSS!
GET TO IT, GUYS! NOW!
I'LL DISTRACT CHESTBEARD!
SO, UH, HEY! YOU GUYS DONE ANY GOOD PIRATING LATELY?
DIG
DIG
DIG
DIG
DIG
YAP! YAP! YAP! YAP! YAP!

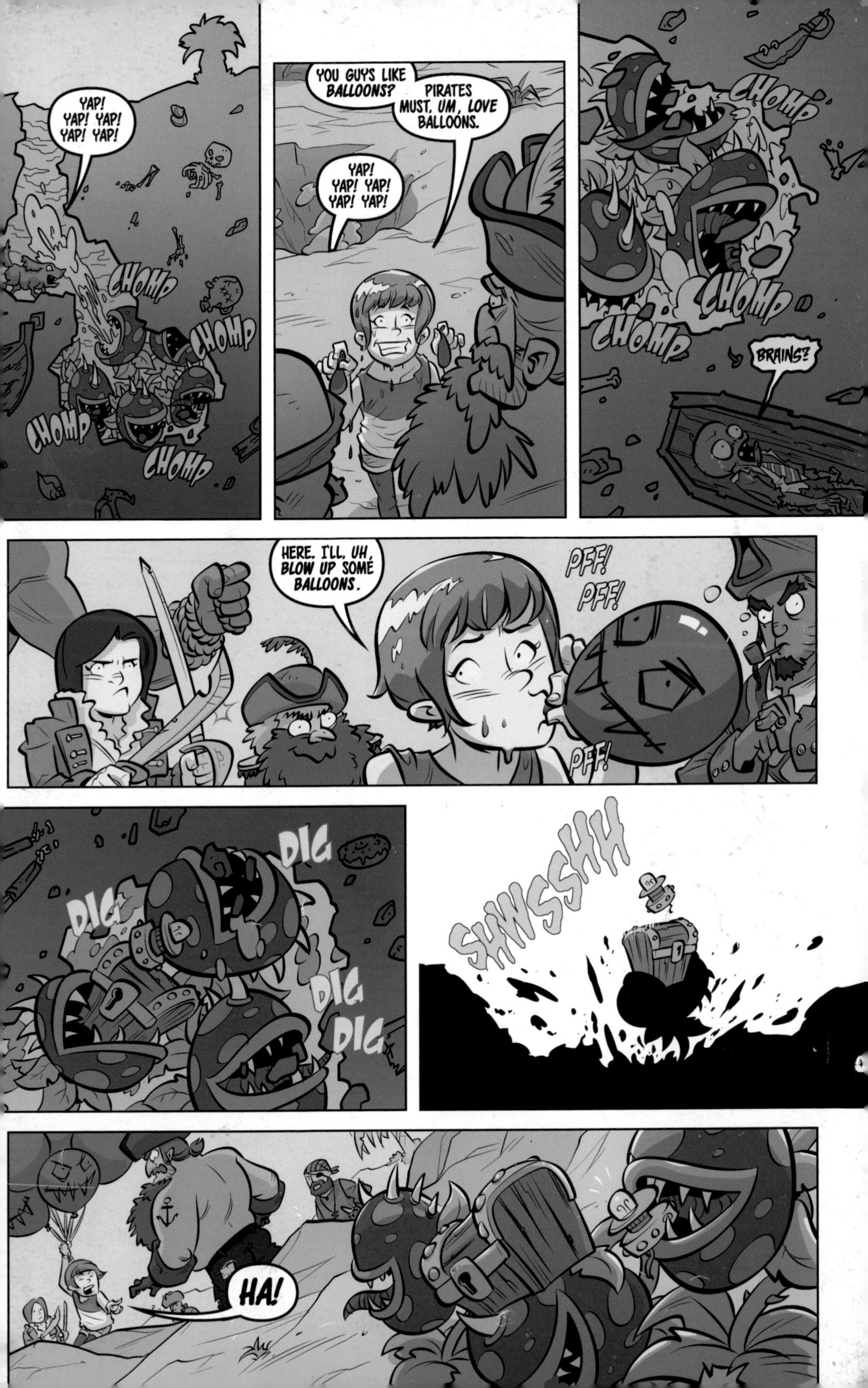
YAP! YAP! YAP! YAP! YAP!
CHOMP
CHOMP
CHOMP
CHOMP
YOU GUYS LIKE BALLOONS?
PIRATES MUST, UM, LOVE BALLOONS.
YAP! YAP! YAP! YAP! YAP!
CHOMP
CHOMP
CHOMP
BRAINS?
HERE. I'LL, UH, BLOW UP SOME BALLOONS.
PFF!
PFF!
PFF!
DIG
DIG
DIG
DIG
SHWSSHH
HA!

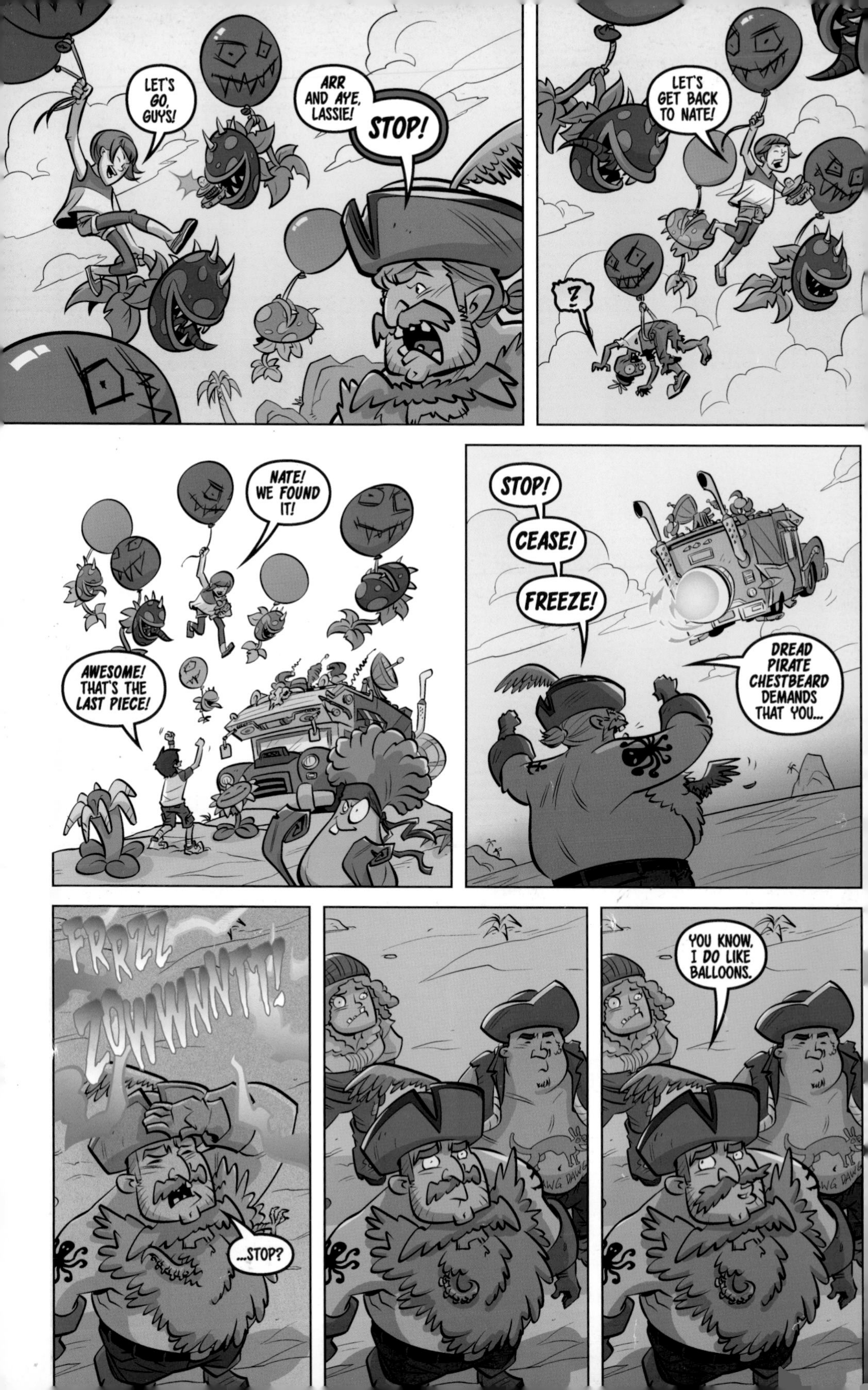
LET'S GO, GUYS!
ARR AND AYE, LASSIE!
STOP!
LET'S GET BACK TO NATE!
?
NATE! WE FOUND IT!
AWESOME! THAT'S THE LAST PIECE!
STOP!
CEASE!
FREEZE!
DREAD PIRATE CHESTBEARD DEMANDS THAT YOU...
FRRZZ
ZOWWNNTT!
...STOP?
YOU KNOW, I DO LIKE BALLOONS.

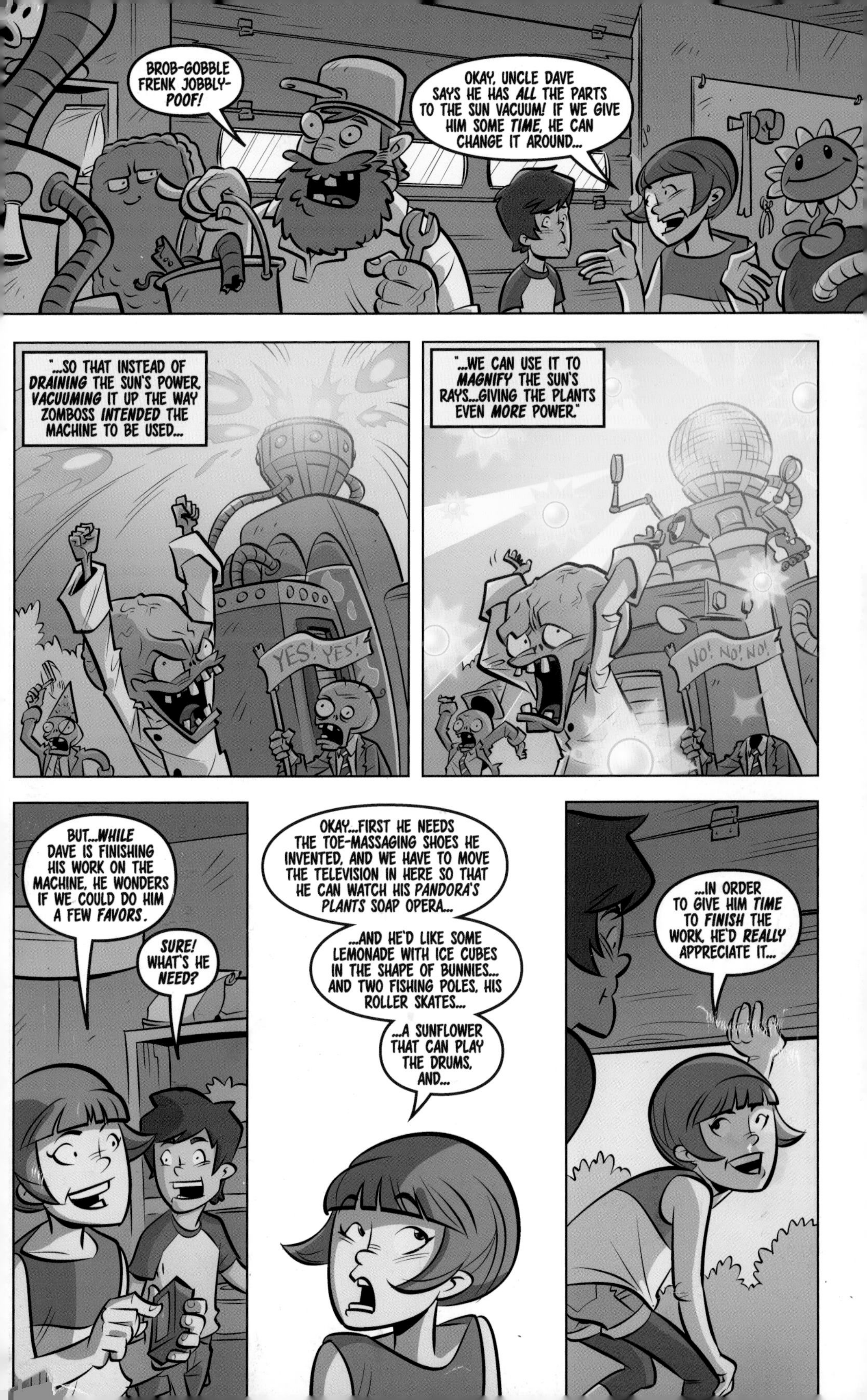
BROB-GOBBLE FRENK JOBBLY-POOF!
OKAY, UNCLE DAVE SAYS HE HAS ALL THE PARTS TO THE SUN VACUUM! IF WE GIVE HIM SOME TIME, HE CAN CHANGE IT AROUND...
"...SO THAT INSTEAD OF DRAINING THE SUN'S POWER, VACUUMING IT UP THE WAY ZOMBOSS INTENDED THE MACHINE TO BE USED...
YES! YES!
"...WE CAN USE IT TO MAGNIFY THE SUN'S RAYS...GIVING THE PLANTS EVEN MORE POWER."
NO! NO! NO!
BUT...WHILE DAVE IS FINISHING HIS WORK ON THE MACHINE, HE WONDERS IF WE COULD DO HIM A FEW FAVORS.
SURE! WHAT'S HE NEED?
OKAY...FIRST HE NEEDS THE TOE-MASSAGING SHOES HE INVENTED, AND WE HAVE TO MOVE THE TELEVISION IN HERE SO THAT HE CAN WATCH HIS PANDORA'S PLANTS SOAP OPERA...
...AND HE'D LIKE SOME LEMONADE WITH ICE CUBES IN THE SHAPE OF BUNNIES... AND TWO FISHING POLES, HIS ROLLER SKATES...
...A SUNFLOWER THAT CAN PLAY THE DRUMS, AND...
...IN ORDER TO GIVE HIM TIME TO FINISH THE WORK, HE'D REALLY APPRECIATE IT...

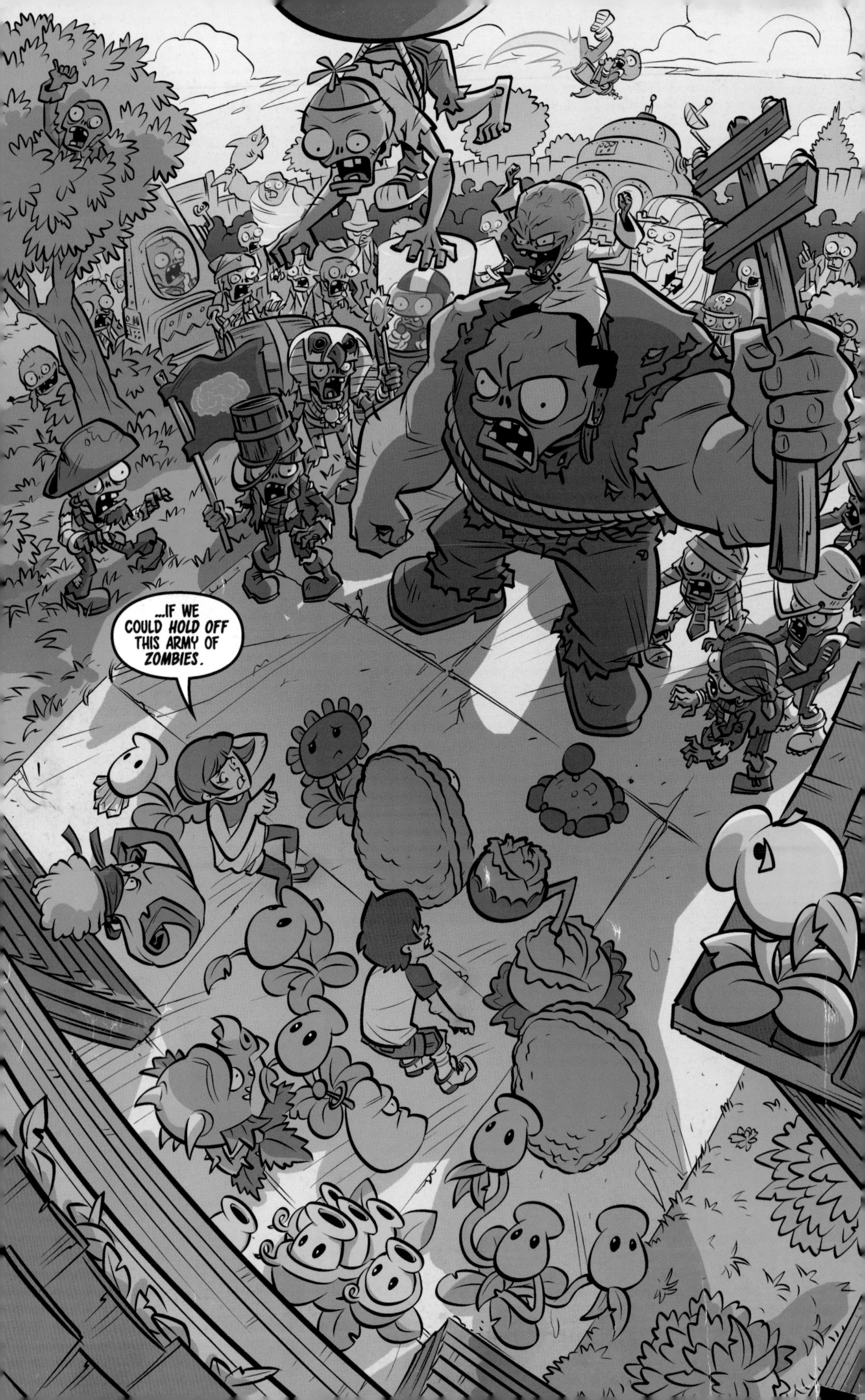
...IF WE COULD HOLD OFF THIS ARMY OF ZOMBIES.

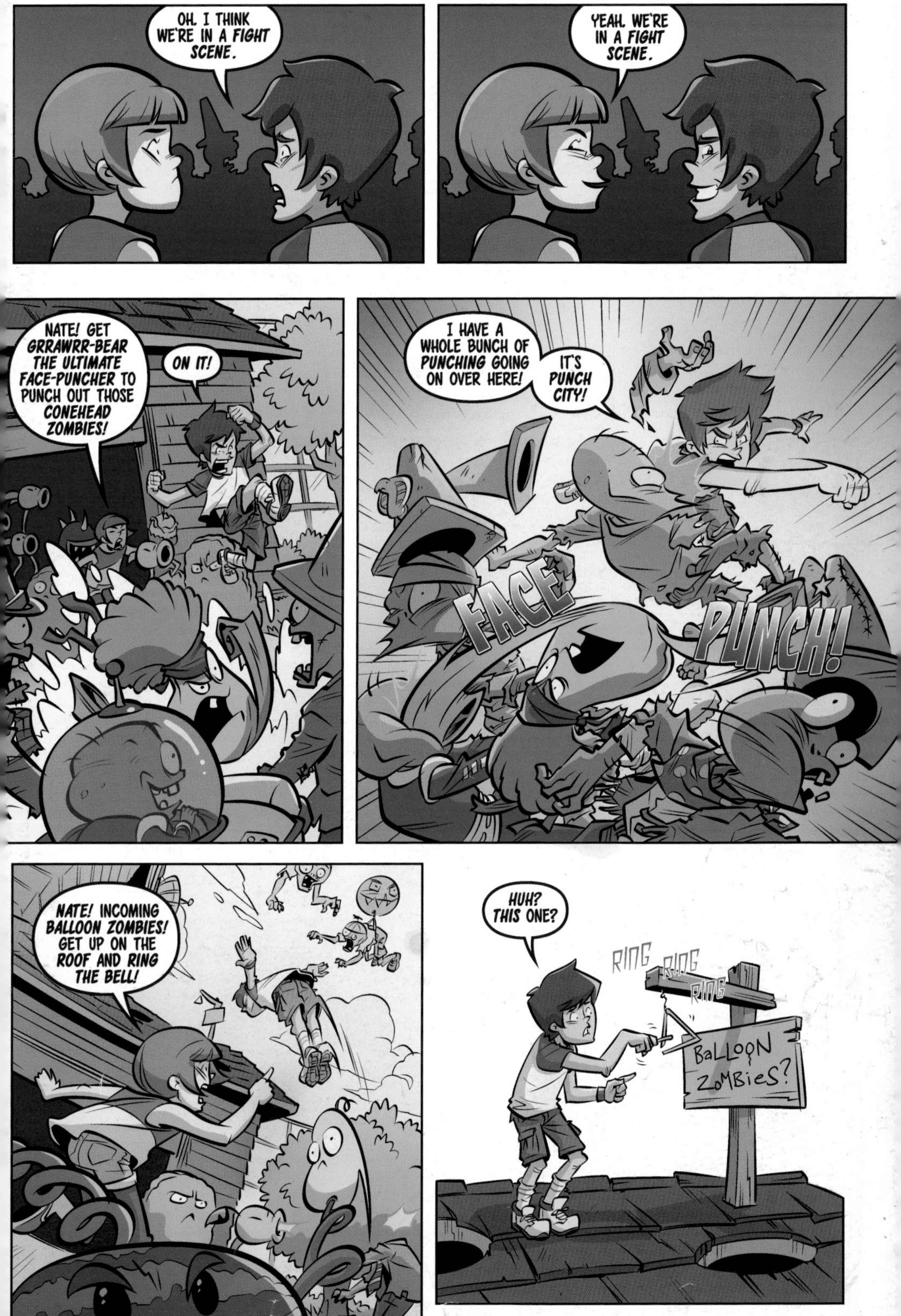
OH, I THINK WE'RE IN A FIGHT SCENE.
YEAH, WE'RE IN A FIGHT SCENE.
NATE! GET GRRAWRR-BEAR THE ULTIMATE FACE-PUNCHER TO PUNCH OUT THOSE CONEHEAD ZOMBIES!
ON IT!
I HAVE A WHOLE BUNCH OF PUNCHING GOING ON OVER HERE!
IT'S PUNCH CITY!
FACE PUNCH!
NATE! INCOMING BALLOON ZOMBIES! GET UP ON THE ROOF AND RING THE BELL!
HUH? THIS ONE?
RING RING RING
BALLOON ZOMBIES?

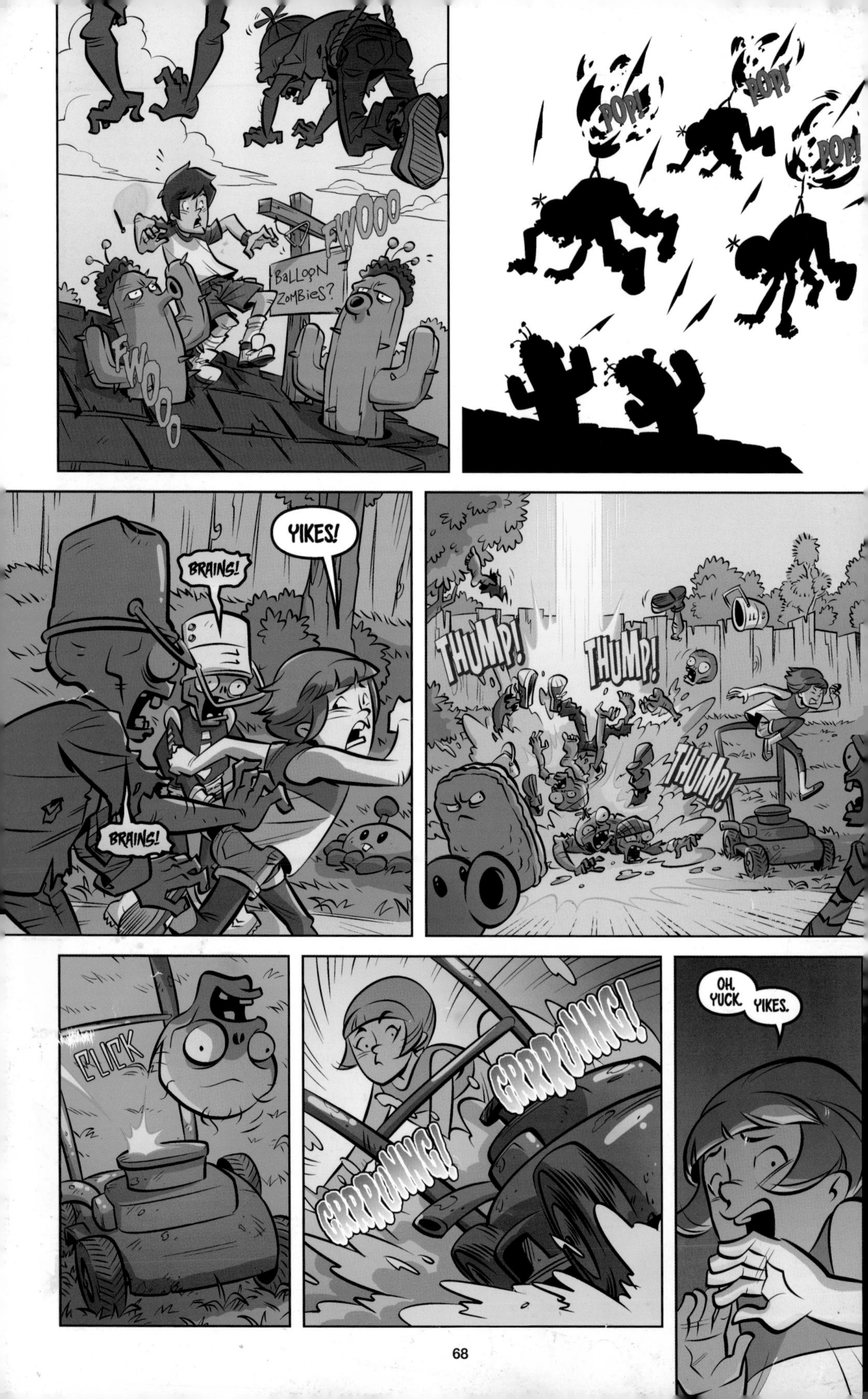
FWOOO
BALLOON ZOMBIES?
FWOOO
POP!
POP!
POP!
YIKES!
BRAINS!
BRAINS!
THUMP!
THUMP!
THUMP!
CLICK
CRRRUNNG!
CRRRUNNG!
OH, YUCK.
YIKES.

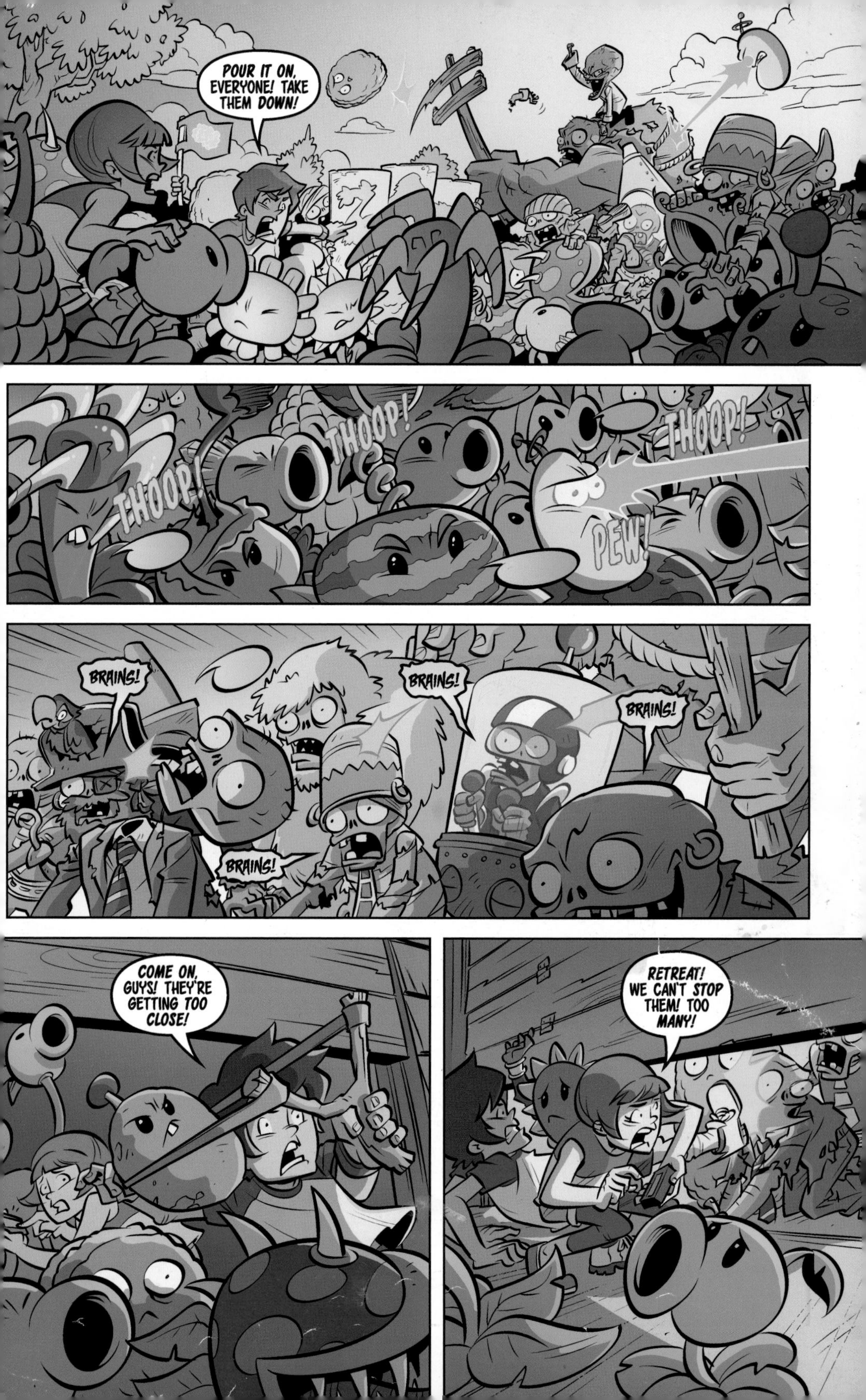
POUR IT ON, EVERYONE! TAKE THEM DOWN!
THOOP!
THOOP!
THOOP!
PEW!
BRAINS!
BRAINS!
BRAINS!
BRAINS!
COME ON, GUYS! THEY'RE GETTING TOO CLOSE!
RETREAT! WE CAN'T STOP THEM! TOO MANY!

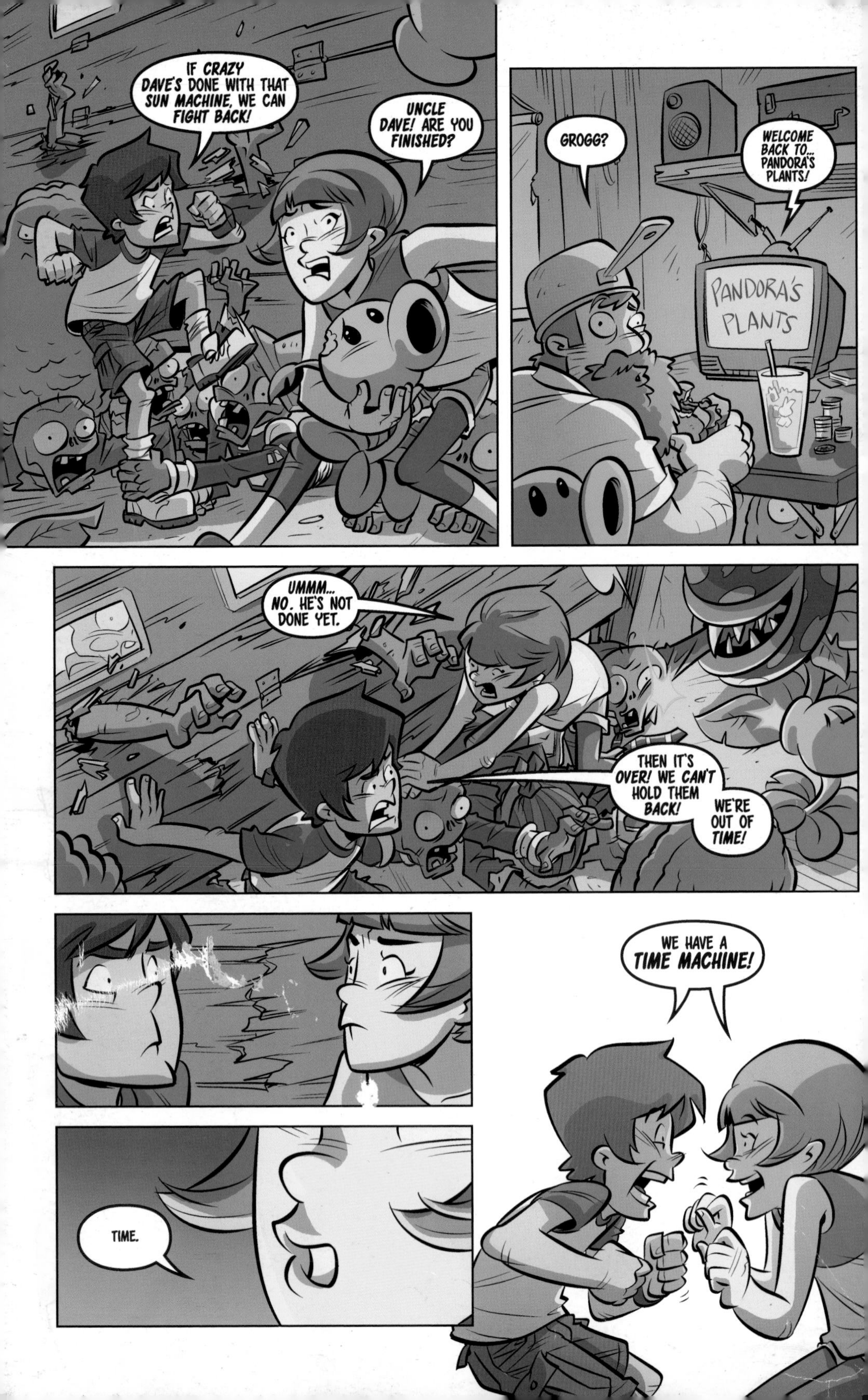
IF CRAZY DAVE'S DONE WITH THAT SUN MACHINE, WE CAN FIGHT BACK!
UNCLE DAVE! ARE YOU FINISHED?
GROGG?
WELCOME BACK TO... PANDORA'S PLANTS!
PANDORA'S PLANTS
UMMM... NO. HE'S NOT DONE YET.
THEN IT'S OVER! WE CAN'T HOLD THEM BACK!
WE'RE OUT OF TIME!
TIME.
WE HAVE A TIME MACHINE!

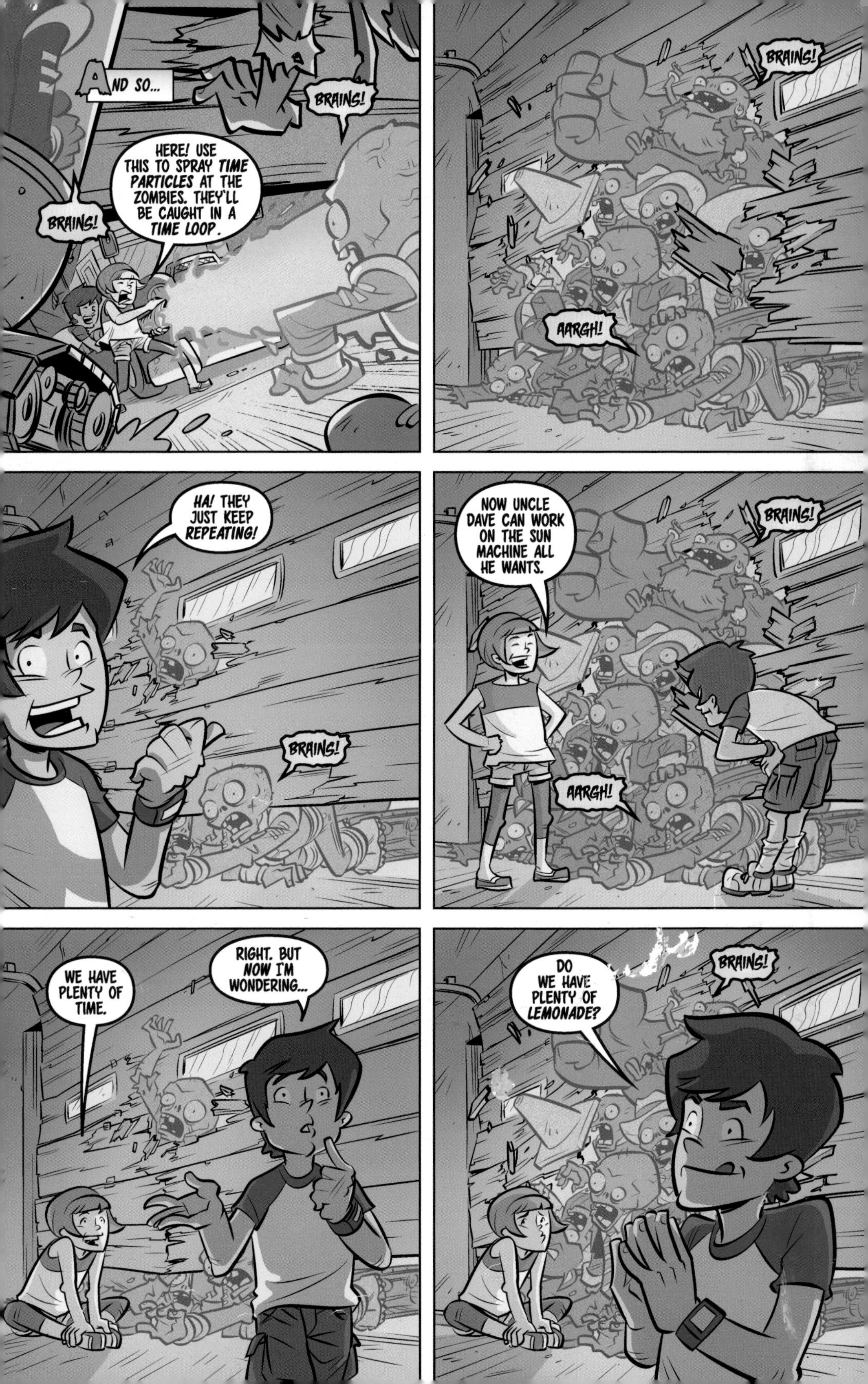
AND SO...
BRAINS!
HERE! USE THIS TO SPRAY *TIME PARTICLES* AT THE ZOMBIES. THEY'LL BE CAUGHT IN A *TIME LOOP*.
BRAINS!
BRAINS!
AARGH!
HA! THEY JUST KEEP *REPEATING!*
BRAINS!
NOW UNCLE DAVE CAN WORK ON THE SUN MACHINE ALL HE WANTS.
BRAINS!
AARGH!
WE HAVE PLENTY OF TIME.
RIGHT. BUT *NOW* I'M WONDERING...
DO WE HAVE PLENTY OF *LEMONADE?*
BRAINS!

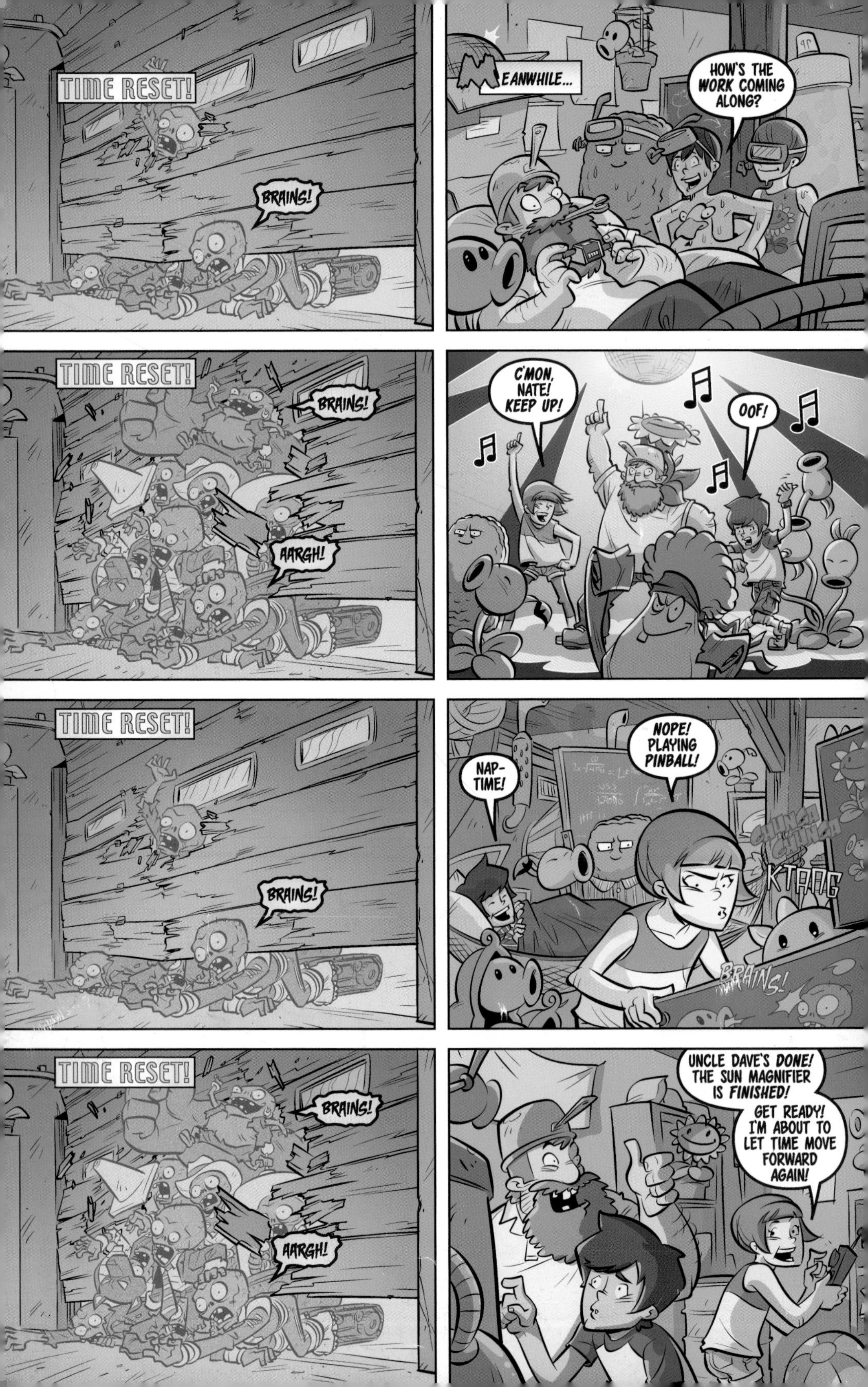
TIME RESET!
BRAINS!
MEANWHILE...
HOW'S THE WORK COMING ALONG?
TIME RESET!
BRAINS!
AARGH!
C'MON, NATE! KEEP UP!
OOF!
TIME RESET!
BRAINS!
NAP-TIME!
NOPE! PLAYING PINBALL!
CHUNGA CHUNGA
KTANG
BRAINS!
TIME RESET!
BRAINS!
AARGH!
UNCLE DAVE'S DONE! THE SUN MAGNIFIER IS FINISHED!
GET READY! I'M ABOUT TO LET TIME MOVE FORWARD AGAIN!

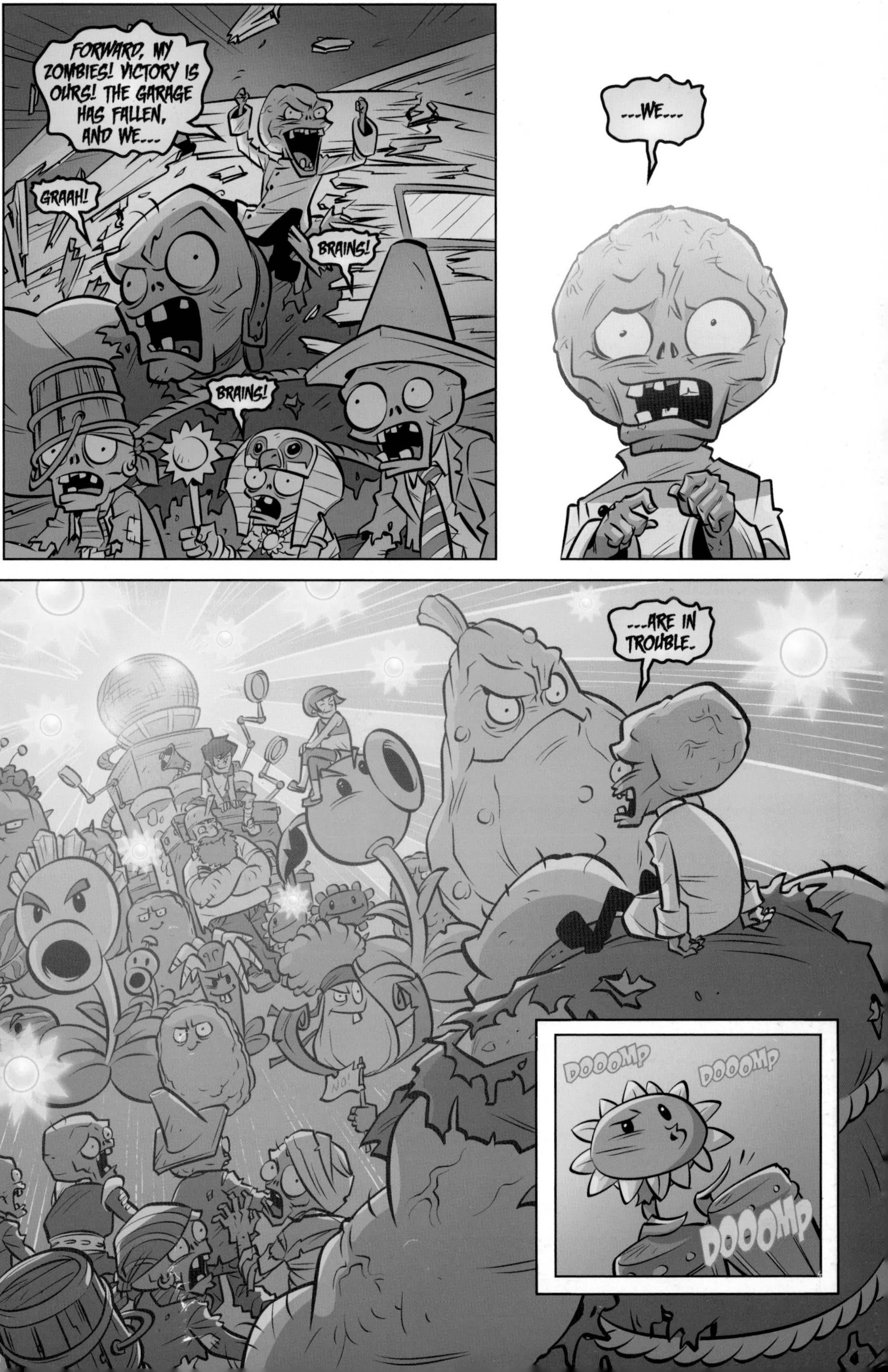
FORWARD, MY ZOMBIES! VICTORY IS OURS! THE GARAGE HAS FALLEN, AND WE...
GRAAH!
BRAINS!
BRAINS!
...WE...
...ARE IN TROUBLE.
DOOOMP
DOOOMP
DOOOMP

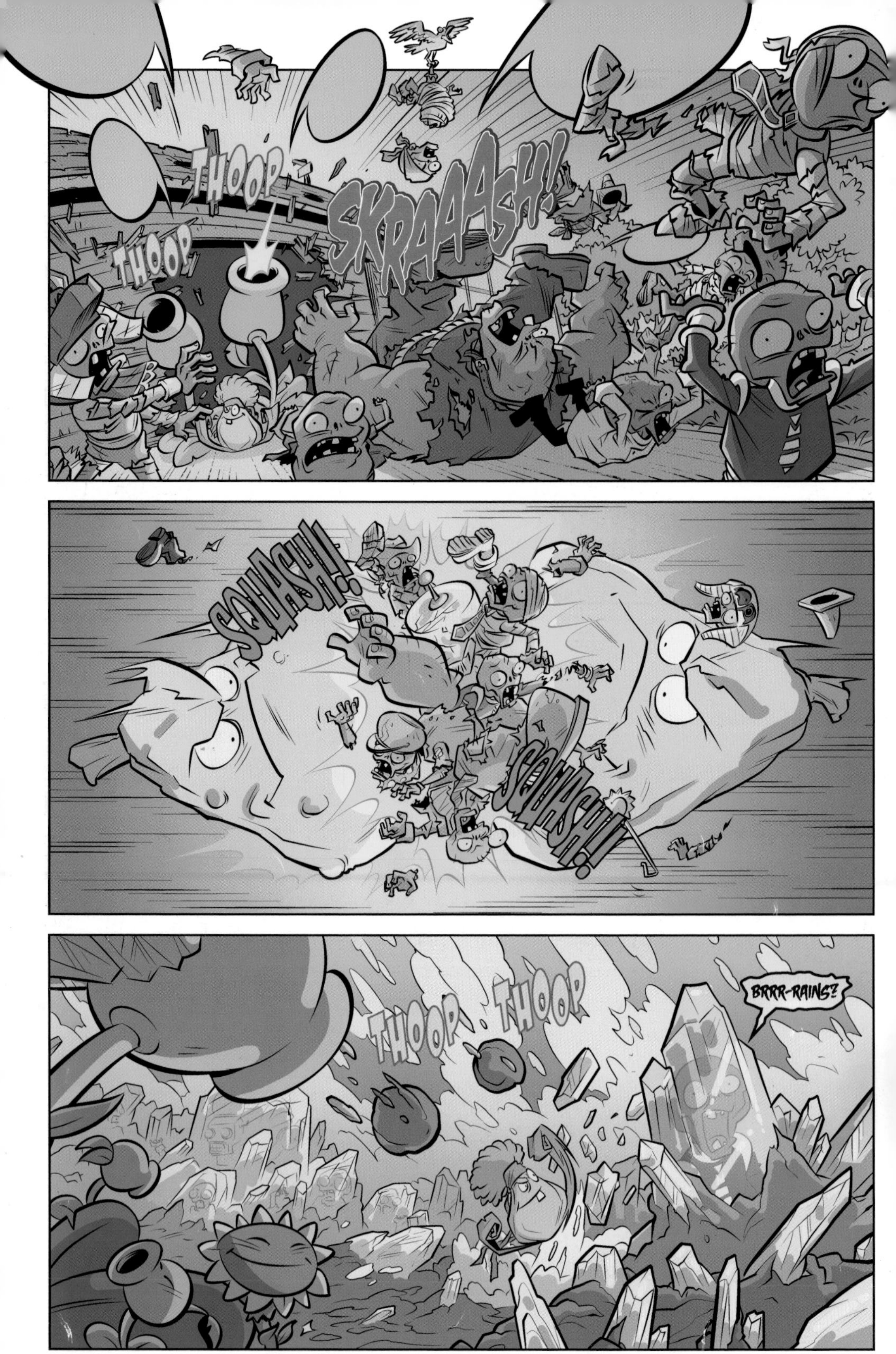
THOOP
THOOP
SKRAAASH!!
SQUASH!!
SQUASH!!
THOOP THOOP
BRRR-RAINS?

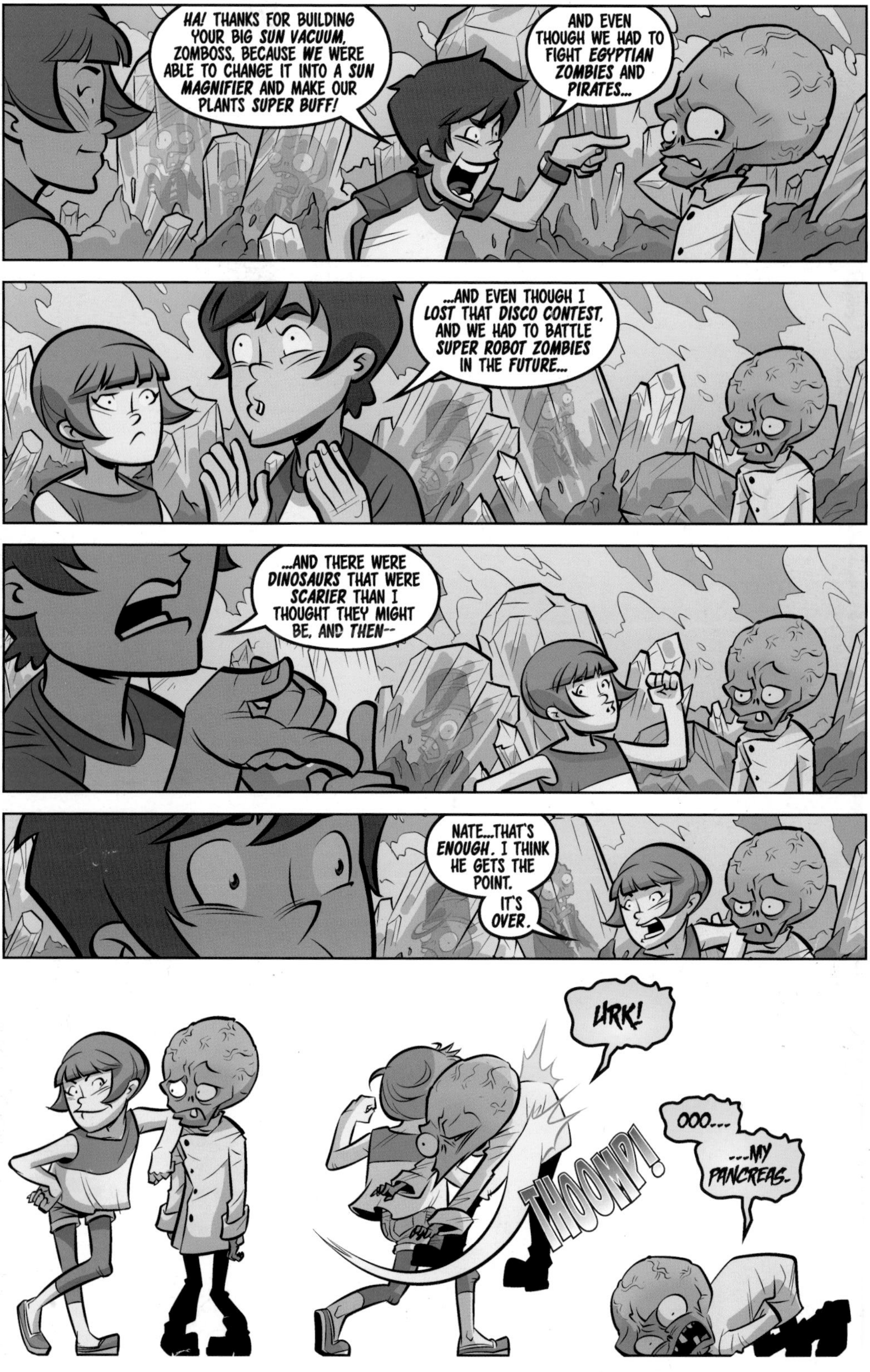
HA! THANKS FOR BUILDING YOUR BIG SUN VACUUM, ZOMBOSS, BECAUSE WE WERE ABLE TO CHANGE IT INTO A SUN MAGNIFIER AND MAKE OUR PLANTS SUPER BUFF!
AND EVEN THOUGH WE HAD TO FIGHT EGYPTIAN ZOMBIES AND PIRATES...
...AND EVEN THOUGH I LOST THAT DISCO CONTEST, AND WE HAD TO BATTLE SUPER ROBOT ZOMBIES IN THE FUTURE...
...AND THERE WERE DINOSAURS THAT WERE SCARIER THAN I THOUGHT THEY MIGHT BE. AND THEN--
NATE...THAT'S ENOUGH. I THINK HE GETS THE POINT.
IT'S OVER.
URK!
THOOMP!
OOO...
...MY PANCREAS.

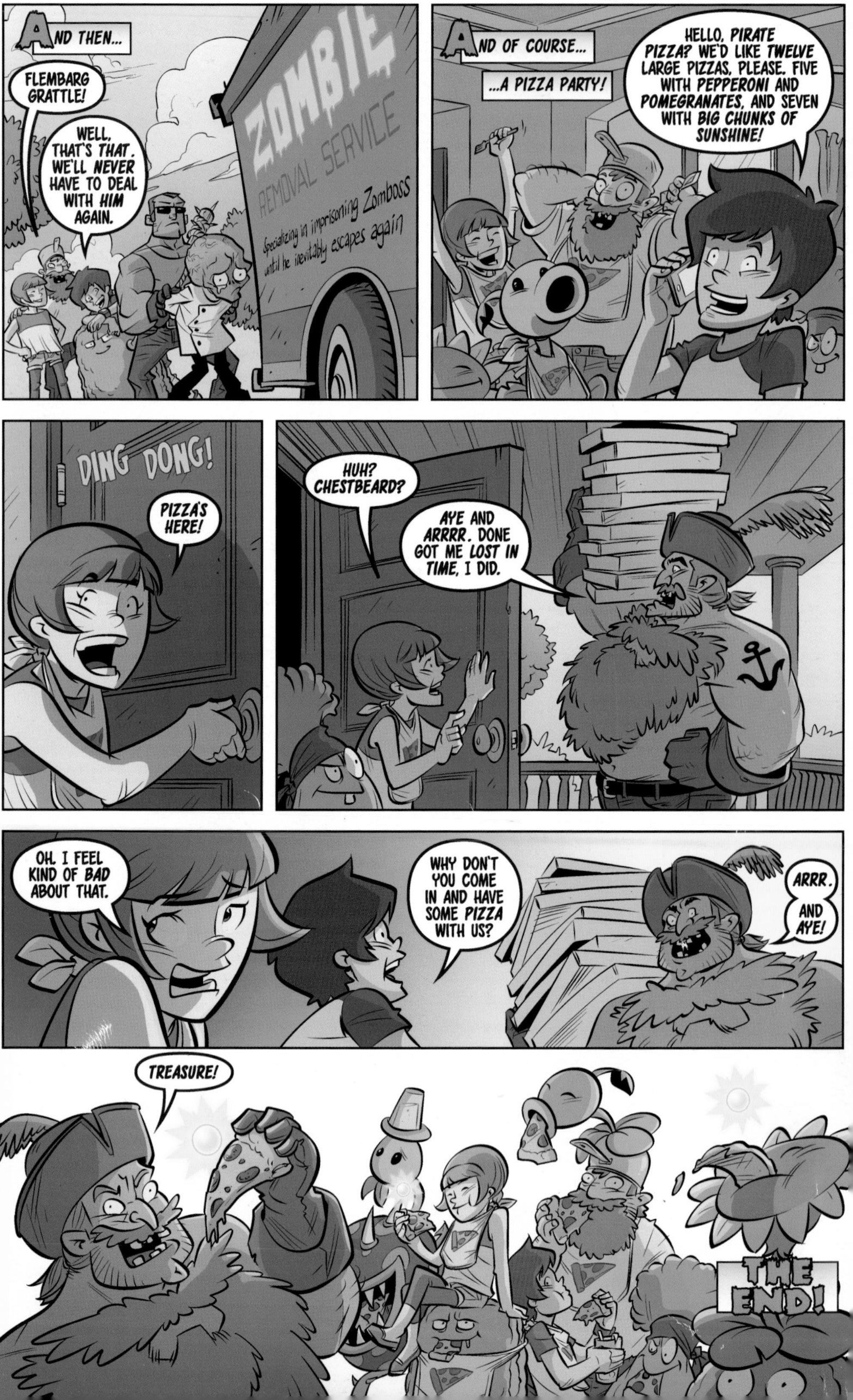
AND THEN...
FLEMBARG GRATTLE!
WELL, THAT'S THAT. WE'LL NEVER HAVE TO DEAL WITH HIM AGAIN.
ZOMBIE REMOVAL SERVICE
Specializing in imprisoning Zomboss until he inevitably escapes again
AND OF COURSE...
...A PIZZA PARTY!
HELLO, PIRATE PIZZA? WE'D LIKE TWELVE LARGE PIZZAS, PLEASE. FIVE WITH PEPPERONI AND POMEGRANATES, AND SEVEN WITH BIG CHUNKS OF SUNSHINE!
DING DONG!
PIZZA'S HERE!
HUH? CHESTBEARD?
AYE AND ARRRR. DONE GOT ME LOST IN TIME, I DID.
OH, I FEEL KIND OF BAD ABOUT THAT.
WHY DON'T YOU COME IN AND HAVE SOME PIZZA WITH US?
ARRR.
AND AYE!
TREASURE!
THE END!

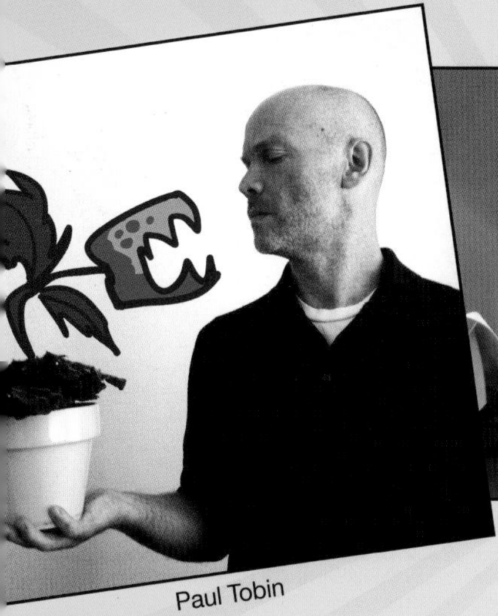

Paul Tobin

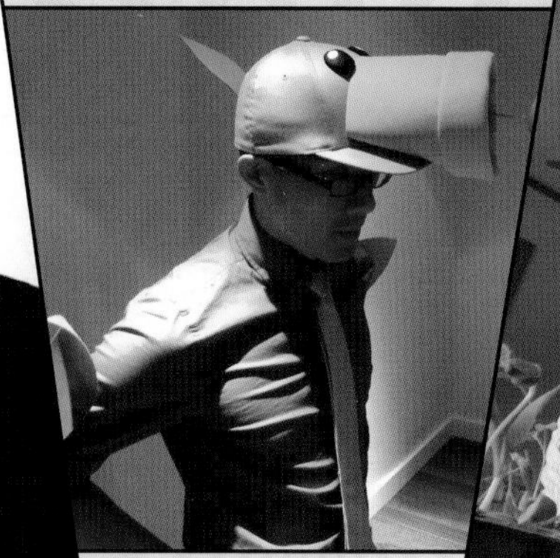

Ron Chan

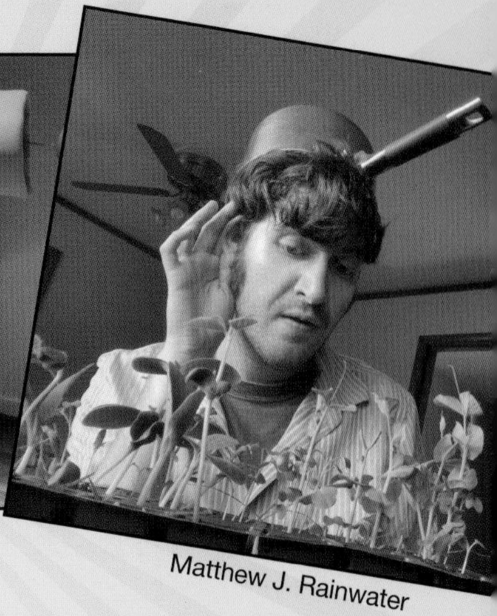

Matthew J. Rainwater

CREATOR BIOS

PAUL TOBIN is a critically acclaimed bald guy who had his first encounter with zombies when he watched the 1973 film *Children Shouldn't Play with Dead Things* on late-night television during one of the first times his parents ever left him alone. They returned to find him cowering in the kitchen with a knife. Paul eventually recovered enough mental stability to go on to write hundreds of comics for Marvel, DC, Dark Horse, and many others, including creator-owned titles such as *Colder* and *Bandette*, as well as *Prepare to Die!*—his debut novel. Paul's favorite zombie-fighting plants are the Cattail, the Snow Pea, and the Spikerock.

RON CHAN is a cartoonist, storyboard artist, and illustrator born and raised in Portland, Oregon. He graduated from the Savannah College of Art and Design in 2005, and is now a member of the Portland-based art collective Periscope Studio. His comic-book work has been published by Dark Horse, Marvel, and Image Comics, and storyboarding work of his includes boards for 3-D animation, gaming, internal development, user-experience design, and advertising for clients such as Microsoft, Amazon Kindle, Nike, and Sega. He really likes drawing the Bonk Choy.

Residing in the cool, damp forests of Portland, Oregon, **MATTHEW J. RAINWATER** is a freelance illustrator whose work has been featured in advertising, web design, and independent video games. On top of this, he also self-publishes several comic books, including *Garage Raja* and *Trailer Park Warlock*, both of which can be found at MattJRainwater .com. Matt is knee deep into *Plants vs. Zombies 2* but has yet to venture into the Far Future and Dark Ages worlds. His favorite zombie-bashing strategy utilizes a line of Bonk Choy with a Wall-nut front guard and Threepeater covering fire.

ALSO AVAILABLE FROM DARK HORSE!

THE HIT VIDEO GAME CONTINUES ITS COMIC BOOK INVASION!

PLANTS VS. ZOMBIES: LAWNMAGEDDON
Crazy Dave—the babbling-yet-brilliant inventor and top-notch neighborhood defender—helps young adventurer Nate fend off a zombie invasion that threatens to overrun the peaceful town of Neighborville in *Plants vs. Zombies: Lawnmageddon*! Their only hope is a brave army of chomping, squashing, and pea-shooting plants! A wacky adventure for zombie zappers young and old!
ISBN 978-1-61655-192-6 | $9.99

THE ART OF PLANTS VS. ZOMBIES
Part zombie memoir, part celebration of zombie triumphs, and part anti-plant screed, *The Art of Plants vs. Zombies* is a treasure trove of never-before-seen concept art, character sketches, and surprises from PopCap's popular *Plants vs. Zombies* games!
ISBN 978-1-61655-331-9 | $9.99

PLANTS VS. ZOMBIES: TIMEPOCALYPSE
Crazy Dave helps Patrice and Nate Timely fend off Zomboss' latest attack in *Plants vs. Zombies: Timepocalypse*! This new standalone tale will tickle your funny bones and thrill your brains through any timeline!
ISBN 978-1-61655-621-1 | $9.99

PLANTS VS. ZOMBIES: BULLY FOR YOU
Patrice and Nate are ready to investigate a strange college campus to keep the streets safe from zombies!
ISBN 978-1-61655-889-5 | $9.99

PLANTS VS. ZOMBIES: GARDEN WARFARE
Based on the hit video game, this comic tells the story leading up to the events in *Plants vs. Zombies: Garden Warfare 2*!
ISBN 978-1-61655-946-5 | $9.99

PLANTS VS. ZOMBIES: GROWN SWEET HOME
With newfound knowledge of humanity, Dr. Zomboss strikes at the heart of Neighborville . . . sparking a series of plant-versus-zombie brawls!
ISBN 978-1-61655-971-7 | $9.99

PLANTS VS. ZOMBIES: PETAL TO THE METAL
Crazy Dave takes on the tough *Don't Blink* video game—and challenges Dr. Zomboss to a race to determine the future of Neighborville!
ISBN 978-1-61655-999-1 | $9.99

PLANTS VS. ZOMBIES: BOOM BOOM MUSHROOM
The gang discover Zomboss' secret plan for swallowing the city of Neighborville whole! A rare mushroom must be found in order to save the humans aboveground!
ISBN 978-1-50670-037-3 | $9.99

PLANTS VS. ZOMBIES: BATTLE EXTRAVAGONZO
Zomboss is back, hoping to buy the same factory that Crazy Dave is eyeing! Will Crazy Dave and his intelligent plants beat Zomboss and his zombie army to the punch?
ISBN 978-1-50670-189-9 | $9.99

PLANTS VS. ZOMBIES: LAWN OF DOOM
With Zomboss filling everyone's yards with traps and special soldiers, will he and his zombie army turn Halloween into their zanier Lawn of Doom celebration?!
ISBN 978-1-50670-204-9 | $9.99

PLANTS VS. ZOMBIES: THE GREATEST SHOW UNEARTHED
Dr. Zomboss believes that all humans hold a secret desire to run away and join the circus, so he aims to use his "Big Z's Adequately Amazing Flytrap Circus" to lure Neighborville's citizens to their doom!
ISBN 978-1-50670-298-8 | $9.99

PLANTS VS. ZOMBIES: RUMBLE AT LAKE GUMBO
The battle for clean water begins! Nate, Patrice, and Crazy Dave spot trouble and grab all the Tangle Kelp and Party Crabs they can to quell another zombie attack!
ISBN 978-1-50670-497-5 | $9.99

PLANTS VS. ZOMBIES: WAR AND PEAS
When Dr. Zomboss and Crazy Dave find themselves members of the same book club, a literary war is inevitable! The position of leader of the book club opens up and Zomboss and Crazy Dave compete for the top spot in a scholarly scuffle for the ages!
ISBN 978-1-50670-677-1 | $9.99

PLANTS VS. ZOMBIES: DINO-MIGHT
Dr. Zomboss sets his sights on destroying the yards in town and rendering the plants homeless—and his plans include dogs, cats, rabbits, hammock sloths, and, somehow, dinosaurs . . . !
ISBN 978-1-50670-838-6 | $9.99

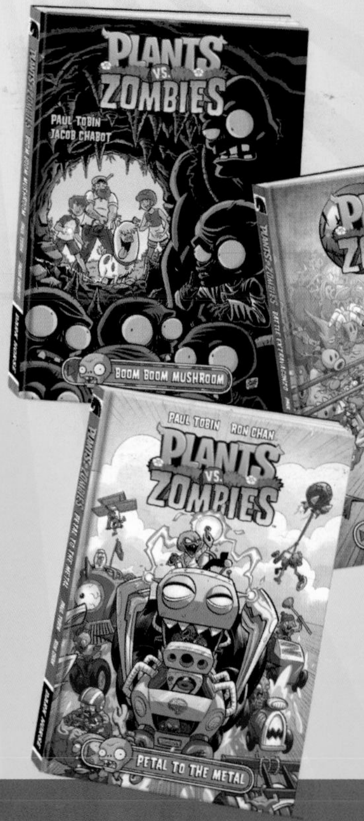
PLANTS VS. ZOMBIES
PAUL TOBIN
JACOB CHABOT
BOOM BOOM MUSHROOM
PLANTS VS. ZOMBIES
BATTLE EXTRAVAGONZO
PAUL TOBIN RON CHAN
PLANTS VS. ZOMBIES
PETAL TO THE METAL

AVAILABLE AT YOUR LOCAL COMICS SHOP OR BOOKSTORE To find a comics shop in your area, visit comicshoplocator.com. For more information or to order direct visit **DarkHorse.com** or call 1-800-862-0052

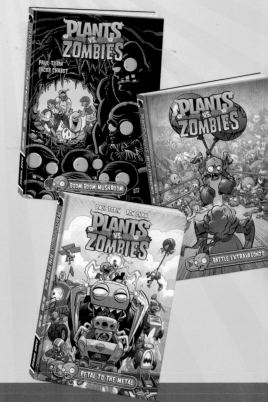

MORE DARK HORSE ALL-AGES TITLES

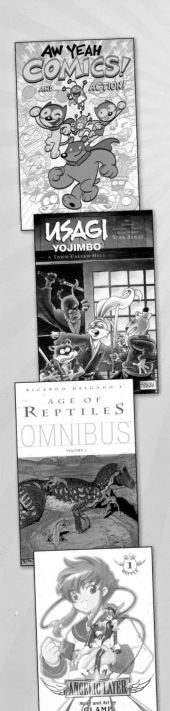

AW YEAH
COMICS!
AND... ACTION!

AW YEAH COMICS! AND . . . ACTION!

Cornelius and Alowicious are just your average comic book store employees, but when trouble strikes, they are . . . Action Cat and Adventure Bug! Join their epic all-ages adventures as they face off—with the help of Adorable Cat and Shelly Bug—against their archnemesis, Evil Cat, and his fiendish friends!

ISBN 978-1-61655-558-0 | $12.99

USAGI
YOJIMBO
A Town Called Hell
Stan Sakai
SAKAI

USAGI YOJIMBO

In his latest adventure, the rabbit *ronin* Usagi finds himself caught between competing gang lords fighting for control of a town called Hell, confronting a *nukekubi*—a flying cannibal head—and crossing paths with the demon Jei!

Volume 25: Fox Hunt
ISBN 978-1-59582-726-5 | $16.99

***Volume 26: Traitors of the Earth* | $16.99**
ISBN 978-1-59582-910-8

***Volume 27: A Town Called Hell* | $16.99**
ISBN 978-1-59582-970-2

Ricardo Delgado's
Age of
Reptiles
Omnibus
Volume 1

AGE OF REPTILES OMNIBUS

When Ricardo Delgado first set his sights on creating comics, he crafted an epic tale about the most unlikely cast of characters: dinosaurs. Since that first Eisner-winning foray into the world of sequential art he has returned to his critically acclaimed *Age of Reptiles* again and again, each time crafting a captivating saga about his saurian subjects.

ISBN 978-1-59582-683-1 | $24.99

1
BATTLE
ANGELIC LAYER
Story and Art by
CLAMP

ANGELIC LAYER BOOK 1

Junior-high student Misaki Suzuhara just arrived in Tokyo to live with her TV-star aunt and attend the prestigious Eriol Academy. But what excites Misaki most is Angelic Layer—an arena game where you control a miniature robot fighter with your mind! Can Misaki's enthusiasm and skill take her to the top of the arena?

ISBN 978-1-61655-021-9 | $19.99

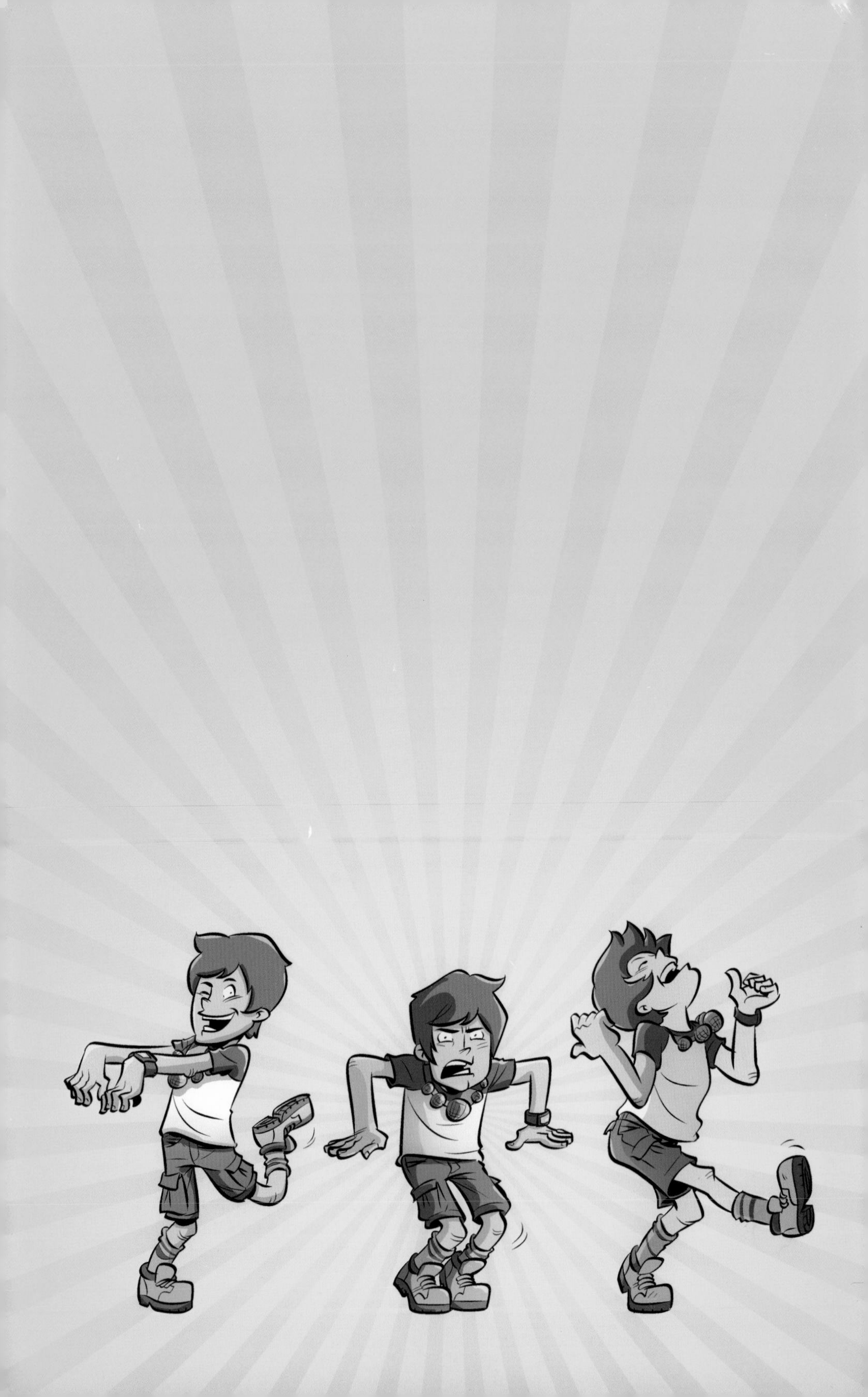